Fields

A West Indian story

by
Lloyd Beharry

www.publishnation.co.uk

For my parents

CONTENTS

Chapter One
West Africa c.1820

A musket ball whizzed through the air and landed with a dull thud into the sentry's left eye, splattering his blood and blobs of brain and sending shards of his skull spinning overhead. His body folded up tamely, and an upswell of fluid from within choked off a warning cry and turned it into a barely audible gurgle of death.

It had been quiet.

Not graveyard quiet, but quiet for a morning in the dense forest surrounding the village.

No birds twittered; no crickets chirped; no pigs grunted as they foraged in the undergrowth. Only the occasional plop of an overripe fruit disturbed the silence as it hit the ground.

The look-out had stood erect, alert, and almost to attention on a plateau of rock, overlooking the village. Only his head moved. First, to the left, then it paused. After a few seconds, it swept slowly to the right, assessing everything within sight. Then, it paused again. His nose sniffed the air as if filtering it for any noises, smells and movements that did not belong, and his eyes, like a lighthouse beam, peered into the distance, intent on detecting the presence of any intruder. Satisfied that all was well, his head began its sweep again. This went on until he was replaced by another guard, just as watchful, just as dedicated.

These were worrying times for the village because someone had told someone that they had heard that marauding bands of men had been attacking and killing or

1

capturing people before razing their villages to the ground. Not wishing to take any chances, the Village Chief had posted a sentry on the edge of the tree line, night, and day, to warn them of any impending danger.

Not far away, just above the river, a boy sat on a rock. He was caressing the head of an injured swallow which had been used for target practice by some child or other. He stroked the bird's head with his index finger and made soothing noises while the animal lay crouching and cowering in the palm of his hand, its wings wrapped tightly around its meagre trembling body.

The boy lay his hand flat on the rock and nudged the bird with his finger until it hopped from his palm and stood tottering on the rock before it limped away, lurching from side to side like a drunk. Then, after a few flaps of its wing, it took off. The boy's eyes followed it as it left the ground in erratic, ungainly flight. He watched it dip towards the river as if it was going to plummet into the water, then he sighed and smiled as the bird rose again in a jagged arc towards the sky. The bird dipped and rose, dipped, and rose, and the boy's mouth opened and closed, opened, then closed, as the bird rose in a steady upward trajectory until it became a black dot which disappeared into the sun.

The boy smiled, then he frowned. He wished that the children wouldn't injure such innocent creatures. It wasn't as if they were trying to kill them for food, which might be understandable if they were starving. But there was no shortage of food in their village. Besides, the old people had told how swallows were protected by *Mawu-Lisa* - the female-male twin deity worshipped by the Fon and Ewe people of the region - because the poor things only flew over their village to escape the fierce heat of the great desert to the north which burned their wings and caused them to fall into the hot sand which roasted them to death; so the

2

old people had said. Sometime back, when he was much younger, the boy had overheard two men discussing the merits of the swallow as food.

'Too many bones', said one, as he whittled away at a piece of wood.

'Too little meat', said the other, spitting in disgust as if it was the bird's fault.

'Tastes like shit', they both had agreed.

The boy lay back on the ledge of rock, his black torso glistening with droplets of water as he dried himself under the mid-morning sun. He looked up at the expanse of sky, bluish-purple in the centre and bluish grey around the edges, like a sucked gobstopper. In front, tufts of wool slowly floated past without purpose. He yawned and thanked *Mawu-Lisa* for having created the earth and all the good things in it, just as his grandmother had taught him to do before he went to sleep.

He shut his eyes and began to drift off to the familiar sounds of bodies plunging into the river, spouting plumes of water upwards that fell back with a whoosh and a splash; children giggling as they chased each other in a game of tag along the river bank and into the thin line of trees, just beyond which lay the village; once tagged, they ran out again onto the riverbank, shouting and laughing; Women chattering away as they squatted by the water's edge, soaking, soaping and beating the dirt out of their family's clothes with wooden bats hewn from fallen trees, their dresses folded over their laps to protect their modesty.

It was just another day in the life of the village. Just another day after the men had gone about their business of hunting and gathering food or building and repairing shelters, and the old and enfeebled had been arranged in such a way that they could see out another day of their existence in as little discomfort as possible.

Suddenly, the smell of gunpowder, mixed with burning thatch and fresh blood, choked the boy, and sparked a fire in his brain. He sat bolt upright and threw his head so far back that his face was set parallel to the sky; he ground his teeth and squeezed his eyes, which caused a drop of water from each one to roll down along his temples and splash silently into the sands below.

From just beyond the trees, came the slapping sound of musket fire; the begging, pleading, screaming, and wailing of people; the cackling of scattering poultry; the grunting of hogs and the braying of asses as they bolted in all directions. The dissonance deafened him. After a short while, as the stinging in his brain dissipated, he righted his head and looked around. Sounds had become muted and he was looking through hazy eyes at a mime veiled by smoke. He peered all around. He could just make out strange men dragging women by their hair along the ground and the women screaming and flailing their arms like tree branches in a storm, their legs wide open and their heels digging into the sand in a vain attempt to resist the assault. He saw children running helter-skelter to evade the men, but their skinny legs and short strides proved no match for their pursuers' spade-like hands which scooped them up and held them as they wriggled like tadpoles.

Not far away, just above the trees, the boy saw thick black smoke billowing upwards like many swarms of locusts.

'Jump, Amadi!' A voice in his head said. 'Jump now!'

Under the water, Amadi felt his chest getting tighter and tighter as he struggled to breathe. He remembered once seeing a cow being squeezed by a python, its deep baritone lowing ascending the musical scale until it reached a whining castrato as the python contracted its muscles. Then, there was silence. He knew that he could hide no

4

longer from the python and decided to take his chance with whatever was running riot above. He pushed towards the surface, desperate to release the tightness around his chest. As his hands cut the water and made a tunnel through which he climbed, he could hear noises muffled by the water, whose sweetish taste was growing more and more salty and brackish. He broke the surface, exhaled, swallowed the air quickly, and glimpsed pandemonium on the shore just beyond the water, which had changed from its normal dull muddy grey into a pinkish-red.

Before he could dive again and buy some time, he felt something land on his shoulders and tighten around his neck. Python. He was yanked forwards and he realised that he was being choked by a rope which was getting tighter and tighter, slowly shutting out the light. Just as oblivion approached, the noose began to slacken, and the light slowly got brighter and brighter. He coughed and spat. He could breathe, but he couldn't move. He was sitting up on the shore with his hands trussed up behind him. He tried to bring them forward, but they wouldn't budge. He looked around and saw the men, mostly white, but some black, binding the hands of the captives and yoking them. They went about their work with urgency, pressing their knees into the backs of the struggling captives while they tied their hands behind them. Sometimes, they paused for a split second, cracked them across the head, and continued the binding, all in one symphonic movement.

Once the captives were secured, the captors marched them through the trees and into the centre of the village which was full of people, some with blood running down their heads and faces, and some with limbs hanging at unnatural angles, evidence of the breaks, fractures or dislocations caused by trying to flee or defend themselves. He saw the huts, the source of the black smoke; they were smouldering, almost all burnt to the ground. He saw the young able-bodied boys and girls and the young children all being subdued in one way or another. And he saw the old and infirm looking on bemused, untouched, perhaps because they were of no interest or threat to the assailants. The men yanked him up and yoked him. He tried to turn left, and then right, but like a bull harnessed to a plough, his field of vision had narrowed so that he could only see ahead as if looking into a tunnel. One by one, they were yoked and put to stand in a line, one behind the other.

His captors shoved him forward to join the others and he could hear mothers shrieking and calling out for their children, repeating their names more rapidly when they heard a familiar voice above the din, somewhere behind, somewhere in front, which told them that their precious ones were alive. He, too, tried to locate his six-year-old sister by shouting her name, but all he could hear were the screams and lamentations of voices he did not recognise.

As the captors pushed the procession out of the village, he thought about his grandmother, wizened and helpless, and now on her own back there with nowhere to shelter. Who, he wondered, would oil the dry skin of her emaciated limbs, and mash her food so that chewing would not inflame her toothless gums? Who, he asked himself, would lift her featherweight form and put her to sit outside their hut, as was his daily duty, so that she could watch village life go by between catnaps? At least she was alive, he conceded, as alive as she had ever been, since that night when a crocodile came in the blackness and took away her only son, his father. He and his sister had been nurtured by her because their mother had died also, while giving birth to his sister. Now, in her old age, she would be deprived of the care and joy she received from having her grandchildren around her and, like the other old ones left behind, she would soon wither away and die, like plants bereft of water. The brigands forced the column of captives through rocky terrain, inhospitable swamps, and thorny bushes that ripped and tore at their bodies; they drove them on with an urgency that was unknown in village life. They beat the women with straps when they fell; they whipped the children with switches for crying and screaming, and they whipped and beat the men for no reason other than to keep them in line. Those who were too weak to go on and had collapsed with little hope of ever being resuscitated, were shot in the head or decapitated. This was not done as an act of kindness, but simply because it saved time so that the captors could make another foray into the bush for another batch of unsuspecting human loot.

Finally, after a long weary trek of many days, the brigands brought the procession to a halt, and whatever relief this might have been for the broken and bedraggled captives, it was soon replaced by a ghastly terror. In front of them, there was an unending expanse of roiling, angry, foaming water, like nothing they had ever seen before. Their eyes widened and their mouths opened, and they shrank back while their captors, having seen hundreds of times how the inland dwellers reacted to the ocean, laughed, and laughed. On higher ground, all along the shore, there were forts looking out to sea, manned by heavily armed guards. There were also many large covered pens clustered together higher up on the shore, all crammed full of people taken from different villages. The captives were shoved into their new accommodation, men and boys in pens, separate from women and girls.

Amadi was fourteen; he was a man. He tried to speak to other men, some older and some younger, but nobody spoke his tongue. He saw no one from his village or tribe, just strangers united only by their sense of fear and

7

puzzlement. And night after night, his sense of desolation grew as he listened to the roar of the ocean's waves as they hit the shore and tried to climb its gradient, only to fizzle out in weary defeat.

Night after night, too, some of his captors came to his pen. As they fiddled with the locks of the gates with unsteady hands, they laughed, and their lisping tongues and alcoholic breaths shushed each other in mock propriety. When he heard the chains of the gate rattle, he tensed up his body and pretended to be sleeping as he waited for the clammy, expectant hands, and he silently prayed that he would not be the one chosen. One night, he felt fingers grab his ankle before they began snaking along his shin, tentatively at first, then more quickly. He held his breath as the fingers paused and lingered for a moment, unsure, before darting away. He exhaled slowly so as not to make a sound, the weight of all his worries decanted in that single breath. A short distance away, he could hear the struggle and the half-muffled cries as bodies were bundled up before being taken away. When he heard the gates being locked, he breathed freely, grateful that he had not been selected, but he knew that there was always the next night - and the one after that, and the one after that. Sometimes, after hours had passed, he could hear the chains again, then the thud of the bodies as they were dumped on the ground, limp, bloody and almost lifeless.

Sometimes, never.

Night after night, too, the brigands visited the women's pens. Once they were in, they groped around on the ground, shaking with excitement until they felt a foot; then an ankle; a shin; then a knee over which their hands climbed, spider-like, until they reached soft flesh, which they squeezed and caressed, savouring and slavering, before coming to the fork in the road where the two paths met and the bush began. Sometimes, there was no bush, but they still pushed ahead despite the cries of protest and the screams of pain.

One morning, Amadi heard the gates to his pen open, this time without stealth. The guards came in and shackled them before marching them out into the glare of the sun. They squinted and gradually opened their eyes, and what they saw caused their mouths to fall open in a gape. There, sitting imperiously in the water, seemingly unmoved by the anger of the ocean's waves and unperturbed by the thousands of black beetles shuffling about aimlessly in chains along the shore, was a giant monster with three long barbs on its back linked by webs of cloth which flapped and thumped as the winds hit them, like the wings of a giant white crane taking off.

As the brigands whipped and goaded the captives towards canoes parked at the water's edge, the captives squirmed and dug their heels into the sand, afraid of the unending, unknown waters and the giant ship anchored some distance away. In what must have been a choice between the devil and the deep waters of the ocean, an occasional captive wrestled himself free and jumped in, never to surface again. When the rest finally reached the ship, they were forced below into the hold where they were locked in chains and placed either supine or up against each other in spooning intimacy with no room to move, like dates packed tightly in a box. The busyness and the noises coming from above, and the way the ship lurched forward, told Amadi that they were leaving.

As the journey ground on, he lay there in the dark wondering where they were being taken. He had heard the stories of villages being attacked and of people being taken

9

away, but the pedlars of such news had never said whether such acts had been done by man or beast, as those who had disappeared had never returned to enlighten anyone. He concluded that the brigands did not intend to kill them, something which they could have done back in the village. No; they wanted them alive. Why else would they have marched them for such a long way and fed them for such a long time ashore, and why, during their journey, would they feed them and go to the trouble of forcing them to dance on deck at intervals, before securing them again below?

From time to time, too, their berths were washed down with quicklime. Deckhands, whose mouths and noses were covered with cloths to protect them from the caustic substance, emptied the liquid and scrubbed and scraped to get rid of the accumulated waste produced by hundreds of bodies defecating, urinating, menstruating and sweating in a small space. This ritual did little to alleviate the stench but made it worse by agitating the caked mess and giving it new, malodorous life. While this was done to keep the captives safe and healthy, sickness and death were never far away. To breathe was to invite both, as both spread disease which caused vomiting and dysentery and added to the loathsome conditions. There were periods when the dysentery led to the uncontrolled evacuation of the bowels and stomachs, during which times there was the frequent unlocking of chains in the hold, the retreating of heavy footsteps and the scuffling on the deck above followed by a splash, as if something heavy had been thrown into the ocean. Sometimes, the unlocking was frantic and was accompanied by splashes in quick succession. Sometimes, above all the ship's noises and the pleas of pained humanity, Amadi could hear an occasional screaming and begging before he heard the thump and the hollow splash made by water being displaced. Sometimes, too, somewhere, deep in the dark hold, he could hear two captives sighing as they spread their forms a little, grateful for the extra space. The journey seemed without end. Locked in the hold and espying sunlight only occasionally, Amadi felt as if he was under water, as if he was being suffocated, as if he was trapped on all sides in a small box. No matter how he widened his eyes, he could see nothing. He could only hear the soft low moans of despair; the movements of discomfort; the cries of physical pain, and the silence of abandonment. And try as he may, he could not rise above the water into the light because there was a confusion within himself which filled his head. All he could do to contain the python was to suck in as much air as he could and release his breath slowly. But that exercise also had its disadvantages, as taking in air meant absorbing all the noxious smells.

The feeling was worse during storms, for while the turbulent waves whipped up a sea spray that splashed into the hold and refreshed him, they simulated at the same time a familiar sense of drowning, as his lungs swelled and pushed against their confines. Storms in the mid-Atlantic lasted for many days and nights and no sooner would one abate, than it would be followed by another, sometimes much worse. There was no feeding, no cleaning nor any exercising during such an assault because of the need for the crew to stand steadfast at their stations. The only thing the captives ingested was saltwater, which caused dehydration, hallucinations and delirium.

The ship, too, seemed to feel the strain. It rocked and rolled in the rough seas, its timbers creaked and groaned, and its sails flapped in the high winds as though nature itself was remonstrating against it for carrying such a

11

cargo.

After many days and nights had passed, there was a strange calm as if the sea and the winds had fallen asleep. Then there was frantic activity above as men scurried about and shouted instructions to each other, followed by something heavy dropping into the water. The captives barely reacted because they were either too weak or too long past caring.

Or dead.

Chapter Two
The British West Indies

A flotilla of little crafts made their way out to greet the Slave Ship as it lay at anchor in the deep waters of the Caribbean Sea, some distance from land. Ketches, yawls, sloops and large canoes churned up trails of white foam as they pushed their way through the azure waters and came to rest alongside. Their passengers – pink and tanned white men in starched white suits and white sunhats, climbed aboard to have a sneak preview of the cargo of exotic goods brought from distant lands.

Amadi and the other captives, sodden, exhausted and dispirited, were later put into canoes and taken ashore. No one struggled and no one jumped into the sea because no one had the strength. They were shoved into pens under superfluous guards, where they spent the night on the earthen floors in a heap.

The next morning, they were fed, washed, scrubbed, and rubbed down with oil so that the naked parts of their bodies glistened and gave a false appearance of good health. Their eyes, too, which would normally have reflected their debilitation, came alive because of their sense of wonderment at being on land and their curiosity about the reason for all the pampering.

They were then taken out of their pens and led into a square, where they were paraded. Not far away, there were the white men of the day before, jotting things down in their books and mumbling to their assistants. The ringing of a bell caused the men and their assistants to rush towards the captives, their claws extended like falcons swooping on their prey. They poked, fingered and fondled them. They looked them up and down like punters sizing up whores. They opened their mouths and checked their teeth as if they were horses. They grabbed at parts of their bodies as if they were meat on a butcher's slab and then, when they were satisfied, they exchanged money.

The captives knew then that they were being sold; but to what purpose, they were still unclear.

A tall, well-built white man strode up to Amadi. He had a scar running from the tip of one eye to the corner of his mouth, which gave his face the semblance of a scowl. He was followed closely by his bent, weedy looking assistant who shuffled around like a mongoose - all the time eyeing Amadi up and shrinking back whenever their eyes met.

'Check his ankles and wrists,' Scarface said to his assistant. The assistant nodded, then he obeyed, all the time warily looking at Amadi. The mongoose nodded again, and Scarface grunted and wrote something in his book.

'Lift his arms and spread them out.' The assistant nodded again, then obeyed. Scarface grunted and wrote.

'Poke him in the belly.' He ordered.

The assistant hesitated. He looked at Amadi to make sure he was securely tethered, then he looked at Scarface as if awaiting further instructions. Scarface answered by looking upwards at the sky and rolling his eyes. The mongoose, in no doubt as to what would happen if he wasted any more time, raised his hand, palm upturned, and thrust it into Amadi's midriff. Amadi contracted his abdominal muscles just in time as the bony fingers hit and bounced off. The mongoose's face took on a look of horror and he thrust again and again until the force, combined with the long months of deprivation, penetrated Amadi's defences and made him exhale. The mongoose looked at Scarface, twisted his mouth, and shrugged his shoulders in a gesture which suggested that the evidence provided by this procedure was inconclusive.

Ignoring his assistant, Scarface curled his upper lip, which seemed to release the tension on his eye, and he said to himself,

'Hmm. A bit weak and gangly, I must say. But he's tall and whole, and we can build him up.'

Scarface wet the tip of his pencil with his tongue and wrote down in his book: 'Lot 79.' With his assistant scurrying behind him, he strode across the square to the women's auction, but this time he did his own shopping. The procedure was much the same as that for the men, except that there was much more fingering and fondling like feeling mangoes at a street market before buying. He approached a nubile young woman whose oiled skin radiated false health. He swallowed as he savoured the fullness of her bosom and the breadth of her hips under her thin cotton dress. He cast a furtive glance around, then he bent down and quickly shoved a hand under her skirt and grabbed her bottom.

'There'll be none of that, Mr. Burnett. You know the rules,' said the Ship's Master.

Scarface bought her along with Amadi, who was sold as 'Lot 79: Male slave named John.'

For transportation to their respective Plantations, the slaves were placed into cages atop cattle-drawn carts which meandered at a pedestrian pace along roads and tracks that had been carved out more through regular usage rather than by design. John looked out of his cage and saw that both sides of the track were paved with an unending wall of tall grass with thick stalks, the likes of which he had never seen. This, he later discovered, was the sugar cane plant, a source of untold wealth to those throughout the world who farmed it.

After some hours, they were set down in an open square where people were busy carrying out various activities. John saw men repairing carts, shoeing horses and mules and sharpening long knives; women, helped and hindered by children, were fetching water in pails and fresh produce in baskets, stitching bags and packing boxes, or cooking. They were all as black as he, and they were supervised by white men with whips.

In another part of the square, under a shed, he saw a black man squeezing a pair of bellows which shot air into a forge from which angry flames leapt high into the air. Slowly, the flames subsided and turned black lumps of coal into glowing blobs of red. Not far away, he saw another black man hammering away at a rod of iron on an anvil before shoving it into the smouldering coals until it, too, glowed like a red menace. The man's face was devoid of expression, as if repetition of action had robbed him of thought or feelings. John's attention, rapt throughout these operations, was distracted by a scuffle that ensued when two muscular black men tried to hold one of the slaves down. It was a token resistance, fathered only by the instinct of self-preservation. The men soon overpowered the slave and spread one of his clenched hands flat on the ground before forcing his palm open. A third black man poured water onto his palm. Then, the anvil-man, like a High Priest with his ceremonial dagger held aloft, advanced and placed the glowing iron dead centre. Upon contact, there was a hissing sound, an escape of smoke and the smell of searing meat. The slave, no more than fifteen, gritted his teeth, contorted his face, and let out an ululation which shattered the air and seemed to cause even the anvil-man's face to take on a look of something like emotion. During and after the branding, some slaves screamed and one or two of them wept, wet themselves and defecated before fainting.

When his turn came, John closed his eyes and clenched his teeth. He did not scream, even though the pain was like nothing he had ever experienced. He tensed his muscles and imagined that he was *bela* the elephant, whose hide it was difficult to penetrate. He gritted his teeth until he heard the hiss and smelled the burn, then he relaxed his muscles, opened his eyes and looked at his palm. It was still glowing but, clearly visible were the red letters 'BB', which covered half of his lifeline, most of his headline and touched his heart-line. This stood for the name of his owner, Bradley Burnett, he of the scarred face and wandering hands, the Planter and Master of Plantation Hope.

John got up and turned his back to the others as if stretching his muscles. He lifted his hands into the air, still fettered at the wrists, and he wiped each eye on a naked arm and licked the drop of blood that had issued from his bitten lip.

He was put to work in the cane-cutting gang from which hardly a day passed without a slave or two attempting to escape. From dawn to dusk, they were forced by ever-watchful overseers to slash the cane stalks with cutlasses before bundling them up for transportation to the mill. They started at four in the morning, slashing the cane stalks and bundling them; they had a short break at nine, after which they slashed and bundled until one in the afternoon, when they had another break for lunch. The breaks were short, barely enough for them to gulp down the rationed pickled fish or meat and stodgy root vegetables, such as yam and cassava. Then, the overseers hurried them into resuming their toil. In eighty degrees Fahrenheit under the sun, for fifteen hours a day, they slashed amid a confusion of razor-sharp steel blades, which flashed and glinted in the sunlight as they fell the long erect stalks of the sugar cane plant.

Then they bundled.

To do this, they had to bend down, tie the heavy bundle with the long cane leaves, grab hold of it and hoick it on to their heads using an action like a weightlifter's clean-and-jerk. That done, and to ease the burden, they wiggled and waddled and picked their way across the fields, which were full of sharp cane stumps and deep cavities, until they came to the dam where the oxen-drawn carts were waiting. The carts were high - above six feet - so that they had to hoist the bundles above their heads before dumping them in. John was glad that he wasn't as short as some of the others, whom he often helped to hoist and dump. He was never sure which was harder – the chopping and bundling, or the hoicking, fetching, and hoisting. It was an idle thought, though, as they both comprised the drudgery of the cane-cutter's life.

What compounded their job was rain. Sometimes, it rained for days without remission and rivers and streams all over the land flooded their banks and gave birth to new veins and arteries. The topsoil that was not washed away into the rivers was turned into fields of sludge in which the slaves slipped and slid as they moved, wincing, and sometimes screaming, as they twisted a joint or broke a bone.

From this purgatory, made worse by the absence of recompense, many tried to escape at the cost of life and limb while their masters sought to control them by three basic measures – flogging, torture-and-dismembering, and death, though this last was only exercised when slaves threatened violence or caused injury or death to others. Its practice, as a routine, did not make economic sense.

When Bradley Burnett's father retired to enjoy his riches

in England, Bradley inherited Plantation Hope but not his old man's sense of business, and it didn't take him long to earn a reputation for drunkenness and depravity. He regularly co-habited with the women slaves, which yielded many progenies - tanned, with blondish-brown curly hair and cat-like coloured eyes. Their existence incurred the opprobrium of the Planters who said that 'Bradley's Bastards', as the children were known, were neither fish nor fowl and should be kept under lock and key and not allowed to roam free. It was an affront to Planter dignity, they felt - as though that man, Bradley Burnett, was sticking two fingers up at them.

His overseers took their lead from him and treated the slaves with unparalleled cruelty and licentiousness. As a result, there was an inordinate number of deaths at Plantation Hope, and slaves were laid up in the sick house for weeks on end with serious injuries, not just to themselves, but also to the finances of the Plantation.

Like most slaves, John was often flogged, not for any reason except to keep him up to his work. He took his punishment with fortitude, and while he was not of a rebellious nature, he had often felt like doing what the slave, Amos, had done. During a savage beating, the cause for which John could not understand, Amos had grabbed hold of the overseer's whip and tugged sharply, causing the man to tip off his horse and land heavily onto the ground. Three other overseers had to wrestle Amos to the ground to prevent him from wielding his cutlass; then they hog-tied and took him away. That was the last that anyone had seen of him, but whispers suggested that he had been taken to the whipping post and tied and beaten until he died.

After a few years cutting cane, John had been transformed from a gangly teenager to a muscular adult, standing just about six feet with broad shoulders and sturdy limbs and he could have hit out at any overseer who ill-treated him; but he knew that such resistance led to nothing but dismemberment and death. He had heard many stories of slaves who had disappeared, and he had seen some others wandering about without an arm or a leg.

Morale on the Burnett Plantation was so low that production suffered, and this forced Bradley to borrow money from other Planters to replace dead or lost manpower. His main lender was Henry King, the owner of Plantation Albion, who was known to all as 'King' Henry, not because he looked anything like the corpulent historical figure of that appellation, but because he owned and managed the largest, the wealthiest and the most powerful Plantation in the region.

'I'm getting fed up with this Bradley. It's the third time this year,' King Henry said.

'I'll pay you back once I've sold the crop, Henry.'

'What crop, Bradley? You're more interested in fornicating with the slaves than in planting cane. Your behaviour is a disgrace.'

'I promise to change, Henry, if you help me this time.'

'You keep saying that every time and nothing happens. And, what about all these half-caste sprogs you've got littering the countryside. I nearly ran over one while out riding the other day.'

'They're not all mine, you know; others have been at it, too. Others have been screwing their slaves and pretending that they are purer than pure.'

'Maybe, but that one looked just like you.'

'Was it a boy or a girl?'

'A boy; about sixteen.'

'Was he tall and good-looking?'

'About five-eight,' King Henry grunted.

'That might have been Simon,' Bradley said, allowing himself a little smile. 'Was he good- looking?'

'What the hell has that got to do with anything?' King Henry exploded. 'It's not a bloody laughing matter, Bradley. You're supposed to set an example. Nobody's saying you shouldn't have fun but breeding the slaves the way you do is irresponsible. Why can't you use some protection?'

'I've tried, Henry, but it takes too long. You must plan for it and soak the skin down so it becomes supple before you can put it on. It's all right if you have a wife or a regular piece, but I do it on the spur of the moment, mostly when I'm drunk.'

'And what about disease? Have you thought about that?'

'Of course - when I'm sober; but you know what it's like after you've had a few and you feel the urge.'

King Henry shook his head. 'I am not surprised that your estate is in the shape it is. You and your men breed the slaves, then you keep them in the field throughout their pregnancy. No wonder so many of them die.'

'That's not strictly true, Henry. They work until they're seven or eight months, then they do lighter work.'

'And that's alright?'

'It's the best I can do. Do you know what happens on the Gladstone estates? They give birth in the fields!'

'Don't talk to me about the Gladstone estates. You can do better if you and your men controlled yourselves. Also, the more you ill-treat the slaves, the more they will run away.'

'My overseers are the ones to blame.'

'They follow your example. The Planters are all pissed-off with you. 'The rotten apple,' is what they call you. And I'm leaving out the other, more colourful, adjectives.'

'They should talk; they're no angels themselves, Henry.'

21

'I know, but at least they are discreet.'

'I promise it will get better, Henry.'

'It had better. The commission of MP's from England will be here next month to investigate complaints about the ill-treatment of slaves and a host of other things. The anti-slavery movement is growing and people like you aren't helping. They'll be going through everything we do with a fine-tooth comb. You just make sure you clean up your stables long before then, Bradley.'

And King Henry, as always, lent Bradley the money. Other Planters did too, from time to time - not because they approved of him - but because, like banks, if they didn't prop each other up, the whole system could collapse.

John kept his head down for most of the time and did as he was told; that is, until the incident with Peterson. Peterson was the most vicious of the overseers whose regular target was a young man in the cane-cutting gang - two or three years younger than John and just as many times weaker. Nobody knew why Peterson singled him out for special treatment, but gossip had it that it had little to do with work and more to do with something darker. One day, he laid into the young man with his bullwhip causing him to shriek and howl. He twisted and turned and tried to dodge the whip, but Peterson advanced closer to make sure he wouldn't miss. John stopped chopping, put his cutlass down, took three strides to where the man was cowering and stood between them, facing Peterson. He stretched his arms out as if to shield the man, looked Peterson in the eye, and said, 'No more, no more.'

Peterson's arm froze in mid-air, the single tail of his bullwhip trailing along the ground like a long flaccid penis. He stared back at John, his mouth wide open, his eyes ablaze.

The air all around became gravid with expectation. The

other workers in the fields, whose own overseers had been distracted by the incident, slowed down what they were doing and peeked under their arms. There was barely a sound; only the slow, lingering, tick-tock of anticipation. Within minutes, a group of overseers came over from adjoining fields and bundled John off to the whipping post. They put him to face the post, tied his hands to it above his head and spread his legs out, so that he could not manoeuvre his body in trying to dodge what was to come.

Deprived of one pleasure, Peterson was about to be compensated by another. He took a long look at the tethered John and licked his lips. Like a golfer practising his swing, he took a firm hold of the handle of his whip and flexed the muscles of his right arm. He slowly brought his arm straight up to mid-day, bent his elbow, and took a deep breath before snapping his arm forward. The body of the whip came alive and tore the air with a loud cracking sound. John crunched his muscles and winced even though there had been no contact. Peterson repeated this a few times, smirking all the time in the knowledge that anticipation sometimes has greater impact than actuality. When he was satisfied that he had got his swing right, he adjusted his stance and began.

With every lash that landed on his back, John prayed:

'Oh, Mawu-lisa, send God *Shakpana* to give him smallpox, so that he will stop beating me.'

But the whip continued to crack and tear into his flesh, and when he realised that the God of Smallpox had deserted him, he resorted to a device which he had used since childhood to escape from anything unpleasant. He fantasised about something else. Now, he thought of *bela,* the elephant, trampling Peterson into the ground before picking up his broken body with its trunk and tossing him high into the air. He saw in his mind an image of *kiniun,* the

23

lion, sitting and chewing contentedly on Peterson's whip-hand, having earlier attacked and disembowelled him. He conjured up an image of *sita,* the carpet viper, striking out at him and leaving two vampire-like holes on his foot, through which its venom would gush and cause blistering, swelling and bleeding, before snuffing his life out.

With each lash, came less pain. Then Peterson stopped. Close to unconsciousness, John thanked his three animal friends, but he couldn't see his back which looked every bit like a well-ploughed field over which a disc-harrow had crisscrossed, leaving deep furrows. He was laid up in the sick house for over a week, during which time the numbness gradually wore off before the pain returned with an intensity that left him screaming. This incident, excruciating though it was, represented good fortune for him, for, had it not been because of Bradley's need to hold on to his fast-dwindling stock of slaves, John could have been dismembered or killed.

Despite Bradley's promise to King Henry, the cruelty and debauchery at Plantation Hope, being endemic, continued, and his business faced financial ruin. The crop had failed because of poor husbandry and neglect and the other Planters called in their loans, which Bradley could only repay in slaves. He paid off King Henry with two hundred slaves, among whom was John.

One night, not many months later, Bradley Burnett, penniless, depressed and pox-ridden, hanged himself from a mango tree, the victim of his own profligacy. It was as though his sole purpose in thirty-six years of life had been to demonstrate to others the evils of intemperance. Suicide by hanging was not unusual, but nobody in the vicinity had witnessed a white Planter dangling from the end of a rope. Crowds of freemen, with largely expressionless faces, gathered in silence around the tree until the police arrived and dispersed them.

It was the time of year when the weather should have been placid; when cool, refreshing breezes should have been wafting through a temperate night. But that night the winds reached gale force and roared through the sugar belt, soughing, whistling and howling as they whipped through the trees and cane fields. Some said that the freak weather was nature's angry lament at the passing of Bradley's tortured soul.

Others said it was the sound of Planter Society breathing a collective sigh of relief.

Chapter Three

Plantations of varying sizes with exotic names such as, 'Albion', 'Adventure', 'Diamond' and 'Pilgrim's Rest', were dotted all along the fertile coasts of the British Caribbean territories - from British Guiana on the northern coast of South America through Trinidad, Barbados, Jamaica and a number of smaller islands in the Caribbean Sea, to British Honduras in Central America. Their purpose was to extract the juice of the sugarcane plant and convert it into sugar which was then sent to England. There, West Indian sugar met Indian tea in a prized fusion that graced the nation's tables and greatly profited the Coffee houses of the time. Sugar was a commodity that enriched all involved in its production and sale, except the slaves. Most of the sugar Plantations and, therefore, their slaves, were owned by people who lived in the United Kingdom and who left the management of these units to others, whose sole task was to make money - which they maximised by reducing costs to a minimum.

Albion was owned and managed by King Henry's father who left it to his three children when he died. The succession, however, was not without its problems, as Henry explained to his friend, Thomas Oliver.

'It's not an easy decision to make, Tom.'

'What do the others think?'

'I don't know; I really don't.'

'Haven't you contacted them?'

'I have; but I haven't heard anything.'

'Albion is a great asset; why wouldn't they want it to continue?' Asked Tom.

'It's not as simple as that.'

'Seems to me that you have three options.'

'Three?'

'Yes. One - you can sell it and divide the proceeds among the three of you. Two – you can leave it to be managed by an agent while you live a Bohemian lifestyle abroad, indulging your passion for research, or whatever.'

'Bohemian indeed!' Henry said, with a smile. 'And what's the third?'

'You can manage it; the three of you.'

Henry stroked his chin and took out his pipe and a pipe cleaner from his desk drawer. He was in an experimental stage, as the cigarettes he had smoked since his teenage days had left him with a rattling cough which he suspected irritated others more than it did himself.

'For me, selling would be a bit of a betrayal. Not only of all the hard work the old man put into Albion, but also of those who depend upon us for their living.'

'But once you sell, it will no longer be your concern,' said Tom.

'I know, but I can't just leave the slaves to someone unscrupulous who might abuse them. And while the Bohemian life has some appeal, I can never be an absentee landlord, like John Gladstone.'

'Why not? He is rich and powerful,' said Tom.

'At what cost? His agent puts the slaves to work every waking minute, with little food or rest in between, and with little concern for their welfare.' Henry was sitting on a straight-backed chair with one leg crossed over the thigh of the other. He was poking around in the bowl of his pipe with the pipe cleaner, which he threw into a bin with disgust when it seemed not to work. He then decided to bang the bowl on the heel of his boot somewhat harder than was necessary to dislodge most of the calcined deposits that had accumulated. 'Do you know that when his slaves are finished a day's work at one estate, they are moved to another to continue working?'

'You mean two shifts?'

'I mean two shifts.'

'Even in cane-cutting?'

'Especially in cane-cutting,' Henry replied.

'But he has often claimed that his Plantations are a model,' said Tom.

'As well he might, Tom. But it's not because of any first-hand experience. He sits on his arse in Scotland and lets morons like John MacLean manage his plantations and do whatever they want to the slaves. Gladstone is more concerned with his bank balance than the welfare of his slaves.'

Sitting opposite in an armchair, Tom watched Henry's face getting redder. He remembered that time when their headmaster had told William Peters, a clever and likeable ten-year old in their class, that he had to stop attending the school. When Henry heard that it was because the boy's father had died and his mother could no longer afford the school fees, he shouted, 'Unfair! That's unfair!' Then he went into a sulk for days.

'I can't believe that Gladstone doesn't ever visit his Plantations,' said Tom.

'He hasn't set foot on any of his Plantations, so he is totally dependent upon what his managers feed him.'

'You mean all that stuff that he told Parliament about slave-houses being made of hardwood frames, roofs covered with shingles and first-class medical facilities, are fictitious?'

'You don't have to take my word for it, Tom. Just pay a visit to Plantation Success and you'll see for yourself - if they allow you to visit the slave quarters!'

'Well, Henry, it seems that you have only one option left.'

'I know.' Henry filled his pipe and lit it up; he sucked on its bent stem and puffed out a stream of smoke which floated towards Tom. 'Sorry, Tom,' he said, as he waved the smoke away.

'Not at all, Henry. That smell reminds me of the freshly sawn timber when we used to play around the sawmills along the banks of the river as children. Remember how we used to hop from log to log?'

'Bloody wonder we never fell into the water and got crushed by the logs,' said Henry.

'We never realised how dangerous it was.'

'Days when we had no fear and no responsibility,' Henry said, looking into the distance.

'Do you know what the others might prefer?' Asked Tom.

'That's the problem. Father had hoped that Norman, being the eldest, would have followed in his footsteps, but when I went to see him in Hampshire before returning from England, he said he wanted nothing to do with sugar. Nothing at all; not even to put it in his tea.'

'That's a bit extreme,' said Tom.

'He said it's like drinking the blood of slaves.'

'Has he always been like this?'

'When we were growing up, I heard him arguing many times with father, and some of their arguments were quite heated. Elspeth and I often listened from under a bed, with her hand over my mouth.'

'What did they argue about?'

'Oh, things that hardly made sense to me. Norman often used language like 'un-Christian' and 'exploitation', which were Dutch to me. He left for England when I was about eight or nine. Mother often read his letters to us from her sick-bed.'

'Did you visit him regularly when you were there?'

'Once. At his Church in Hampshire. He struck me as a reasonable person, kind and generous in spirit, but he didn't say much about the old man; talked more about Mother. We were like strangers, but he did ask me about my plans after Oxford.'

'What did you tell him?'

'Couldn't tell him what I didn't know. I mentioned the possibility of teaching or doing research, and he seemed to think it was a good idea. He also suggested a period of travel as a way of broadening my horizons.'

'Seems as though he was trying to steer you away from Albion,' said Tom.

'Not directly; I don't think so. But he did talk about how stifled he felt growing up in an environment where he was expected to follow father without question, and about the iniquities of slavery and the plantation system.'

'Are you still in touch?'

'I did write to him after Father died, asking about what I should do with Albion, but I haven't heard a thing. I guess he's quite content running his ministry and not wanting anything to do with sugar.'

'And Elspeth?'

'Oh, you know how it is. She was never in the running, really. Not a job for a woman, the old man used to say. Mind you, I think she would make a good Planter; she's strong and determined,' Henry said.

He went quiet for a while and smiled. Then he continued.

'She practically brought me up because of Mother's illness, you know. She shows the same qualities in her campaign against slavery - following the abolitionists all over the place and latching on to their every word. I hear from her now and then from different parts of the world, but no reply to my letter about Albion. Neither of them would come near a sugar plantation, I'm afraid.'

'They seem to feel the same way as you do.'

'I'm afraid so, Tom, except that I'm the one left holding the baby.'

'It looks as if you have only one option, then.'

'It does, doesn't it?' Henry said.

'But if you do decide to manage Albion, how are you going to fit in with the other Planters, given your views?'

'It's more a question of how they will fit in with me. I think Albion is powerful enough to lead the others. Slavery is an iniquitous system, I know, but it will change sooner or later.'

'And in the meantime?'

'In the meantime, I'll stay and do what I can to run an efficient, but humane, business.'

'But...'

'I know... I know..., Tom, but I can't just set the slaves free. Where would they go? How would they live? They will only be caught and enslaved elsewhere. In any case, if Albion does anything radically different, like paying for labour, it will cause the collapse of other smaller Plantations and destroy many other lives, and I wouldn't like that.'

'It's a real dilemma,' said Tom.

'Not really. I could run Albion and still impose some of my values. There is no reason for slaves to be tortured and starved.'

'The others won't like it if you step out of line.'

'What will destroy the system they treasure so much is their own stubbornness, not my changes.'

'You'll be embarking on a mission then?'

'Call it that if you wish. Why not join me? You were always up for a fight, and your agricultural background would be a real asset.'

'But knowing that lot, it could get quite brutal; much

more than log-rolling.'

'All the more reason for us to stand together, like old times.'

'Hmm…,' said Tom. 'If you're the same person I grew up with, you'll need someone to temper your zeal.'

Chapter Four

Albion continued operations with King Henry at the helm and Tom Oliver responsible for field and factory operations. It was not long before Henry embarked upon radical changes which were designed to improve the welfare of the slaves, but which sent waves throughout the sugar belt that made him very unpopular with the Plantocracy.

Field slaves lived in crowded mud-floored, rat-infested hovels on the periphery of the cane fields, on land that was not suitable for sugar cane cultivation. Here they grew whatever food they could to sustain themselves, but only tubers such as, yams, sweet potatoes and dasheen survived in the rocky ground, and these formed the mainstay of their nutrition. They were also allocated rations of imported pickled and salted pork, beef and fish but this was often the bare minimum necessary for their sustenance. When King Henry doubled their rations, one of the Planters complained to Tom Oliver.

'Our slaves are now clamouring for the same, Tom, but if we followed, we would soon go bankrupt!'

'Think of it this way, man,' replied Tom. 'More food would give the slaves greater strength and energy, which would improve production and profits.'

'Horse shit!' Said the Planter.

While men-slaves like John were put to work in the fields to harvest the sugar cane, most of the women and children spent long hours clearing the fields of rocks and stones and keeping them free from weeds, always under the watchful eye of an overseer. For many, especially the younger women, their day was much longer. After working in the field, cleaning and weeding and generally satisfying the overseers' sadistic pleasures, they were then expected to gratify their sexual ones. Sometimes, such indulgence did not wait for the end of a day's work but took place during work, in the fields.

McKay was an overseer, a squat fellow with ginger hair and a quick temper, who spent most of his money and leisure time in the whorehouses and Chinese gambling dens in the city. He often turned up drunk for work and took his foul temper out on the slaves. One day, he beat up a young woman for resisting his advances and left her on the ground unconscious and bleeding. The other slaves surrounded him and there is no telling what they would have done, had King Henry not been passing nearby. He stopped his horse, dismounted, broke up the crowd, sent the woman to the sick house and dismissed McKay on the spot. News of this spread throughout the sugar belt and enraged the other Planters, who decided to deputise Robert Watford, owner of Plantation Waterloo, to discuss the matter with King Henry.

'Henry, I know you're new, but you can't dismiss an overseer just like that.'

'You should have seen what he did to the woman!' Said Henry.

'I can imagine. We all know McKay, man, but dismissing him summarily in front of the slaves sends out the wrong message and undermines our authority.'

'He's lucky I came along when I did. The slaves might have killed him because they were so worked up.'

'That's as may be, but he is one of ours, so we must protect him.'

'Bob, I have warned McKay many times for his drunkenness, brutality and absenteeism.'

'I know, Henry, but you've got to understand how things

34

work.' Watford said. 'Your father would have handled things with a softer touch if you get my meaning.'

'In what way, Bob?' Henry asked. 'What kind of softer touch?

'Well, he might have moved McKay to another section of the field until things had quietened down a bit; or he might have given him a stint in the mill, for instance,' Watford said.

'And who's to say he wouldn't have done the same thing again?' Henry asked.

'If he had, then your father would have asked one of us to take him in exchange for one of our more stable overseers. In this way, we are able to contain protests while protecting our own people.'

'So, McKay would have been free to carry on his violence elsewhere?'

'No, no. We would have spoken to him about his behaviour.'

'And how long would this game of musical chairs have continued? Until he killed somebody? Or would you then have moved him to one of the other islands?'

'Come, come Henry, you're exaggerating the problem.'

'No, Bob, I'm dealing with the problem instead of passing it on. McKay has no place working with people. He's a drunk and a rapist and he has no respect for human life.'

'But they're slaves, man! Where's the harm in a bit of fun. If he maims or kills them, then that's another matter. Can't have him destroying our property, eh!'

'I know one of you will employ McKay, but that's a matter for you. There's no place for that kind of person at the Albion I want to build.'

'I don't think you really understand how things work Henry. We have all got to stick together by doing the same things. But we'll talk again.'

When Henry related this to Tom Oliver, Tom said:

'You've gone and done it now, Henry. They'll be watching everything we do from now on.'

'I hope they copy us!' Henry replied, with a smile and a glint in his eye.

'What else have you got up your sleeve, Henry?'

'Nothing, really. Why do you ask?'

'I know you, and I can see it in your face. Come on - out with it.'

'Well, since you ask...I'm thinking of making Sunday a day of rest for the slaves.'

'Are you crazy?' Tom exploded. 'The Planters hate you enough as it is, what with the McKay thing and the increased rations. But this? This is madness!'

Henry said nothing for a few seconds, then he looked at Tom and said, 'I think it is inhuman for anybody to work for seven days without a break.'

'As do I, Henry, as do I. But I just think that now is not the time to do it!'

'Do you think I should discuss it with them before deciding?'

'I can't believe you! Do you think that will help? You know what they will say!'

'But surely they can see the wisdom of such an arrangement.'

'Don't be so naïve, Henry. All they will see is one day's loss of production. One day's loss of profits.'

Naïve or not, Henry disregarded Tom's advice and floated his novel idea at a meeting of the Planters. And all hell broke loose.

The heathens knew nothing about the significance of the Christian Sabbath, they said, and that being the case, there was nothing wrong with them slaving for seven days.

What on earth, they demanded, did the owner of Albion think he was playing at? When Henry pointed out that the day off was meant as a day of rest so that the slaves could regain their energy, they accused him of being a 'dangerous fucking liberal'.

Later, he said to Tom: 'Perhaps it wasn't wise to discuss it with them after all.'

After his brief flirtation with consultation, King Henry declared Sunday at Albion as a day of rest, an act much welcomed by the slaves but one which confirmed to the Planters that there was an enemy in their midst.

As time went by, King Henry applied his reforming zeal to some other practices that had taken root in the Plantation system. In many cases, pregnant women were kept working in the fields right up to full-term and gave birth on the ground, often in the mud. King Henry introduced a system whereby when a woman's pregnancy was confirmed, she was removed from the fields after five months and given more sedentary tasks indoors like sewing and mending bags so that she wouldn't run the risk of miscarriage.

Another commonplace practice was the treatment of those who had become disabled or rendered unable to work for any other reason. Such people were deemed a liability and were evicted from the Plantation. Deprived of the security and support of the Plantation system, they were left to fend for themselves, but many found it impossible to cope on their own and died prematurely like domesticated animals cast out into the wild.

However, King Henry decided that he would keep them on at the Plantation and give them other work to do, such as, chores in the children's gangs, in transport, or in the mill - depending on the nature and extent of their disability.

'After all,' he said to Tom, 'Most of these injuries are

work-related and we can't just chuck them out like that.'

Cane-cutting was a frantic operation, and the pace with which the slaves were driven by the overseers meant that there were many accidents, some minor, but most disabling. One day, as John was busy chopping away, he felt a sharp pain at the back of his foot. When he turned around, he saw blood spurting from his heel and another cutter mumbling apologetically. John looked on, fascinated, as a red pool collected on the ground and bubbled away as if it were cooking, before it slowly sank and disappeared into the grey-black soil. His eyes rolled about in his head and he collapsed and lost consciousness. He was rushed to the sick house where he was sewn up and kept for over two weeks, after which Doc Munro deemed him disabled, not just because his Achilles tendon had been severed but because the blade of the cutlass had also chopped through his heel bone, which rendered him 'unsafe and unfit' for work in the cane cutting gangs.

Some weeks later, as King Henry was riding along a track in the fields, he noticed a broad-shouldered muscular man with a pronounced limp surrounded by children who were pointing at his foot and giggling. They followed him every time he tried to limp away, and they giggled and pointed; pointed and giggled. When King Henry returned to the office, he said to Tom:

'I saw big John with the kids in field twelve. What's he doing there, Tom?'

'It was the only place I could put him after his accident,' replied Tom.

'What about the mill?'

'Too dangerous. Could cause accidents – the way he walks.'

'Hmm… he looks unhappy', observed Henry.

Tom arched his right eyebrow but said nothing.

'The kids are running behind him as if he is the Pied Piper, but they seem to be poking fun at him,' Henry said.

'Well, that's one way of getting rid of the field rats, I suppose,' said Tom.

'Seriously, though,' said Henry, 'his experience at the hands of Bradley and his lot was terrible and it can't be a nice thing to have a bunch of children laughing at your disability.'

'I know. But it's a difficult one. I can't put him with the women or with transport.'

'Hmm,' said King Henry, 'I was thinking...Philip is getting too old to handle the horses on his own and he could do with some help.'

'But John doesn't know anything about horses.'

'He could understudy Philip, and if he does well...'

'I don't know...,' mumbled Tom. 'I really don't know...'

'Well, try him out and let's see.'

The next day, in a move that caused him great disquiet, John was sent to work at the stables. He wondered if this was what his life was meant to be – a slave to be beaten and chastised; to be put to work under the fiercest conditions which disabled him and caused him to be dumped - the shames of all shames - in the children's gang. And now a tender of animals! He mused that this latest might be an improvement on the previous one, but even though he loved animals, he had never been near a horse before and he was afraid of those bulging eyes, the tongue that snaked out from between those large yellow teeth - and those strong powerful hooves. He recalled that when he was a boy he had once freed a wolf cub from a cluster of nettles that had enmeshed it, but, well...this was a different matter.

The slave who looked after the stables was called Philip. He was a stooped old man with a full head of white hair and a long white beard which reached down to his chest. His cheeks were sunken, not only because of his age but also because he had lost most of his teeth. He squinted when he spoke, not out of habit, but because one eye had been completely covered by the eggshell of a cataract and the other was half-masked by the same affliction. He had been a slave since he was a boy and had worked in the fields until his increasing fragility had rendered him a liability there.

'Come, let me show you the horses,' he said.

John followed him towards the stables, still not sure.

'This is Herod', Philip said, as he patted a roan on the cheek and allowed it to lick his hand. 'He is quiet and doesn't give any trouble.'

They walked to the next box.

'This one is Tomahawk. He is frisky and likes to jump up on the ladies,' Philip said, as he caressed the horse's face.

'You have to be careful of this grey,' Philip said, walking towards another box. 'His name is Agouti and he likes to bite people…sometimes he bites the other horses, too.' Philip rubbed the animal's head but was careful not to let his hand wander any lower.

This was all new to John. There were ten horses in all, and Philip proudly rattled off their names and described their personality as though they were people. This was going to take some getting used to, he thought, and gave an involuntary shudder at the thought of Agouti's teeth sinking into his flesh.

Finally, as they approached the last box, Philip said, 'And this is The Black Thunderbolt. '

The colt standing in the stall was jet black and stood seventeen hands high. His ears were pricked and his eyes alert as he looked inquiringly at John.

'He is only three, and he is everybody's favourite, but

only Massa Henry rides him. Remember that. We call him 'Blackie', Philip said, as he rubbed the horse's head.

Blackie neighed and nodded his head a few times. And John, without hesitating, reached out and patted the horse on its head. Later, in his quietude, he tried to rationalise why he had acted so impulsively by abandoning the fear and caution which he had felt towards these strange animals and indulged in such an act of overfamiliarity. He could find no explanation.

What fascinated him more than the horses, were the stables in which they lived. For each horse, there was a spacious stall whose walls were painted with a glossy finish; the floor was covered with a grass matting upon which they could roll around in comfort; there were lanterns outside each stall so that they would not be afraid of the darkness of night; and even the uprights in the boxes were all padded for protection against injury, in case they smashed into them. And, for some reason, there were no rats running around the stables.

John and Philip shared a white-washed outhouse with two wooden cots next to the stables. It was spacious, far more than anywhere in which John had lived in captivity, and even though there were no mattresses, the cots were far enough off the ground to avoid the attention of rats. The mud floor was covered over by wooden planks, with just the odd space revealing strips of earth, so that when it rained, the underfoot conditions remained largely dry. There, when they had finished their chores, they ate, smoked, and chatted by candlelight. Here, they told each other about their experiences - of places from which they had been wrenched and of people from whom they had been separated. Philip was from a different tribe, but the circumstances of his abduction were similar, except that he still seemed aggrieved that it had been carried out with the help of his own tribesmen. He showed John his brand, 'VJ', which was on his shoulder. He said he was sold to King Henry many years earlier after his owner, Vernon James, had died.

'The Massa might change, but the mark will always stay,' he said softly.

John showed him the brand on his palm and described his experiences under Bradley Burnett at Plantation Hope.

'They say that man was the devil himself,' Philip said. 'I was lucky to come to Albion. We are still slaves, but King Henry is kind.'

He explained how he had been captured when he was ten and put to work for a few years as a water boy for the cane cutters before being put to cut cane himself.

'That was hard work, man,' Philip said.

'Yes,' replied John, 'but at least it is man's work. When they put me to work in the children's gang, I felt like killing myself - all those annoying children following me around and staring and laughing at my limp.'

'Maybe they were just curious,' said Philip.

'Maybe, but I didn't like it. I'm glad King Henry put me here. I might not know anything about horses but what I know is that anything is better than working with children.'

'And I'm glad they sent you to help me,' said Philip. 'I'm getting too old to fetch and carry and I'm getting blind. Sometimes, when Tomahawk gets too frisky, I can't handle him. But don't worry, I will teach you all I know about horses.'

Philip taught him all about the body parts of horses and how they functioned, and how the animals thought and behaved. He even explained what it meant when they did things with their bodies, like what Blackie was trying to say when he nodded his head a few times in quick succession or pricked his ears or pinned them back, or when he pawed the ground. He explained that horses were born to run and if stabled for too long, they became moody and fractious.

John did not immediately grasp the implications of this until one day, when the old man led Herod out of his box, put on a saddle and bridle and said, as he tightened the girth, 'Now, mount up.'

'But…but I don't know how,' stammered John.

'You will soon learn. It's easy with Herod.'

Philip brought a stool and put it next to the horse. He demonstrated how John should mount up and, having tried and fallen off a few times, John was finally sitting on top of the horse, looking quite uncomfortable. He had seen the overseers on horse-back and he had thought how masterful they appeared as he looked up at them, but now, from his perch, now that he was there, he realised how far away he was from safety and he felt that he would break something if he fell. Another thing that surprised him, was how big the animal's head was. But that was not all. Herod, though he was docile, had a habit of throwing his head back every few strides and John knew that any contact between the horse's head and his own could be disastrous, so he sat with his spine ramrod straight and his head tilted back, a posture which amused Philip.

'Relax, man, you have to relax,' he instructed. 'Horses can feel you, you know.' John let his shoulders drop a bit, but he never relaxed his grip on the reins.

'Relax your knees too. Don't squeeze the horse's belly too much. How would you like it if somebody squeezed your belly?'

John's eyes took on a look of pain as he recalled Bradley Burnett's mongoose assistant poking him in the gut. He eased his knees off a bit.

Philip showed him how to get Herod walking and, in the days that followed, he also showed him how to get him to canter and gallop. John's enthusiasm knew no limit and there were times when Philip had to remind him that exercising the horses was only one of his many duties. He grew in confidence and Philip reported to Tom that he was getting on well with the horses. Tom reported this to King Henry, who said:

'Never know till you try, Tom.'

One day, John said to Philip, 'I think I'm ready for Tomahawk.' Philip looked at him and smiled.

'At least I want to... to try...,' John said, trying to row back on his overconfidence by introducing a touch of humility.

'Ok. But you must be careful when you approach a mare or filly. If you don't control his head, he's going to try to mount them while you are still sitting on his back, and I don't think you'll like it. If you want to look at the sky,' Philip chuckled, 'there are more comfortable ways of doing it.'

John rode Tomahawk and reported that he was no trouble at all. Philip smiled and shook his head.

Agouti, though, was a different proposition. He was named after the tailless South American rodent because he had got his tail entangled in a wire fence while he was frolicking in a field as a frisky yearling, and his frenzied attempts to free himself had resulted in the lower part of his tail becoming so badly damaged that it had to be docked. One day, as John was harnessing him, he bit him on the upper arm. It was not an entirely unfriendly gesture, though it hurt like hell for a few days and the teeth mark, embedded in a band of red, remained for much longer. This happened every time he tried to harness the horse. The horse seemed to think it was an act of fondness, but John was mindful of the damage those powerful jaws could do, so he set about trying to work out ways in which he could solve the problem. As the biting occurred when Agouti was being harnessed, John focused on this and he soon worked out that if he could have an attachment put at the end of the bridle, like a kind of muzzle, this might solve the problem. He explained his idea to Philip.

'I'm sure the blacksmith can make something. But there is still one problem,' Philip said.

'What's that?' Asked John.

'He's still going to bite you when you try to put the thing on him.'

'That's true. I didn't think about that.' John agreed.

This problem occupied his mind for days. Then, after some weeks of trying to solve the problem and being bitten by Agouti, he announced to Philip:

'I've got it! I've got it!'

Philip looked up and smiled.

'What is the one thing that Agouti likes most?' John demanded.

'Biting?' The old man answered.

'No, no!' Protested John, 'The other thing, man.'

'Oh,' replied Philip. 'You mean sugar?'

'Sugar!' Exclaimed John. 'You notice when you give him sugar how he takes his time tasting and eating it without seeing or hearing anything else?'

'Yes, but I can't see how it's going to help.'

'Well,' said John, 'When he is concentrating on the sugar, I could creep up and harness him.'

Philip listened. He bit his lip as if considering what John had said, then he nodded in understanding. 'Show me,' he said.

John grabbed a handful of sugar and gave it to the horse, who greedily snatched the sugar, along with his hand. He cried out and pulled away, wringing his hand in pain. Philip fell to the floor and rolled around, doubled up in laughter. Amidst his giggles, he said:

'You must watch closely next time. When I give him sugar, I don't use one hand. I spread both palms together so that he can't bite me because his mouth isn't big enough.'

His hand still smarting, John said, 'I'm going to put the sugar on the spade and then feed it to him.'

'That's a good idea,' Philip said, as he stifled a laugh.

Chapter Five

John cocked his head and listened to the distant thunder of galloping hooves. He guessed that there were three horses – no, no – four – yes, four horses approaching, and that the speed with which they were being pushed meant they would soon be upon him. He was getting quite good at this game, considering that he had only been working with horses for a few months. He had sent out four horses for general duties, but they must have been commandeered for another purpose, he thought to himself. Every time this happened, the horses would return blowing harder than a blacksmith's bellows, with their sweat - a yellowish-white foam, like vanilla ice cream, billowing out from under their saddles and between their legs.

The lead horse, Blackie, was ridden by King Henry. The other riders were a motley group of white men of different shades of tan and puce who held different positions of importance in the Plantation's hierarchy. Their khaki shirts and shorts and parts of their faces were covered in mud and they blew harder than the horses. One of them, a Field Assistant called Tubby Spencer, was purple in the face and he gasped and wheezed as if he was in the throes of a heart attack.

John looked on as Tubby began his dismount. He felt sorry for the horse, who looked relieved as Tubby decanted his seventeen-stone carcass from its back onto the ground. He wondered why Tubby didn't ride a mule instead. True, they were slower than the horse but they were much sturdier and shorter so they could take his weight while allowing him to mount and dismount with greater ease.

Still, it wasn't his business; and perhaps Tubby preferred a faster conveyance so that he could jiggle off some of his flab as the horse moved.

The riders peeled off sheets of mud from their clothes and faces, threw them onto the ground and stamped vigorously in trying to dislodge any caked mud that might have got stuck to the bottoms of their rubber boots. The four tracker-dogs, their tongues lolling out, panted as if they were asthmatic, but they kept close to the horses until one of the riders signalled for them to stand down. Freed from their responsibilities, they rushed to the river, less than fifty yards away, where they noisily lapped up the water. The horses would have to wait for a drink as they had to be cooled down with buckets of water and wrapped in their blankets first.

'Saddle up another three, John; I'll sit this one out,' King Henry said out of breath. 'Two run-aways. Seen anything?'

'No, Sah, Massa Henry,' John replied.

'Getting too old for this,' King Henry said to no one in particular. He was about forty-five, tall - about six something - with blue-grey eyes and fair, mousey-coloured hair. He was slim, but the bulging biceps which strained against his shirt sleeves and the absence of any trace of fat around his neck and torso suggested that chasing after escaped slaves on horseback should not have been too taxing.

The men slapped their clothes with their hats and created a dust cloud which made them choke and splutter, then they walked in the direction of the Great House, where King Henry lived.

John brought out three fresh horses and saddled and tethered them in wait for the return of the riders, then he washed down the spent horses one by one, covered them with their blankets, gave each of them a bucket of water and a bundle of hay and left them in the sun to dry. The last one was Blackie. John plunged the cloth into the bucket and swirled it around so that it soaked up the soapy water. He wrung it to expel the excess liquid before slapping it onto the flank of the colt, the mixture of soap and the sweat of the animal producing a grey-white lather which was slightly slimy. John flicked it away. He repeated this until the green grass on the ground was speckled with mushrooms of froth, the tiny bubbles of which popped silently and disappeared into the earth. The colt stood still, occasionally nodding and neighing as if he was enjoying the ritual. Sometimes, when John bent down to soak the cloth in the bucket, Blackie nuzzled him and caused him to lose his balance.

After completing this part of his chore, John sat down on a stool, took out a half-smoked cheroot from the top pocket of his shirt, lit it up and inhaled. He shielded his eyes with his open palm and looked up at the sun, which was almost directly overhead. It was an unconscious gesture as time was of no great importance and the routine tasks, like those he had to perform every day, had a life of their own. He finished smoking, threw the butt onto the ground, and picked up the brush. Blackie whinnied. John started to brush the horse's dry body with short brisk strokes punctuated by long sweeping ones, until the horse's coat gleamed in the sunlight as if it were a cloak of pure polyvinyl chloride. John stood back and admired him. There were ten horses in his care, but Blackie stood out among them. He had strong hindquarters, and a handsome head out of which peered eyes that showed an understanding bordering on intelligence, and ears that moved as if to express his thoughts, his every mood. John often heard the white men talking about the colt.

'Pure Thoroughbred, you know.'

'Bred for speed and stamina.'

'Can't get better than that.'

'Blah, blah, blah... racehorse.'

In addition to being even-tempered, Blackie could run fast. Philip had told John that only the previous year, he had left the opposition standing in the King's Cup, a horse race of great status among the Plantations which highlighted the celebrations that were held all over the land after the harvesting of the sugar cane crop. The 'crop-over', as it was called, was a bacchanalian festival of horse and mule races, music and dancing, and rum-drinking and fornication. It was a day off from work - one of the few in the lives of the slaves.

The grooming over, it was time for Blackie's feed. John filled a nosebag and put it around the horse's neck then he patted him on his flank as a signal for him to start eating.

The riders returned, clean, refreshed, and ready to continue their quest. King Henry had had a change of clothes; he was wearing a red shirt over white trousers and he looked relaxed, which suggested that his labours were done for the day. The others mounted the fresh animals, Tubby's face expressing gratitude that John had given him a shorter horse and had also put a low bench next to it.

'Remember now,' said King Henry, 'don't go into the river. If they disappear there, let them be. I can't afford to lose good men. But if you catch them, there must be no violence.'

The men rode off, accompanied by the four rested dogs which yapped and yelped with gusto in anticipation of the chase.

The chase was often futile but on those rare occasions when the runaways were caught, the standard practice among plantation owners was to thrash them so close to death that they were no more of any use. Often, they were tortured, dismembered, or hanged, which was a cost to their owner, but one which they were prepared to pay as a deterrent to the disobedience, revolt and rebellion which were always present. Each Plantation was expected to follow these agreed practices, but the forms of discipline at Albion were less harsh even though King Henry made a great show of pursuing escaped slaves and often boasted that his men had caught and disciplined runaways in the time-honoured fashion.

John looked on at the departing posse of Planters. He stood up, hunched his shoulders, slung a towel over one, picked up his buckets and hopped towards the river.

Once, an exclamation mark.

Now, a comma.

He reached the bank of the river and climbed down the slope to the wooden landing. His heel was feeling stiff and painful this day as it always did on very hot and humid days. He rested his buckets and sat on the edge, letting his bare feet dangle in the cool soothing water. After a few minutes, the muscles in his jaws, always tense when he walked, started to relax. The current was a bit strong and the water eddied as it moved silently along, taking bits of wood and trees it had picked up along the way. Occasionally, there was a dead fish propelled by the current as if it were alive, though its white belly, floating uppermost, testified to its defunct state. A four-eyed fish appeared stationary against the pull of the current, its top eyes perched on its head like a swimmer's goggles, the lower ones seeking out any prey below the water line. Above, there was not a cloud in sight; only a pair of swallows, coursing along on some invisible roller-coaster, disturbed the expanse of purplish-blue. In the water, just below the opposite bank, a cluster of hollow reeds swayed, nudged by the water, and massaged by a gentle breeze.

John spent much of his time here because the river evoked memories of a time and a state of contentment long past. He lit up his cheroot stub, inhaled and closed his eyes. He listened to the tweets of the birds and the gentle soporific lapping of the river against its banks. He dozed off for a while, and when he opened his eyes, he noticed that something in the idyll had changed. Two of the hollow reeds, which had become detached from the cluster, were moving along with the current. This, of itself, was not unusual, as reeds were always being uprooted and taken downstream. What was different about these, though, was that even though they had been uprooted, they were moving vertically to the water. He sighed and shook his head. It was going to be a long day for Tubby Spencer and the others slave hunters.

The river was a favourite route of escape for the slaves. It was long, so it was not easy for the hunters to predict at which point they would enter, nor where they might be when the current was fast. But it was also deep, and only the strongest swimmers survived. Many of the runaways who the Planters assumed had successfully escaped, had instead been dragged under by the strong current only for their bloated bodies to be discovered days later floating somewhere along the route of the river, all fish-nibbled and bird-pecked.

The river was even more perilous for the Planters on horseback because only the sturdiest horse was able to cope with the depth and the strong current, and even if they somehow managed to survive, their riders would be so tired that they would have no advantage of speed over the fugitives. Above all, the river masked the scent of the slaves and frustrated the tracker dogs, causing them to run around in circles as if they were chasing their own tails.

The objective of the runaways was always to reach the mountains, which offered the safety of an impregnable citadel, but it was a long and tortuous journey because, by using the river current to help them along, they had to move away from the mountains towards the flat muddy shores of the ocean. In order for them to get to the mountains, they would then have to double back by picking their way through the mosquito-infested mangrove swamps and the deep, soft, squelching mud that could suck a man under, slowly, inch by inch, unselfishly allowing him enough time to scream, to reflect on his life, and to pray, if he was so disposed, before the potage of grey mud began to seep into his mouth and then his nostrils and, finally, as an act of mercy, to cover his eyes so that he could not witness his own passing.

Long and arduous though this escape route was, it protected the runaways from the posse, for no white man in his right senses, having heard tales of how the muddy graveyard showed no partiality towards beast nor man, black nor white, would risk himself or his horse in that morass.

Once in the mountains, the slaves were relatively safe as they could easily spot and repel any pursuers with rocks and pieces of wood. But a successful escape into the mountains was one thing. Survival in the thin air, where little grew and only the hardiest of reptiles and the odd goat managed to live, was quite another.

Chapter Six

No one had ever taken the time to teach John anything, so he was grateful for Philip's patience; and Philip, who had no kin, was glad for his company because John was gentle, respectful and willing. He was also a natural with the horses. The two men had a tacit agreement on the division of labour. Philip swept out the passageways and repaired the tack while John fetched water from the river, mucked out the stables and exercised the animals. John also did the heavy lifting and held the more unruly horses while Philip extracted stones from their hooves.

They did the cooking on a fireside covered by a shed next to the outhouse. It was a simple oblong thing with two holes for the pans and an opening below for the firewood. It was made of mud, which became rock-hard like pottery after the heat of the first fire had evaporated all its water; maintenance of the structure thereafter being done by the application of cow dung to keep it moist so that it would not fracture.

King Henry lived in the Great House, which was about a hundred yards from the stables. While there were some Planters who criticised him for being too soft, he was very popular among others and those of the social class who ran the country. He regularly hosted parties which were attended by most of these important people and, on one occasion, the guests had included the Governor, the Surveyor General for the region, the Commander of Her Majesty's Armed Forces, and the Commissioner of Police. Discussions, as always, centred on current problems, such as rebellions, security, the rising cost of slaves and other commodities, the growing tide of anti-slavery sentiment both at home and abroad and strategies for tackling them - all aimed at securing and perpetuating the Plantation system. Never far from the ruminations of such august gatherings was what abolition would mean to the labour supply and what contingency plans might be put in place if the slaves were to leave the plantations in large numbers.

News of a party at the Great House was always greeted with anticipation by John and Philip because one of the maids would usually bring some left-overs for them the next day; not that either of them was a bad cook, but there was only so much that even the most skilled and creative chef could do with pickled meat and ground provisions. The leftovers from the Great House consisted of meat and bread, fresh vegetables from King Henry's well-tended gardens and a variety of cakes and puddings.

The highlight for John, however, was Maria, one of the maids who sometimes brought the food. She was about twenty, some ten years younger than he; she was petite, about five three, pretty and chatty - very much the opposite to John, who spoke with economy and whose limp had reduced him to a surly five-seven-or-eight from his previous six feet. Whenever she brought the food, Philip would take a cake and make some excuse to leave the outhouse, mumbling about something or other that needed doing at the stables, for which John was grateful.

On one of these days, following a party, John was returning with his buckets after communing with the river. His limp was more pronounced because the coolness of the river's water had not done much to ease the soreness of his foot. As he approached the outhouse, he heard voices - one of them distinctly female. His heartbeats quickened at the thought of seeing Maria, so he plunked down his buckets, straightened his clothes, preened himself, and tried to correct his limp as much as he possibly could. He pushed back his shoulders and tried to stand erect, something which he achieved for a moment or two before reverting to his natural slouch, then he propelled himself forward, all the time gritting his teeth and clenching his fists because of the pain. He reached the door and steadied himself, something which was not easily achievable given the throbbing in his chest and the rushing around of his blood, but when he opened the door, his heart sank, because he realised that the woman who was chatting with Philip was not Maria. Even though she was dressed in a maid's uniform and had her back to him, he knew, because she was taller and slimmer than Maria and the way she spoke was different. As he shut the door, she looked at him then she began to turn away, but she looked back quickly and stared for a few seconds before turning and addressing Philip, 'Don't forget, King Henry wants three horses in the morning, including Blackie.'

Then she left.

'Hee, hee,' tittered Philip. 'She is too smart, that one.'

'Who is she?' Asked John.

'Her name is Elizabeth, but they call her Queenie.'

'She speaks like an English woman,' said John.

'Oh, yes,' said Philip. 'But it wasn't always so. She used to work in the fields where she was beaten up by a wicked overseer called Mac-something or other, so King Henry sacked him and moved her to the House to look after his sick wife. That's how she learnt to speak English like that.'

'She looked at me in a strange way.'

'Oh, she does that to all slaves. After King Henry's wife died, she became in charge of his household and all the house slaves, so she thinks she is better than slaves like us.'

'No,' John mumbled, 'it's not that; it's something

different.'

For a few days, John's behaviour changed; he said less than was usual, even for him, and he brooded, sometimes forgetting to do things, sometimes doing the wrong things, and sometimes taking a long time to do others.

Philip understood; he understood that there was a place in a slave's mind that was locked away, a secret cache of memories and emptiness, which only he could enter, and which could sometimes colour his mood without him being conscious.

'It's time, you know,' he said to John one morning.

'Uh? Time for what?' John asked abstractedly.

'Time for you to do what you have been dying to do,' Philip replied. John shot him a quizzical look.

'Time to ride Blackie,' Philip said.

'But... you said that only...'

'Yes, only Massa Henry rides him for work and races. But we've still got to exercise him, you know.'

This, as Philip had hoped, wrenched John out of his trance-like state. While nothing John did could ever be described as jaunty, it would be fair to say that he walked up to Blackie's box with something akin to a spring in his impaired step. When Blackie saw him, he whinnied and tossed his head about. John took him out, patted him on his flank and rubbed his head. He threw a saddle on his back and tightened the girth, which was easy, because Blackie stood still like a little child who knew that this was a precondition to him being allowed out to play. Putting on a bridle, though, proved a bit tricky, as the horse kept nuzzling John as if he was telling him to hurry up with the last bit of his attire. John led him out and mounted him, then he moved him off at a canter with a click of his tongue. There was no need to use the boot or the whip, as the horse understood his signals and obeyed the slightest pull on the reins.

After a short while, they reached the left bank of the river and John double-clicked him into a gallop. They breezed along the full length of the bank against the flow of the water and headed towards the mountains, the horse's long black mane flowing in the wind, occasionally flying into John's face and tickling him. When they reached the foothills of the mountains, John dismounted and sat in the shade of a star-apple tree, smiling, while Blackie grazed nearby. He fell asleep and dreamt that he was lying upon rocks under a clear sky, listening to children laughing and playing, women chatting, and bodies plunging into the water. And of a wounded bird taking off into the sky in fits and spurts and disappearing forever into the vast unknown. When Blackie nudged him awake and he opened his eyes, he looked perplexed.

The sun had already begun to wester, and the sky had started to take on an apricot hue. He jumped up and mounted Blackie, who galloped back along the river's bank, flowing in symmetry with the river and swerving to avoid holes and rocks in the ground to keep John on an even keel. John sat motionless looking at the water as if he was trying to see what lay beneath. He was trying to recall his dream, but it flitted between light and darkness like a will o' the wisp, whispering and teasing, *now you see me; now you don't, now you see me; now you don't,* as the hand of his mind tried to grasp the gossamer snatches of illumination, which seeped through his fingers and disappeared like mist. Suddenly, he felt himself jolted as Blackie's rhythm, hitherto elegant and graceful, became jagged and irregular. He realised that in going into the cobwebbed arsenal of his memories, he had unconsciously stiffened his upper body and rounded his shoulders, which had transmitted his deep sadness to the animal like an electric current which paralysed the horse for a few strides. He quickly corrected his posture by taking a few deep breaths. He opened his shoulders, and, in a combination of apology and reassurance, he patted the horse's head. Blackie snorted, lengthened his stride, and sailed in the air - a flying phenomenon without wings.

When they arrived back at the stables, John went about his chores with speed, trying to complete all his tasks that had been delayed because he had been away for so long with Blackie.

'What do you think makes him special - different from the others?' Philip asked.

'I don't know... you mean... apart from his speed?'

'Yes, I can see how you change when you ride him. It's like you're in a different place. Like you're dreaming. Like when you see Maria.'

John lowered his eyes and shifted his stance. The slight trace of a smile that had begun to play around his mouth when Maria was mentioned, quickly gave way to a frown.

'I don't know what you're talking about,' he said.

'I might be going blind but I'm not stupid; I can feel these things. Now tell me about Blackie.'

Relieved, John said, 'When I sit on him, I feel like I'm part of him. I don't look down and think about how far away the ground is from where I am sitting, like I do when I sit on the other horses. It's like I'm standing on it - on the ground – if you know what I mean. When I want him to go left or right or to trot or gallop, I just think it and it happens. It's like I'm the one who is moving. I don't know if you understand...'

He looked at Philip. The old man said nothing; he just smiled, put a hand on John's shoulder and squeezed gently.

Chapter Seven

The sugar cane plant takes about six months to a year to mature. During its growth cycle, it is watered and kept free from insect or other damage until it reaches maturity. Then the fields are set on fire. Why, one might reasonably ask, would anybody want to commit such an act of seeming stupidity by burning something that they had so tenderly and lovingly cultivated?

Burning gets rid of the sharpness of the leaves and makes it easier and safer for harvesting without injury. it also gets rid of poisonous snakes such as rattlers, which inhabit the fields because of the richness of rodent and insect life found there. However, the primary reason for burning the fields is that fire improves the sucrose content of the sugarcane stalks, thereby ensuring that the sugar yield is maximised.

Slaves were forced into a burnt field as soon as it had cooled so that the cane could be cut and sent to the mill as quickly as possible before the sucrose degraded. There, the stalks were crushed by rollers powered by animals, and the resulting juice was then boiled until it was reduced to crystals, which were then bagged and stored in warehouses for shipment to England where they were refined for British domestic use and for export.

But sugar cane was not all that the workers reaped. Fields on fire discharge carbon monoxide, methane, nitrogen and sulphur oxides into the atmosphere, and the inhalation of these noxious elements give rise to a variety of respiratory ailments which cause protracted suffering and early death. At a time when environmental and welfare concerns were non-existent or trumped by the need to maximise profits, slaves were the canaries of the coal mines; they were the guinea pigs, the mice and the rats of the science laboratories.

The end of the harvesting signalled many celebratory activities, culminating in horse and mule races at the local racetrack. The riders of the animals in these races were all white and included Planters, overseers and local whites from Plantations all over the country. The competition was fierce, and the highlight of the day's racing was the King's Cup, which not only rewarded the winner with a substantial purse but bestowed upon the winning Plantation a fame far more valuable than money. The race was run over a mile and a half (two laps of the small track) and was open to horses of all ages. It had been won by 'The Black Thunderbolt' the previous year. ridden by King Henry, and he was entered for the forthcoming race. However, a repeat of that performance was doubtful as rumour had it that there were two horses on other Plantations that were even better. Plantation Plymouth had a speedy three-year-old called 'Fleetwood' and Plantation Buccaneers' Cove had an inmate called 'Hercules', which had stamina in abundance. If this duo threatened Albion's superiority, what happened to King Henry dealt it a deadly blow.

Some months before the event, King Henry was riding out in the cultivation when his horse reared up and threw him onto the ground. People could not believe that such a thing could happen to a master horseman until a worker, who was in the vicinity, said that he had seen a monster rattlesnake, with fangs longer than a cutlass blade, standing taller than the horse and threatening it, which caused the horse to panic and throw King Henry on to the ground. King Henry later denied that there was any snake in evidence and that it was a freak accident which resulted in him breaking an arm and his spine, leaving him paralysed below the waist. The prognosis, which shocked and saddened everyone, was that he would never walk again. Thereafter, he was confined to a wheelchair, from which he continued to run Albion with the help of Tom Oliver. The worker, who had claimed that he had seen the giant snake, was consigned to light duties in and around the factory because of his mental state.

While King Henry accepted, somewhat philosophically, that his disability was down to fate, one problem dogged him. Who would ride Blackie in the King's Cup?

Tom had recommended one of the younger overseers, a capable horseman named Robert Wyatt, a descendant of a long line of horsemen who had served the Plantocracy at one time or another. On the first occasion that Wyatt tried to ride Blackie, the horse refused to move, even though Wyatt had booted him till it hurt them both. The next day, the horse consented to move off, but ignored Wyatt's urgings for him to canter. On the third occasion, Wyatt cantered the horse then tried to get it to gallop by booting and booting it, but the horse stubbornly refused to change pace. In frustration, Wyatt cracked the whip across Blackie's withers and the horse bucked and kicked until it dislodged him and caused him to fall flat on his backside.

'That's it!' Wyatt said to Tom, tossing his whip on to Tom's desk.

'What's the matter?' Asked Tom.

'That stupid horse is a devil! It can't win a three-legged race.'

'That horse won the Cup last year in record time.'

'Someone must have rubbed cow-itch on its balls to speed it up,' spat Wyatt.

'Don't talk nonsense,' said Tom.

Tom reported this setback to King Henry, who pursed his lips and said nothing. He was staring into the distance.

'Well, what do you think, Henry?' Said Tom.

'About what? Oh, sorry, Tom, I wasn't with you for a moment there.'

'About entering Tomahawk, instead.'

'You're joking, Tom!' King Henry said.

'Why? Young Wyatt gets on well with him.'

'Maybe, but you know how coltish he gets when he sees a filly or mare. He just wouldn't pass them.'

'Tomahawk is fast – not as fast as Blackie, I agree – but fast enough to go to the front and not be distracted by the women's backsides,' said Tom.

'If what they say is true, then the pigeon-catcher at Pilgrim's Rest and the juggernaut at Buccaneer's Cove would eat Tomahawk for breakfast.' Henry replied.

'Perhaps we should stay out this year, then.'

'Out of the question! We've never missed a King's Cup,' said Henry.

'There's always a first time.'

'Not for the King's Cup, there isn't. No. No! Albion isn't going down without a fight.'

'I know how important it is, Henry, but I can't see what else we can do. It's better to stay out than to get beaten. The other Planters would understand that it is because of your injury.'

'I really don't give a damn what they think, Tom!'

'Well, if Blackie can't run and Tomahawk is not the answer, what can we do, Henry? Henry? You've got that look in your eyes again! What plot are you hatching now?'

'You know, Tom, there might be a way out,' King Henry said, biting his bottom lip and frowning as if an idea was beginning to form in his mind. 'Yes, I think there just... might... be.'

'What's that, then?' Asked Tom.

Henry stirred his coffee and wiped the spoon on the edge

of the cup before putting it to rest upon the saucer. He sat back in his wheelchair and stared at Tom.

'John. John can ride Blackie,' he said, looking past Tom as if the rest of his plan was materialising from the air, somewhere beyond Tom's shoulder.

Something had sucked the blood from Tom's face.

'Well, Tom, what do you think?' Asked Henry.

Silence.

'Tom?'

Tom ran his fingers through his thick black hair; he rubbed a hand along a plump cheek and looked Henry straight in his eyes. 'Now, who's joking, Henry?' He stammered.

'I'm dead serious, Tom.'

'I can't believe it! This is ridiculous, even from you!'

'I know how it sounds, Tom, but I think it can be done.'

'But how? Slaves are not allowed to attend the races, much less ride a horse!'

'But free men can.' Henry said.

'I don't understand.' Said Tom. 'John's a slave.'

'I know. But there's something I've been thinking about for a while...'

'What's that?'

'I've been thinking of giving him his freedom.'

'Well, you own him, and you can set him free. But this...this is a different thing altogether. The Planters would go mad. There will be riots!'

'To hell with them, Tom. I'm tired of talking to them. I'm tired of worrying about what would upset them. It's always about them, them, them!'

'But you've got to be practical, Henry. Putting John to ride is one thing; losing after such a grand idiotic gesture would be far worse. It'll make us a laughing-stock.'

'Who says we're going to lose?'

'John's too heavy. At a guess, I would say he's about a stone heavier than any overseer who would be riding. We have always looked for the lightest riders but someone with John's build will only handicap the horse.'

'Not Blackie. John has a special bond with him that must be worth at least a stone. Have you ever seen him on Blackie? Does the horse ever look like he's carrying a burden?

'No, I must admit.'

'Also, even though John's hands are like spades, when they touch Blackie's reins they become like velvet. He'll carry the weight and beat them.'

'Even if he does, it will cause an almighty outrage. Think about it – a slave beating all the white overseers and Planters!'

'That would make a pleasant change, don't you think?' Said Henry.

'You can laugh, Henry, but they wouldn't find it funny. They'll see it as a betrayal.'

'So be it, then.'

'There are some practical problems, too,' said Tom. 'As a freeman, John can go to the races, but how long is he going to last in the jockey's room before there is a riot? The jockeys are all overseers or Planters, and your racing silks won't change their attitudes towards a black man, slave or free.'

'We'll have to think of something, then.'

'It had better be good, Henry. Otherwise, John will be left at their mercy.'

'I won't allow that. I'll think of something.'

'Try to picture John dressed in your colours in the same room with them. That should help.'

'Nobody would touch him. They wouldn't dare!' King Henry said.

'I hope not,' said Tom. 'He's just an innocent.'

'You don't seriously think that I'm doing this without thinking about his welfare, do you, Tom?' Henry asked earnestly.

'No, no, Henry. That's not what I mean. All I'm saying is that they might go for him - when the person they really want is you.'

'Oh, they'll come for me all right. Those bastards.'

'I don't like their attitudes either, Henry, but we have to show solidarity with them as long as we're growing sugar.'

'And I do. Don't I? Except when it sticks in my craw.'

'But what's the solution?' Asked Tom.

'The end of slavery.'

'But you're convinced that it'll happen soon. It's what you want, isn't it?'

'Yes and no.'

'You're confusing me now, Henry.'

'It's simple. If slavery ends by law and the slaves were set free, there would be no guarantee that they would remain and work for us.'

'But how can it be avoided? If I were a slave and I was set free, I would run like hell – far from a system that had oppressed me!' Said Tom.

'But if we paid them for their work - and not force them to work for nothing - they might stay. In other words, we should put an end to slavery ourselves and retain some goodwill,' said Henry.

'But payment would reduce profits. Albion might be able to survive, but many of the others would fold up,' said Tom.

'That's true, but they might have fewer strikes, sit-downs, go-slows, escapes, arson, loss of lives and all that. As things stand, Albion loses far less through such activities than the other plantations, don't you agree?'

'I do. But it's not easy to change such a system

overnight.'

'Perhaps. But think about what the alternative might be - the end of slavery imposed by Parliament; a labour force vacating the land and leaving us high and dry because they resent us; Plantation upon Plantation going out of business for want of labour, and, even if the freed slaves choose to stay, they will be free men and women with a grudge, always plotting and looking for some way to pay us back.'

'It's an impossible situation, Henry.'

'Difficult, yes; but not impossible, Tom. Imagine the trust we could earn if we were to put an end to slavery ourselves – the kind of co-operation we could get. Imagine how people like us must have felt during the days of slavery in Rome and Egypt. They must have had conversations just like this. They must have been just as frustrated, but still, they must have kept chipping away at the edifice until it crumbled, just as we are doing.'

'So, John riding Blackie is symbolic? Another way of chipping away at the edifice?'

'Not deliberately, no. I can't ride him, and nobody else can. This is how change happens. This is the dialectic.'

'The what?'

'Oh, sorry Tom. It's philosophy – where two opposites come together and result in a fusion. A bit like grafting plants.'

'That's a dream, Henry. It doesn't always work with plants and I don't see how it will work with people.'

'Maybe. But dreams do come true.'

'Try telling that to the Planters!'

'Naturally, they would think I am mad. Oh, how I miss those student days when you could discuss ideas without anyone thinking that you are crazy or that you are a subversive,' Henry sighed.

'Don't forget that it was slave money that made it

possible for us,' said Tom.

'You don't have to remind me. That's why Norman and Elspeth avoid me; they think I'm perpetuating the system.'

'And are they wrong?

'Strictly? No. But people do things differently. I can only reform the system by being part of it.'

'They might think that you should have nothing to do with Planters or Plantations.' Tom said.

'Someday, they will understand that one or two reformers are better than none.'

'And do you think that putting John to ride a horse is going to change anything?'

'Not really.'

'Then why do it?'

'I suppose I feel helpless in this bloody thing,' he said, slapping the sides of his wheelchair. 'I just want to remind them that Henry King is crippled and not useless or dead.'

'So, you're only doing it to poke them in the eyes?'

'It should be fun, shouldn't it?' King Henry said.

'Some fun,' said Tom, rising to leave.

'You'll push me around on race day, won't you, Tom?' Henry asked.

'Do I have a choice? No other white man would,' Tom replied.

Chapter Eight

John was hammering tacks into a saddle when King Henry's butler sidled up to him and told him that he was wanted at the Great House. His mouth went dry and his hands became moist. He didn't look up, but continued tapping with the hammer, missing his target a few times, and sucking his teeth.

'Did you hear me? The butler said, raising his voice. 'King Henry wants to see you.'

John looked up at the butler who was about ten years younger and slight of build. His face was lean, and he had a longish pointed nose which seemed more accustomed to poking itself into other people's business than to breathing or sneezing. *Who does this upstart think he is? He might be a house slave, but he is still a slave, despite his white gloves and black jacket*, he thought.

After a few minutes, he mumbled and nodded.

The butler grunted, did a right turn, and flounced off.

John said to Philip, 'I know Massa Henry is vexed about what Blackie did to Massa Robert.'

'But it's not your fault; Blackie just didn't like him,' Philip said loyally.

'I know,' said John. 'But Massa Robert is a white man. And an overseer. And they blame me.'

'But it's still not your fault. He hit Blackie; I saw him do it - and Blackie doesn't like to be hit,' Philip said.

'Massa Henry might tell me to leave Albion.' John said, not really listening to Philip.

It was a cool day as John walked towards the Great House, but beads of sweat appeared on his forehead and rolled down his face. He wiped them away with one hand, while his other hand, sweaty and sticky, gripped his shabby straw hat tightly. As he approached the heavy wrought iron gates, he saw the uniformed guard standing at attention, his rifle shouldered, and his gaze fixed at a point somewhere in the distance. John gulped. His execution, which he had imagined earlier, somehow became real; but the guard opened the gates and let him in without averting his gaze or uttering a sound. He mumbled a 'thank you' and thought how pink the guard's face had become in the heat, like the colour of a newly born mouse.

He stood in the grounds of the Great House and looked down the long wide avenue that led to the tall, white, multi-storeyed building with its red roof gleaming in the sunlight. It was a privilege afforded few slaves - and one which would normally inspire awe – but one which aroused in John a feeling of trepidation, of dread, given the purpose for which he thought he had been summoned.

He trundled along the avenue which was lined on either side by royal palms whose naked trunks towered into the sky like giant columns and culminated in a canopy of green fronds. Just beyond the lines of palms, *Victoria Amazonica* lilies floated upon wide waterways, spreading their eight-foot wide circular leaves over much of the water, their upturned edges giving them the appearance of vast green flan baking tins. It was claimed by some that they were able to take the weight of a small child, though others of a more philosophical disposition questioned how heavy a small child was. There being no empirical evidence to support this claim, the only testimony to the strength of the leaves remained the variety of bullfrogs and birds which hopped from one leaf to the next in pursuit of insects without sinking into the water or creating so much as a ripple. In stark contrast to the logjam of gigantic green platters covering the water's surface, the flowers of the lilies shot high into the air like an explosion of fireworks and emblazoned the blue sky with a riot of purple and red.

John dragged his feet wearily.

As he approached the Great House, his sense of foreboding grew. He looked up at the glass windows that lined each storey of the house and they stared back at him like the eyes of a demon peering into his troubled soul. He didn't know enough about numbers to count them, but it crossed his mind that it must take the house slaves many days to clean and polish them so that they could glint and dazzle so spectacularly in the sunlight. He crossed the forecourt on feet of lead and went to the back door, the slaves' entrance, upon which he tapped hesitantly, not really wishing to be heard.

After a short while, the door opened, and a gust of antagonism blew into his face.

Standing in the doorway was the butler, all bedecked in black jacket and white gloves. He looked down along his nose at John's bare feet to make sure that he had wiped them. Seemingly satisfied - and his was the kind of face that could never express complete satisfaction - he stuck his chin in the air and signalled with a crooked index finger for John to follow him, seemingly content if John elected not to do so. He led John into the drawing room on the ground floor and ordered him to wait there as he minced over to a door at the opposite end of the room and disappeared. John swallowed. Any time now, he thought;

any time now he was going to know his fate.

He stood and looked around at a world he had never seen before, at a world he had never dreamt existed. He looked at the spacious room, about four or five times the size of their outhouse, whose waxed wooden floor sparkled like no wood he had seen before. He looked in awe at the plush curtains which cascaded down in folds from the high ceiling like a red waterfall coming to rest in a pool upon the shiny floor. In one corner of the room, stood a grand piano whose black and white teeth grinned at him as if it knew something that John didn't. Just above, sitting on a rack, was a book opened at a page which was scrawled with strange symbols, as if a little child had been doodling with a stick in the sand. In the centre of the room, was a suite of deeply buttoned, red, leather-upholstered furniture, which seemed to be inviting him to slump down and rest his weary bones. He moved snail-like around the room, all the time listening for movement from the other side of the door. He stared at the walls - at the faded pictures of people, perhaps of King Henry's antecedents, some of whom wore beards and moustaches and most of whom had benign countenances. There were some, too, dressed in military uniform, like the soldiers who came whenever there was trouble on the Plantation. They wore handlebar moustaches and no expression, and they sat upon horses which all looked alike in sepia, and he thought of his horses and about how different each one looked. He looked up at the ceiling and allowed his eyes to descend along the elaborate ormolu chandelier, with its many arms and candles, which dangled like an oversized crown. He stood on one spot, afraid to move; afraid that to do so might disturb the order of things.

He glanced through the window and saw Queenie

talking to the gardener. Her stance, her hand gestures and the look of contempt and displeasure in her face, suggested that she was not merely talking, but reprimanding the man as if he had interrupted her piano lesson or something similarly unforgivable. The man's head was hung low in abjection like a child being scolded. John saw her look up, and he smiled with an uncertainty born of unfamiliarity. He didn't know whether she had seen him or had done so and was merely ignoring him, because her countenance remained unaltered, except for one fleeting moment when he thought he could detect that strange look that she had given him back at the outhouse. Maybe, in his state of mind, he was just imagining things.

He heard the noise of wheels creaking from beyond the door and he edged back into the position in which the butler had left him, as if everything in the interlude had been imagined, a fantasy conjured up by his over-active imagination. A fantasy of red waterfalls, grinning black-and-white teeth, horses of uniform colour and a woman, black like himself, who spoke the language of white people and who had given him another strange look.

The door opened and King Henry appeared in his wheelchair, pushed by the butler. His legs were covered by a blanket.

'Hello, John,' he said cheerily.

'Morning Massa,' John replied, bowing slightly, barely able to open his mouth.

'You can leave us now, Vicky,' King Henry said to the butler, whose powdered face and downturned mouth reflected a reluctance to leave his Master alone with John.

After the butler had left, King Henry said, 'John, I need to speak to you about something important. About Blackie.'

'Sorry Massa. Sorry Massa. Blackie didn't like Massa Wyatt because he hit him with his whip and Blackie didn't like that at all and he bucked and bucked and threw Massa Wyatt down...,' John said, gasping for breath and passing his hat from one hand to the next, his lips trembling.

King Henry looked at him with knitted brow, then he smiled.

'No, no. That isn't what I wanted to talk to you about, John,' King Henry said, smoothing the blanket on his lap. 'You know the King's Cup is in two weeks, at the end of the harvest?'

'Yes, Massa. Philip told me,' he mumbled.

'Do you think Blackie will win?'

'Oh, yes, Massa. Blackie will win. We have been preparing him.'

'You really like him, don't you?'

'Oh, yes Massa. He is a clever horse.' John shifted his weight from one foot to the next, a bit more relaxed.

King Henry looked at the undisguised joy that radiated from John's face, and said: 'I know, but there's one problem...'

'Massa?'

King Henry cleared his throat, smiled, and glanced down at his covered legs. 'As you can see, John, I can't ride him as I did last year.'

John said nothing; he looked down at the floor. It was common knowledge that the King had lost the use of his legs and couldn't ride Blackie, and that was why Wyatt had been sent to try him out. John wondered how King Henry could remain so calm and show no sign of bitterness, despite what had happened to him. It was during this thought that he heard King Henry's voice as if it were coming from afar, like a voice in a dream, like an echo among the foothills.

'I want you to ride him, John.'

A million thoughts swirled and darted about John's mind. His eyes took on a blank look and he wondered, *did I think those words, or did King Henry really say them?*

'I want you to ride Blackie, John.' King Henry repeated. This time, the message and its source were clear.

'But...but Massa... only ...'John whispered.

'John, from today you are a free man. You can do what you want. You can leave Albion. You can go to the village or the town and find work. You can even go to the racecourse to watch the racing. You can do what you want, John. From today you are no longer a slave. But I want you to stay at Albion and I want you to ride Blackie.'

A story is told in the Bible about a disabled man who had been bed-ridden for thirty-eight years and who Jesus had healed, commanding him to "rise, take up thy bed, and walk." The man, instead of walking as he had been instructed by the Lord, left his bed, and bolted down the road, shouting and screaming with joy.

There was no such reaction from John. He was transfixed as though a lightning bolt from above had penetrated his body and riveted him to the ground. It was as if an ice-cold blast of wind from the Arctic had frozen his muscles and caused his tongue to swell and fill up his mouth.

The only life he had known as an adult was the life of a slave and, while he had been glad to be rid of cutting sugar cane, his work with the horses - especially Blackie - was the epitome of happiness. No one bothered him. No one shouted at him. No one flogged him. He couldn't imagine a life outside that provided by the safety and security of the Plantation system.

Gradually, very gradually, the lightning bolt receded; the thaw began, and John started to stir - economically at first

- then more animatedly, as he shifted from one leaden foot to the other. He was like someone coming out of a state of suspended animation. He bent his elbows and opened his hands; he stretched his fingers as far as they could go, like a man shape-shifting into a werewolf; he gasped for air, opening and closing his mouth without making a sound like, a fish out of water. His eyes, too, previously closed, but now fully distended, darted from side to side as his generous lips began to tremble again and his tongue began to move in his mouth.

Sensing his discomfort, and to prevent him from breaking down and blubbering, King Henry said quickly, 'I want you to continue looking after the horses with Philip, John, but now you will get paid.'

John nodded his head, up and down, down, and up, still unable to speak.

'And I want you to ride Blackie in the King's Cup,' King Henry added.

'But it's only …'

'Don't worry about that, John. I want you to ride Blackie for me,' he said, glancing down at his own legs. 'For Albion.'

'Yes, Massa,' John croaked.

As he walked away from the Great House, he kept looking down at the ground, concentrating on which foot he should move next so that they wouldn't tangle and trip him up. This time his preoccupation was different. The imagined threat of eviction from Albion because of the Wyatt incident had given way to something more frightening. He was free. Free. But he wasn't sure what that meant. He walked along the avenue, past the palms; past the lilies; past their flowers; past the guard, and through the gates.

Without seeing.

He entered the outhouse where Philip was sitting on his bunk smoking.

'What happened?' Philip said. 'You look like you've seen a jumbie.'

John wiped the sweat from his forehead and sat down.

'It's worse than that.' And he told Philip about what went on at his meeting with King Henry.

'You know what that means?' Philip said excitedly. 'You're going to be the first black man to ride a horse at the racetrack. You're going to be the first to ride with the white men.'

John held his head in his two hands and groaned. 'What happens if I beat them?' He asked.

'You mean 'when'. Do you think that anything can beat Blackie?' Philip replied, sucking his teeth. 'He's going to mash up that Fleetwood and Hercules!'

'No, I mean they won't like it if I beat them – the other white riders.'

'Don't worry. King Henry will protect you.' Philip said reassuringly.

They spent the next two weeks preparing the horse for the race. John did his other chores and helped Philip as much as he could, but he spent most of his time riding Blackie. Philip instructed him to hold the colt back in the early part of the race and let the others wear themselves out. Then, before turning into the straight, he should wind the pace up until two furlongs out.

'That's when you go for the line. Whoosh! And you will pass all of them.'

John looked at Philip and nodded. He looked at Blackie

and knew that the horse was ready.
He wasn't sure about himself.

Chapter Nine

Race day was on a Saturday, and people from all over the country made their way towards the 'Savannah', as the racetrack was known. The Planters, their senior men, overseers, and their families - all white - arrived in a variety of horse-drawn vehicles. They occupied the grandstand together with other white luminaries such as Police Inspectors, Doctors, high-ranking Civil servants and Educators and they were cordoned off from the rest of the people.

The social stratum below - the Freemen - which comprised mulattos (products of white/black miscegenation) and local whites ('red legs') - occupied the ground area, where they stood or sat on the grass, all spruced up in loud floral patterns.

The slaves, the lowest stratum of society, were absent; they were confined to their plantations, not simply because they were deemed unworthy to be socialising anywhere near their betters, but also because allowing them to mingle with slaves from other Plantations might encourage a cross-pollination of ideas which could foment unrest.

'The Savannah' was a replica of the racetrack at Ascot in Berkshire, England, and reflected the class prejudices of that racecourse where the working classes were seldom in evidence, except where they functioned as servants. It was run by the all-white Turf Club, which organised a fare of supporting low-class horse and mule races culminating in the Class 'A' King's Cup.

Mule races were very popular among the racegoers because they were a source of amusement and were the entree before the main fare. The mule, a crossbreed between a male donkey and a female horse, is a sterile, hard-working animal characterised by its stubbornness. Often, at the off, a mule might dig its heels in and refuse to budge in spite of the efforts of its rider or, when it did condescend to move, it might head in the opposite direction to the others or, then again, it might just buck until it deposited its rider on to the ground.

This slapstick comedy was followed by the 'King's Cup'. The purse was rich, but it was not the only source of possible winnings. There was the matter of reputation, and the victorious horse was not only talked of in fascination but was coupled with its Plantation's name, as in 'The Black Thunderbolt of Albion' - a tribute for which any Plantation owner would have given anything.

King Henry, his legs covered up by a tartan blanket, sat in his wheelchair at the lowest level of the grandstand, closely attended by Tom Oliver. Other Planters came up to him to exchange greetings and to wish him a speedy recovery. He was popular, not only because he was the wealthiest Planter, but also because of his sense of humour and his kindliness. Even though his views on the slave system were detested for being too liberal, there were a few, albeit not many, who conceded that he might have a point and that anything was better than enforced abolition. However, these were not prepared to publicly make common cause with him.

'Ok, Tom, you can leave me now. John needs your help,' he said, fumbling, as he took out his binoculars from their case.

Tom looked at him and said, 'I know I'm going to regret this, Henry.'

The preliminaries over, the runners and riders for the King's Cup were hoisted upon the board. Number eight was The Black Thunderbolt and alongside the horse's name was the name of his rider, J. King. There was mild clapping from the crowd as the horses filed into the parade ring, but when Tom Oliver led Blackie in, the clapping increased in rapidity and volume. The horse strode majestically, his ears pricked and his black skin shimmering in the sunshine like a sunbathing seal, as he looked around at the crowd as if to acknowledge their adulation. When the bugle sounded for the jockeys to mount up, John walked up to Blackie with his head bowed as if he was trying to hide from the crowd. He was wearing a large soft hat, the rim of which hung over most of his face, and a crumpled jacket with its collar pulled up around his neck, which King Henry had provided, and which disguise gave him an unremarkable appearance. Up to that point, nobody paid any attention to him as there was too much going on in the ring. There was a smattering of applause when John removed his jacket to reveal the well-known red and white silks of King Henry, but this soon turned to gasps of disbelief as he took off his hat and revealed his black face. The crowd in the grandstand gasped and stared, transfixed by a mixture of disbelief and alarm at the sight of a black man amidst the white riders. The riders, too, looked at each other in bafflement. It was only when Tom gave John the leg-up that they came out of their trance and were jolted back into animation.

'What the fuck do you think you're playing at, Oliver?' Demanded one of the jockeys.

The crowd booed and catcalled at the sight of a white man holding a black man and they swore and gesticulated – some in the obscenest fashion. Someone threw a bottle in John's direction and they were swiftly arrested by two policemen, which gave rise to even greater howls of protest from the crowd as if the police had acted unfairly. Tom's face went red, and it wasn't just through the effort of lifting the weighty John.

John felt Blackie beginning to get edgy and he hurried him into a canter to get him away from the noise. As he breezed past the grandstand, standing in the stirrups, and feeling at one with the horse, he was oblivious to the invectives, racial slurs and the odd missile being hurled at him by members of polite society. Nor did Tom Oliver and King Henry escape the anger of the crowd, who berated them with a range of expletives including allusions to incest with their mothers. It was not only the whites in the grandstand who were making their feelings known, but also the black freemen and 'red legs', who had become accustomed to an order of things which they felt was in mortal danger of being destroyed, not in some abstract way, but right in front of their eyes.

John followed Philip's instructions and he piloted Blackie to win the King's Cup in devastating style. Of greater importance, though, was the political fissure that the issue had caused in the ranks of the Planters. After the race, some of them came up to King Henry and accused him of being a slave lover and of giving the slaves a stick with which to beat them.

'This time you have gone too far, Henry,' Watford warned.

'You haven't heard the last of this,' said another.

'You are a bloody idiot, King!' Bellowed Lofty Pilgrim of Pilgrim's Rest, flecks of spittle from his mouth showering the air like confetti at a wedding.

And some of those who had previously wished him a speedy recovery, now hoped that he would burn in hell.

King Henry took the reactions of the Planters in the manner of a man who had expected them. What he had done was no act of caprice or impulse; it was no indulgence of whim or fancy. He had long cautioned the other Planters that unless they improved the lot of the slaves, the pressure building up from those outside, and by the slaves themselves, would force unfavourable decisions upon them. At the Planters' quarterly meetings, he had repeatedly tried to persuade them that sugar farming could work for all and that there was no need for the continued enslavement of people.

They had remained convinced that the backing they had from England would keep things in place.

But slave revolts in the British and French colonies had been growing. In one island, striking slaves had caused widespread damage to sugar cane fields and sugar depots by setting them on fire. Some slaves had been killed but so, too, had a Planter and a couple of overseers. King Henry argued that at a time when sugar prices were falling, the last thing they needed was ill-feeling and revolt festering among the labour force. The Planters accused him of exaggerating what was happening elsewhere, and they said that they were confident that the English Parliament, notwithstanding the protestations of a few malcontents, would never abolish slavery.

Some suggested that he was deliberately putting pressure on the Planters to force them to his way of thinking and that his latest act of putting a slave to ride his horse was a mischief that had gone too far. Oliver tried to assuage their fears by explaining that it wasn't deliberate but that it was the result of a chain of random events, such as King Henry's infirmity, the horse's unwillingness to co-operate with Wyatt and its affinity with John, that had conspired to bring about this.

The Planters rubbished his explanations and accused him of being cut from the same cloth as King Henry.

'Looks like we're at war, Henry,' Tom said.

'Then so be it, Tom. I'm getting tired, really tired,' said Henry with an unusual pause between words, as if to demonstrate his tiredness, but there was something in his voice that made Tom feel that he wasn't just talking about the pig-headedness of the Planters.

Blackie's victory over the horses from the other Plantations was celebrated by the slaves, who had not seen the race. It was a victory for their Plantation, their Albion. King Henry provided extra rations for the slaves and they made merry with copious amounts of rum.

For years to come, people from all along the sugar belt would speak in awe about the achievement of Albion's 'Black Thunderbolt'.

And for years to come, too, people would talk in disgust about the other black thunderbolt that King Henry had unwittingly unleashed upon them.

Chapter Ten

John was a hero in the eyes of some, but he was weary of all the fuss and just wished to be left alone. He was a simple man who did what he had to do for someone who had rescued him from a life of misery. Besides, sitting on top of Blackie made everything worthwhile.

Queenie visited the day after the races, and this time she spoke to him.

'Well, well, the hero upset the Planters,' she scoffed.

He did not react, but Philip, who was sitting on his cot, said:

'Whoosh!' And he made a gesture with one open hand passing the other stationary one.

She ignored him and said to John. 'I hear the Planters didn't like it.'

'Whoosh!' said Philip.

'I wish he would shut up,' she said. 'I hear you are a free man', she persisted.

'Yes. Massa Henry set me free.' John said.

'And you thought you could ride the horse and not upset the Planters?'

'I did what Massa Henry told me to do,' John said, hoping that she would go away.

'That's typical of Henry. Always stirring up trouble. I don't know why he can't leave things alone,' she said, as if talking to herself.

'Massa Henry is a good man,' Said Philip.

'John King, eh?' She said, ignoring Philip. 'I suppose you are going to move to a village now, John King.'

'No,' he replied. 'Massa said I could stay.'

'I told him not to do it, but Henry is a stubborn man,' she said, again as if to herself.

John could not work out whether she was talking about King Henry setting him free or getting him to ride the horse, but he wondered why she was so concerned about the feelings of the Planters rather than being happy that another slave had been set free or that Albion had won the race. He knew that house slaves thought that they were superior to other slaves, but her scathing, reprimanding manner was something quite different. There was something else. What did she mean by *telling* King Henry not to do it? He pondered for a while, but just couldn't be bothered; he was tired of the whole affair.

'Hee, hee, hee,' Philip chuckled after she had left. 'She is a smart one. Too smart.'

John paid him no heed; he had become accustomed to the old man's incoherence and was sure that he was losing his mind. Physically, too, Philip had deteriorated rapidly. For as long as John had known him, the old man had never been an imposing figure, but now he appeared to be shrinking before his eyes. His skin seemed to be getting increasingly taut, revealing more and more of his frame and, sometimes, when he walked, he canted like a sloop that had sprung a leak. There were days, too, when he never got out of bed and on those when he did, he just sat around the outhouse and smoked. He had lost the strength to control or groom the horses and all these tasks fell to John. John did not mind; he liked the old man and he felt he should be allowed to pass his last years in peace.

One morning, after he had fed the horses, John mounted Blackie and sensed that something was wrong with him. He was on his toes, which was a sure sign that something was making him uncomfortable. He dismounted and checked each of the horse's legs in turn just to make sure there was no physical injury. He ran his hand along the pastern, then the fetlock and upwards towards the cannon bone. He patted the knee and felt the forearm, but he couldn't detect any irregularity; nor did Blackie react to his gentle probing. He walked him around a few times and his rhythm seemed sound. Satisfied that there was nothing physically wrong, he mounted him and clicked him into a trot to settle him down.

As he breezed him along the riverbank, he detected changes in the atmosphere. He had never seen the river look so benign; it was crawling along like treacle as if overburdened by the weight of its own viscosity. The sun had disappeared, and the sky was heavily overcast by a deepening grey that caused the day to look like night. There was a kind of stillness, too, as if, in a fit of pique, the wind gods had sucked the winds out of the atmosphere and left the leaves on the trees looking dead, with not even the slightest shimmer. Overhead, a few crows circled, occasionally breaking the dead air with their caws. It was difficult to breathe, and John felt his shirt clinging to his back like a damp living thing, moving as he moved.

Under him, he felt Blackie jink occasionally.

'We're in for the mother of all storms, boy,' he said to Blackie. 'We'd better get back and make sure everything is safe.'

He returned Blackie to his box and peeped in on the other horses. He made sure that they were all wrapped up in their blankets, the lanterns were lit, the water buckets were full and there was enough hay. Then he bolted the doors. There was no telling how long the siege might last.

The horses were most vulnerable during a storm as the noises could make them panic in their boxes and cause them to injure themselves. He had often wondered what it was like for them, hearing all those unusual threatening sounds and not being able to see or do anything. He thought of what it must be like for them in their wild state. He supposed that they would seek shelter under trees and the awnings of caves during a storm or that they could run into the wide open if they were startled by a predator. What, he wondered, would it be like to be a horse in the wild. To be able to do whatever you wanted, whenever you wanted. To be able to gaze upon the beauty of a mountain ascending into a clear blue sky; to run amongst forests of green and to be able to experience the orgasmic pleasure of scratching an itch against one of its trees; to roam over hills and sprint down the steep slopes of lush valleys; to feed on fresh grass among carpets of multi-coloured flowers; to drink from cool quenching streams, and to frolic with your own.

To do all this, instead of being locked up and given small lumps of kindness in return for serving others by pulling them in carts or allowing them to sit on your back just so that they could feel on top of the world; to have them pull your mouth left or right, sometimes with iron bits that cut through your flesh; to have them kick you in your belly with a spiked wheel, or crack you with a leather whip to impel you, when all you wanted to do was to stand still and mind your own business. He wondered how many of those fat military men he had seen pictured on horseback in King Henry's house had ridden their steeds in battle. Or did they pose like that just so they could look down upon their fellow men while boasting about how they had deprived the animal of its freedom?

Tropical storms are preceded by a deceptive calm and darkened skies before torrential rain beat down incessantly upon the earth, liquidising it into a dysentery of mud and rheum which swell the rivers and cause them to breach their banks and flood the plains, sometimes swallowing all in their path. Like an orchestra of a thousand musicians executing a Mussorgsky symphony, they are accompanied by the flashing and crackling of lightning and the rumbling, cracking and booming of thunder, which reach an ear-splitting finale that cause the whole universe to ring out and resound in discord. All the time, gale force winds snatch animals and uproot houses, trees, wooden sheds and chicken coops, and whirl and twirl them around in the sky like children's playthings. It would go on for hours and hours and after the tumult plays itself out, what is left behind, amidst the stillness, is a tapestry of death and devastation - the swollen bodies of animals and people lying amidst other everyday objects of human existence.

Having secured the horses, John went to batten down the outhouse so that he and Philip could sit through the impending onslaught. As it was only mid-morning, Philip would still be asleep because these days he didn't stir much before midday. He went in, bolted the door behind him and stuffed jute bags in the crevice at the bottom. He slid the crossbar into its slot then did the same with the wooden windows, shutting out all the natural light. He sat on his bed and felt around on the table next to it for the calabash bowl that held the candle. He lit the candle and its flame gradually grew brighter, lighting up his part of the room.

He looked at the outline of the sleeping form on the other cot, and said, 'Looks like we're in for a bad one, old man; it's like a graveyard out there. Even the chickens have gone dead quiet.'

When there was no response from the old man, he went over to his bunk to see what the matter was. He called him a few times, then he gently nudged him. When there was no response, he stood up and went across the room for the candle so that he could get a better look. In truth, he did so just to confirm his suspicion that Philip was dead; he must have died sometime during his sleep.

As he walked back to his bunk, John's breath was laboured, like that of a Titan holding up the sky. He sat down amidst the gloom and lit up a cigarette. He thought of how fate had conspired to throw him together with the old man; about how much he had learnt from him and of how much he had owed him. He knew that he had fulfilled a need in the old man's life as much as the old man had fulfilled one in his. In the gamut of human relationships, such a symbiosis was as close as people could get without trying to own each other.

Hours had passed since he came in to get away from the impending storm, but it was still very quiet outside. Curiosity got the better of him and he decided to open the door. When he looked out, he saw that the skies were clear, the sun was out, the crows had disappeared, the waters of the river had resumed their friendly babbling and there was a gentle wind blowing and ruffling the leaves of the trees.

Where, he wondered, was the storm?

Philip was buried under the shade of a balata tree in a burial ground reserved for slaves on the outskirts of the Plantation. King Henry and Tom Oliver attended, together with a small group of field and house slaves. The King read a passage from the Bible and said kind words about Philip before committing his body to the earth. John and Maria stayed on after the others had left.

'I thought Queen Elizabeth would have come,' John said.

'No. She said she had too much to do. King Henry has visitors coming tonight.'

'She came after the race, but her behaviour was very

strange.'

'In what way?' Asked Maria.

'She seemed upset that King Henry had set me free.'

'I can't understand why,' Maria said. 'Slaves should be happy when good things happen to other slaves.'

'Perhaps she thinks she is better than slaves.'

'Well, she can't change her colour,' Maria replied.

'She was also rude to Philip,' John said.

'Why? I can't understand how anybody can be rude to Philip.'

'He was jabbering nonsense, but that wasn't new.'

'Maybe she was just tired,' said Maria.

'She seemed more concerned that the Planters were angry.'

'I can't see why. King Henry himself loves to make them angry. Anyway, it's nothing to do with her.'

'And she kept calling King Henry by his first name.'

'I know she doesn't follow the rules, but she wouldn't do that to his face.'

'I don't like her,' John said. 'She is cold, like a fish.'

John looked at Philip's grave. 'They captured him when he was ten and brought him here, you know. They put him to work in the fields, but he wasn't strong, so they flogged him regularly. Then King Henry put him with the horses. He loved them and knew each one like they were his children. He was getting old and blind, though, so he was happy when I came. He treated me like his son.'

Maria squeezed his hand.

It was not easy at first for John to get used to being alone. The chores were not a problem and with careful management of his time, he could easily do all that was needed and still have time to spare. It was when he returned to the outhouse, especially at dusk, that he felt Philip's absence most. He used to enjoy the chatting, cooking, and eating, which all helped to pass the time. He was always amazed that even though Philip never left the stables or the outhouse, he knew all that was happening, not only at Albion, but also at other Plantations. John had asked many times how he knew something or other, and he would either ignore him or go, 'Hee, hee, hee.'

The horses were the most important thing in his life. If one was in pain and he couldn't help, he would stay awake and smoke and walk around the room, which annoyed John because every time the old man took a pull on his cigarette, John would see fireflies flitting about the room through his closed eyelids.

Little things suggested that the horses also missed Philip. Tomahawk did not appear to notice the fillies; he did as he was instructed and didn't go chasing after them with a full-blown erection, as was his nature. Agouti, too, had the chance to bite John on many occasions when he got close to him, but didn't. And Blackie appeared to have lost some of his sparkle; he walked with his head down and was not his alert self and, sometimes, unusually, he did not respond as quickly to John's signals.

Tom Oliver told John that he would find an assistant to help with the horses, but John said he could manage. Tom understood that the embedding of a stranger in the stables at this time would invade John's sorrow, so he decided to postpone it.

Six months after Philip's death, Henry King, slave owner, Master of Plantation Albion, and gadfly to the Planting establishment, died, having never fully recovered from his illness.

As news of his death spread, slaves at Albion cried and wrung their hands in despair.

Tom Oliver wept openly for the loss of his friend and all along the coast, among the other Plantations, the news was received with sombreness. King Henry had been well-known and while his views on slavery had upset many in the white establishment over the years, the balance of opinion was that he had been a just and kind man.

Now that he was gone, and even before his body had been placed in the ground, many wondered about the future of Albion. It was the biggest Plantation in the country and one of the biggest in the region with three thousand acres of land and nearly a thousand slaves. What happened to this behemoth could affect them all. King Henry did not have any children and there was no heir-apparent, and it was well known that his blood relatives, who all lived in England, were thoroughly against the system of slavery, notwithstanding the kindness he himself might have shown to his slaves.

Hundreds attended his funeral, which was held at the Church of England Cathedral in the city where only white people of that faith worshipped. It was a grand affair, officiated by the Bishop himself and attended by no less a figure than the Governor. The Planters and their Managers, too, were there in their droves, many no doubt eager to hear any gossip about the Albion question.

When his Will was made public, it was revealed that King Henry had left sums of money to his brother and sister in England and also to his life-long friend Tom Oliver. He had bequeathed funds to the Church, the Alms House and the Orphanage in the city. He instructed that all his house slaves should be set free upon his death and that they should thenceforth be paid for their labour. This last disposition caused great concern among the Planters as they saw it as setting a dangerous precedent. Slaves were rarely set free unless they had enough money to buy their freedom and, as they did not work for wages, this hardly ever happened. This act of freeing slaves, albeit only house slaves, was something new, and one which could only embolden the rebels on all the sugar Plantations. The Planters shook their heads and tut-tutted and some even cursed. It appeared that even from beyond the grave, Henry King was making mischief.

If this caused the Planters deep concern, what produced something resembling a nuclear explosion, was the final declaration in King Henry's will:

'...the rest of my property – my money, house, horses, slaves, and Plantation Albion - I bequeath to my beloved wife, Elizabeth.'

Questions zipped around the Planters' ears like enraged hornets whose nest had been poked by some mischievous schoolboy. *Who is Elizabeth?* They asked, as they gathered in little groups to discuss the situation; it was as if England had declared war on somebody or other. *Who knew, they asked, that Henry had remarried and had said nothing? Did Henry bring her from England or was she from one of the Planter families in the region?*

When, eventually, it became clear that the Elizabeth of his will was none other than one of his house slaves, chaos broke out among the Planters.

Speculation was rife as to how such a thing could have come about. *Was Henry knocking off the slave woman while his wife was still alive? Who knew what, and didn't say? Did she bewitch him through some obeah brought from that dark place? And when did they get married? This was beyond belief,* some exclaimed. *How could that troublemaker do something like this to his own people?* Some even suggested that it would have been better if Henry had sold Albion and thrown all the proceeds into the Atlantic.

94

They worked tirelessly at the jigsaw puzzle, piecing together every nod or wink they could recall, every innuendo that they may have heard and every intimacy they may have seen, but of which they had taken no notice. *Slaves were property, so there was nothing wrong if Henry was poking one of them. After all, one had every right to ride one's own horse. And the horse in question was quite fetching,* as some of them recalled, having seen her on some visit or other to the Great House. *She was well put together; she was pretty - for someone of her race -* and her body was quite beautifully sculpted. *Who could blame Henry if he found relief in her bed? I wouldn't say no if I had the chance. But did that stupid fool have to go and marry her? Why, oh why,* some asked, as if it was the burning philosophical question of the day, *did he have to buy the cow when he was getting the milk for free?*

Such questions were on the lips of all who had a stake in the sugar industry, and the absence of answers kept many awake at night. '*When Albion sneezes,*' King Henry was fond of reminding them, '*the sugar belt comes down with a cold*'.

They consulted lawyers in the hope of discovering that his marriage had been performed by some voodoo priest and was therefore not legal, or that Henry might have been doolally at the time of making his will. After all, his was the act of a madman. Or might the coroner be able to shed some light on whether Henry could have been poisoned by the slave woman? Arsenic was used to kill rats in the fields and was therefore widely available to anyone who wanted to use it for more devious purposes. Who is to know what went on behind Henry's back while they canoodled at breakfast? Who is to say what effect a drop or two of arsenic in his porridge each morning might have had over time? Or, perhaps, there was something in English law that prohibited a slave or ex-slave or black people or whoever, from inheriting.

The lawyers made inquiries of the Police and Coroner and they feverishly pored over their tomes in search of some precedent that might enable them to contest King Henry's will, but they couldn't find anything to placate the Planters, who were disappointed and dejected but who were determined to make sure that Albion remained in white hands. The alternative was too ghastly to contemplate.

'She is going to set all the slaves free and pay them, and we will be forced to do the same or deal with the discontent that follows,' said one.

'Our slaves wouldn't just escape into the mountains; they will escape to Albion,' added another.

'And we just can't compete. We depend on unpaid labour to make a profit. We just can't survive if we had to pay,' argued another.

After lengthy discussions, the few Planters who owned and managed their estates, and the many absentee landlords who lived abroad, agreed that as no single one of them was rich enough to buy Albion, they would have to form a consortium to do so. After a few months, the Consortium's Accountants had done all the costings and obtained commitments of financing from the banks and they were able to make an offer to Henry's concubine, or whatever she was. After all, they reasoned, running a sugar estate, especially one as big as Albion, was no picnic for a woman, and certainly not a woman of her background. They were more than optimistic about success because with sugar prices falling, even Albion would have little room for manoeuvre.

Three Planters of the newly formed Consortium, together with their lawyer and accountant, visited the new mistress of Albion. They were received with courtesy, but they were uneasy at having to deal with the woman as if she were an equal. As things stood, though, she had something that they desperately wanted, so they had to swallow their pride and try to be cordial. After offering their condolences for her loss, singing the praises of King Henry and making some small talk about this and that, all the time shifting uneasily in their chairs, their lawyer donned his glasses, cleared his throat, and turned to the business at hand. With the help of the accountant, who spread out graphs, charts, and tables of statistics on a desk, the lawyer argued that the costings and projections depicted a bleak future in which Albion, without King Henry's expertise and experience, was likely to founder in the face of falling sugar prices. The Consortium hoped that its arguments, based on false logic and spurious economics, would convince Queenie to sell, so they refrained from mentioning their fear of what would happen if she were to free her slaves.

All things considered then, they were prepared to make her an offer of one and a half times the market price for Albion, 'lock, stock and barrel', as the lawyer put it. The Planters pointed out that it was more money than she was ever likely to see in ten lifetimes. And, as if money, especially such a lot, was not incentive enough to sell, the lawyer sought to cajole her. 'Running a Plantation is no easy business, even for a woman of your undoubted capabilities,' he said.

Queenie listened patiently to the lawyer's spiel, much of which made no sense to her.

'Gentlemen, thank you so much for coming and for your most generous offer,' she said.

Then she paused before continuing, 'I regret to tell you, however, that Albion is not for sale.'

They looked at her, their mouths open without a sound. The lawyer's glasses fell off his nose and stayed dangling from a string around his neck, and The Planters looked at each other in puzzlement. The offer, after all, was a generous one, and one which any sane person would find hard to resist. They bundled up their papers and stormed out, one of them knocking over a chair and leaving it where it had fallen.

Queenie smiled.

She knew deep down that their reaction owed much more to who she was, rather than to her decision not to sell, however irrational.

Chapter Eleven

'Did you know about her and Massa Henry?' John asked Maria.

'Not really,' Maria said, shifting her stance a bit uneasily. 'I only suspected because I heard others whispering.'

'But looking back, it all makes sense,' said John. 'She used to call him "Henry", and she used words like, "I told him." It all sounded strange at the time.'

'Well, she's a rich woman now; she owns all the land and the field slaves.'

'She doesn't own us, though,' said John.

'Thanks to King Henry,' Maria replied.

'Do you think she would set the slaves free?'

'She would have to pay them, and the Planters won't like that.'

'What a thing, eh!' Maria said, shaking her head.

'A slave owning slaves,' said John. 'Maybe Massa Henry is up there laughing,' he smiled.

As the weeks and months unfolded, it became clear that Queenie had no intention of setting the slaves free. Instead, the new Mistress of Albion lorded it over her slaves, who grew increasingly restive. Whenever she rode out in her open-top carriage to visit the fields, all dressed up in her finery and protected from the rays of the sun by a fluffy silk-and-lace parasol, her slaves booed, swore, and called her names. She made sure that her carriage was always flanked by two security men with handguns and that there was always some distance between her and the slaves to minimise the risk of attack. However, one day, as her carriage was passing a field, the slaves swore and pelted her with a variety of missiles, one of which, a stone the size of a golf ball, hit her in the chest. Shaken and peeved at this lack of adulation from her subjects, she summoned Tom Oliver:

'Things have to change', she said. 'All rebels are to be punished by flogging, and runaways are to be put to death regardless of the circumstances. Any 'go slow' among slaves will be punished by cutting their food rations by half.'

'But this will only make things worse,' said Tom.

'I don't care,' she said. 'Things must go back to what they were before.'

'But Henry...,'

'Henry was too soft,' she said.

'Reducing their food will make them weak and affect their work,' protested Tom.

'Do you expect me to feed them when they don't work?'

Tom opened his mouth to say something but thought better of it.

'And, another thing,' she continued, 'Sundays will no longer be a day of rest. They have to work a full seven days to make up for the ones that are disabled or dead.'

Tom kept quiet, grateful that she had come to the end of her edict. As he got up to leave, she said, 'Oh, one more thing: In future, all disabled slaves must be evicted from the Plantation. I am not a charity.'

Tom bit his bottom lip and left.

When the Planters heard about the new policies, they began to feel that their fears had been misplaced. Albion was stepping into line. There was no more wishy-washy liberalism like in the days of King Henry and no more undermining of a tried and tested system that had ensured their continued prosperity. They had even invited Queenie to their quarterly meetings where they endorsed her hard-line policy towards recalcitrant slaves. The need to maintain the system overshadowed such factors as her race and slave background. The repressive excesses of the slave system, so weakened by King Henry's liberal defiance, were now reinvigorated by the policies of his Queen.

'I never thought she would become like that,' Maria said to John.

'Phillip did. He used to say she is 'too' smart. I always thought he meant that she was very clever. Now I realise he meant that she was too clever for her own good. She is going to destroy Albion and Massa Tom can't do anything,' John said.

It wasn't for the want of trying that Tom couldn't do anything. As the person responsible for all field and factory operations at Albion, Tom Oliver tried to contain the descent into savagery by continuing to pay lip service to the pursuit and discipline of runaway slaves. However, Queenie, backed by some of the Planters, set up a special group of armed men that was responsible for tracking down and disciplining them and while her brutal regime could not be solely blamed for the breakdown of law and order at Albion, it did little to arrest it.

Unrest was widespread, and the exploits of slave rebels elsewhere were tapped out in a steady rhythm as if on drums, spreading the message that change of a radical kind was on its way. The Planters, afraid of what this meant, wrote to the legislators in England arguing that slavery should not be abolished because the slaves were happier than they had ever been:

'Their labour is light, and they enjoy great repose. There are schools on each estate for the education of children, and their parents are instructed in the knowledge of their

religious duties.'

The number of revolts and their ferocity grew, and the slaves seemed to have become immune to punishment. Reports of the death of many slaves throughout the Plantations during their violent armed rebellions did not deter others. The vehicle was out of control. Fields of immature cane were regularly set on fire and black clouds of smoke spiralling against the skyline became the unplanned backdrop of the sugar belt. The Planters had to mount patrols day and night to prevent arson and to protect overseers from being dragged from their mounts and beaten, or even killed, in the most brutal fashion.

It was always going to be an uneven fight for the Planters, not only because of the overwhelming numbers of slaves but because of their determination to set themselves free. The colonial army, upon which the Planters had depended for their protection, became less effective as the slaves became better mobilised. In one island 60,000 slaves went on strike. By the time the army had put down the rebellion, 200 had died, but so, too, had 14 white men.

Planters had always been mindful of the need to set aside large amounts of funds to deal with eventualities such as damage caused by hurricanes, floods, drought, plant disease and insect infestations. Now, though, they found that they had to cater for damage caused by man. The destruction of crops and the loss of labour throughout the region hit sugar revenues hard, and many had to dig into their reserves to effect repairs, strengthen security and replace manpower.

Many understood that Albion had come under increasing violence because of the measures introduced by the new regime, but they couldn't fathom why, of all the

Plantations in the region, it had to fall victim to a widespread infestation of a deadly parasite at the same time.

On the one flank, there were violent revolting slaves marching relentlessly on, using their torches to set everything alight as they advanced. On the other, there was a plague of worms tunnelling and crunching through the cane stalks and turning the miles and miles of verdant swathes of sugar cane fields into one vast canopy of dead rust-brown leaves and drooping top stalks - the trademark of the moth borer larvae as it moved from field to field and sucked the lifeblood out of the plants. It was a coincidence that defied rational explanation, and because people were unable to find any logic to explain it, they concluded that it was an act of divine retribution. It was as if God had decided to subject Albion to a Rommel-like pincer movement because He was unhappy at the way Queenie was treating her slaves.

Amidst this carnage, Queenie summoned Tom Oliver to the Great House. When King Henry was alive, he would discuss any field problems with Tom and the overseers on site. The Queen, however, as she had become known among Planters and slaves alike – and not without irony - ruled from the Great House, afraid to venture forth from her fortress for fear of being abused by her slaves.

'Why can't you do something to stop all these riots and go slows?' She asked.

'The army is trying, but all the Plantations have the same problem,' Tom said.

'Not like ours. And now we've got this frigging insect to deal with. We've never had this problem before. What is this damned insect?'

'The moth borer is a worm which drills through the cane stalks and damages the sugar content,' he said. 'This reduces the amount of sugar we can extract.'

Tom thought that this simplified version could be easily understood by the lay-person but, just to make sure, he produced a three-jointed piece of sugar cane stalk which was pockmarked as if someone had used it for target practice with a sawn-off shotgun. For added graphical effect, he showed her the shrivelled form of three stiffened worms, each between 25mm. and 30mm. long, in a bottle filled with formalin. The label on the bottle read *Castnia Licoides' (Giant Moth Borer).*

'Can't you do anything about them?' She asked, curling her lips in disgust.

'We've been trying to control the infestation with chemical sprays, but most of the fields are infected. I'm afraid this crop might be lost,' said Tom.

And, so too, was the Queen.

Tom continued: 'This kind of infestation affects all estates at one time or another and cannot be avoided. In normal circumstances, we would be battling on this front alone. But now we must battle the slaves as well, and I do not have enough people to do both jobs.'

'What can we do then?'

'For a start, you could drop your new measures, which have caused widespread dissatisfaction. What do you expect if you cut rations, hunt them down like animals and force them to work on Sundays? Henry would never have done this.'

'Henry's dead,' she said.

Weeks went by, and there was no let-up in the behaviour of either the slaves or the worms. Albion was under siege and, for the first time in its history, the great

Plantation was facing a loss. Labour was lying idle for want of healthy cane to cut, and as is common in such cases, the Devil found other things, mainly destructive, for them to do. They burnt down barns where sugar was stored, they sabotaged factory and field equipment and they assaulted staff. They got bolder and bolder and, with nothing to do and no one to restrain them, they left their own Plantation and walked long distances to meet with others so that they may plot rebellion.

The numbers were now in charge, and Queenie fell into a deep depression.

One dark night, in desperation, she sent her trusted butler Vicky on a mission of great secrecy towards the sound of the drums which throbbed nightly from sunset to dawn deep in the heart of the forest. Having discarded his black jacket and white gloves in favour of black trousers and top, Vicky furtively picked his way through the backtrack carefully avoiding any prying eyes or chance encounters, until he came to the edge of the forest. He cocked his head and listened out for any movement nearby, but he could only hear the drums in the distance, beating with increasing urgency. He headed through the trees towards the sounds and as he got closer to their source, he could make out the glow of a fire in a clearing just beyond a ring of bramble bushes.

He got down on his hands and knees and crept along the ground to get a clearer look. He slowly parted the bushes and saw the shapes of naked men and women moving like animated cardboard cut-outs as they danced to the beat of the drums, not rhythmically, but in jerky spasms as if under strobe lighting. He swallowed and moved a little bit closer. He saw the dancers holding branches of the black-sage plant and ripping off the leaves with their teeth, before chewing them. They chewed and chewed like masticating cattle, then they swallowed the hallucinatory juice before spitting out the remnants, all the time jerking to the insistent rhythm of the drums, their limbs loose and uninhibited and their heads lolling in abandon as if they were attached to their bodies by hinges.

Around the dancers, there were couples copulating in different positions. Vicky skirted around them, not wishing to alert them to his presence. Even though he had grown up as a house slave, sheltered from the wider world, he knew that it was not wise to disturb people in heat, especially when they were under the influence of the black-sage juice. By the flickering light of the campfire, he could make out the shapes of women lying naked on the ground with their feet, stretched almost perpendicular into the air, quivering like the banged tines of a tuning fork. Women, hands flat on the ground and their legs wrapped around the waists of standing men, being driven into the soil with each pelvic thrust from behind. He could see women's heads bobbing up and down as they gagged and spluttered and imbued rigidity to weapons upon which they would soon be impaled.

He looked around for someone answering the description he had been given; even in that poor light, he told himself, it should be easy to locate a seven-foot-tall man with the stamp of evil upon his face. But there was no such person. He peered into the distance beyond the clearing at the far edge of the forest and he saw a hut thatched with coconut branches, within which there was a dim light flickering. There was something about the hut – a certain aura – that convinced him that it was the hut of Daado, *the obeah-man,* the man to whom he had been charged by his Mistress to deliver a letter. Daado. Vicky shivered at the thought of his name and all that he had heard about him.

He picked his way around the edges of the clearing and headed towards the hut. As he got closer, he noted that there was a band of earth around the hut that was devoid of all vegetation and that there was not even a trace of the ubiquitous and almost indestructible crabgrass that carpeted the rest of the earth beyond. It was as if that ring of land had been rendered barren by fear. As he got closer to the infertile circle, the pall of evil grew more oppressive. Just then, an owl hooted, and Vicky felt his spit dry up in his mouth and a dampness spread between his legs, warm and comforting at first, then cooling, sticky and uncomfortable. Without any thought, he found himself running past the entrance to the hut and throwing the letter into a dark opening, without looking - without breaking his stride. The next thing he knew was that he was hurtling through the forest at breakneck speed, stumbling and snagging his clothes on thorn bushes and scraping and scratching his face, arms and legs against twigs and branches. He had seen no one, but he could feel himself being pelted headlong into the undergrowth, as if by an unseen force. When he reached the end of the forest, he stopped. Gasping, he looked back and listened. There was no noise; only the rhythm of the drums muffled by the distance and the trees. His heart thumped and he grabbed his left breast as if to stop the noise from giving his position away; then, after what seemed an age, he began to lick his dried lips and breathe more easily. Satisfied that nothing or no one was following him, he retraced his steps carefully until he reached the Great House. He hastened through the door, locked it behind him and quickly climbed the stairs to the top floor. He saw his Mistress, sitting in a rocking chair, gently rocking. She nodded when he told her that he had delivered her letter and she kept on rocking, oblivious to his tattered clothing and the marks on his face, which looked like stitches on a wound dotted with blood.

Nor did she see the terror in his eyes.

Days passed as she waited for a response, but there was none. She summoned Vicky and asked if he was sure he had delivered the letter.

'Yes, yes, Missis, I am sure. I am sure,' His confirmation, his pleading tone and his closeness to tears, seemed to satisfy her.

That night, with his teeth chattering and his bare hands clasped so tightly that the blood had drained away to other parts of his body, Vicky begged God not to let her ever send him there again.

A week later, just after midnight, Daado came to the Great House. He did not knock; he did not call out; he just seemed to have materialised from out of the floor in Queenie's room.

Contrary to rumour, he was about six feet tall, muscular, with black chiselled features and fiery, almost deranged, eyes. He might have been described as handsome but for his harelip, which revealed an incisor when at rest. He was the *obeah* man of whom the slaves only whispered and whose name they dared not utter three times in succession for fear of a lingering, excruciating death.

It was not the first time Queenie had met him. She had visited him after she had just become King Henry's wife; she had gone to see him in the clearing among the trees where he lived; and there, in his hut full of bleached bones and polished skulls, around which the grass did not grow nor insects crawl, she had asked for a spell to be cast. At that time, she was a simple house slave, with nothing to offer but herself.

Now, she was the Mistress of Albion; rich, but begging for survival.

Daado had three conditions for casting a spell to save Albion from the moth borer infestation.

'First, I want money. Some people think it is cheap and easy to do what I do. After all, I am merely a middleman; I must pay for higher occult and supernatural services. It is the only way I can get The Beast of the Earth and The Two-horned-Lamb-that-Speaketh-like-a-Dragon to do my bidding. This is how I have become famous throughout the world - and even in this country - for making things happen. I am the envy of all witch doctors, Voodoo priests, missionaries and shamans. But it cost money – lots of it. I don't have to remind you how much it cost me to do that other job for you. The God Damballah doesn't come cheap,'

Queenie nodded her agreement.

'Second, I want twenty acres of prime land.' This, he said, in a matter-of-fact way, was simply a matter of greed. 'Why shouldn't I own land?' He asked rhetorically.

These two conditions were as much a reward for the success of his first spell as for the weaving of the one he was now negotiating.

Queenie nodded her assent again and without waiting for him to make his third demand, she turned her back to him, raised her dress by the hem and bent over. Daado rammed into her, and she relived the first time she had felt him - the bludgeoning, the agony, and then the long drawn out ecstasy that left her weak and broken.

The new deal struck, Daado disappeared like a wraith into the night, as quickly and as noiselessly as he had appeared.

The turmoil moved apace on Plantations all along the sugar belt. Day after day, marauding bands of slaves joined others in burning and destroying all in their path. And at Albion, they were accompanied by the pernicious hordes of worms which continued to sweep through the cultivation, drilling and chomping away like a Roman legion, leaving a trail of death and devastation in their wake. What had not been set on fire out of revenge, was being infected out of spite.

Since Daado's visit, Queenie had taken to sitting at a window in the uppermost storey of the Great House, looking out day after day upon its approaches in the hope that someone - a messenger perhaps - would come running, out of breath, to tell her that, praise the Lord, the insect infestation was over and the crop had been saved. She had met Daado's conditions; she had paid the money, transferred the land to him and she had given herself to him. What more could he want? Whenever she put her hand on her belly, she could feel him deep inside and she knew that this yearning for him would never end because only a fool would try to take back something given freely to an *obeah-man*. She waited and waited. Two weeks went by and every night she could hear the drums; she could hear him calling, calling. And every night, ensnared by his spell, she wanted to go to him, but she dared not venture out.

Still more days passed and there was no news of the end of the insect infestation.

She sent for Tom, who reported that the infestation had become so widespread that there was only one solution.

'We have to flood the whole cultivation.'

'What? And what will happen to the crop?'

'We will lose it.'

'So, flooding the fields will get rid of this frigging insect?'

King Henry had taught her well, Tom noted.

'Yes,' he replied. 'We have to flood for two days.'

She received this news with resignation. Whatever else she might think of him, she knew that when it came to matters of sugarcane agriculture, Tom Oliver had no equal. She had heard King Henry say so many times.

'Can't it wait for a week?' She pleaded with sunken eyes.

'I suppose so. But why the delay?'

'I have my reasons,' she said.

'But not a day longer. We must take urgent action; we can't risk the borers finding their way into the nursery fields or we will lose not only this crop, but the next,' said Tom.

She sighed.

As he was leaving, he looked at her sitting in her chair, her shoulders slumped, and her head bowed. He did not much care for her, especially since she had changed Henry's policy towards the slaves. Now, he remembered how much his friend had loved her, and he couldn't help but feel sorry for the tattered figure before him.

After dinner that evening, as Vicky laid on his bunk reading his Bible, the bell in his room rang. That sound, even though it might be his Mistress simply summoning him to make a cup of tea, now filled him with dread. *Could she be calling me to send me back to that place? Please, God, don't let it be,* he begged. But when she told him that he was going to travel alone on another mission of secrecy, in the opposite direction and away from Daado's forest, he looked upwards and whispered a thank you.

Late that night, under the light of a full moon, he journeyed by horse and trap to a deserted place ten miles along the coast. On his way, he passed a churchyard in which a tall eucalyptus tree stood, guarding a pointy-headed wooden church which appeared to be asleep. Just beyond, where bits of broken glass on the ground glinted in the moonlight, he saw the silhouettes of gravestones sticking out from the earth, marking the spots under which reposed many who had once seen themselves in life as indispensable. He cracked his whip to quicken his horse past this sepulchral tableau and as he did so, he mused at how terrified he would have been of all this, to the point of pissing himself, had he not had that experience in Daado's forest.

He headed towards thicker vegetation and took a path on the right. Here, in a hut deep in the bushes, lived the widow Elvira, a toothless crone who, so it was said, could predict the future by reading the entrails of a chicken. She had survived four husbands, all of whom had died in mysterious circumstances.

Vicky turned off the main path into a long bumpy track that led up to the hut. He stopped the trap outside the hut and tied the horse to a tree. As he entered, he was overcome by the cloying smell of scalding flesh, the source of which soon became evident. Hunched over a fireside, talking to herself, and cackling like a spotted hyena, in the way that witches are said to do, he saw the widow Elvira. She was engrossed in plucking clumps of feathers from a dead chicken before shoving her sharp claws into its anus and scooping out its innards. She paused, looked around, and ordered Vicky to take off his shoes, then she pointed for him to sit down on a rickety stool. He obeyed.

As she walked towards him, jerking like a car whose chassis was bent, she threw the bird's entrails onto the mud floor, just in front of his naked feet. A few bits and pieces pitched in different directions, but the mass remained where it fell. Vicky recoiled; he held his breath and stared at her – at her matted hair and deranged eyes - and he wondered how his Mistress had come to know such people, people who were either crackbrained or downright evil. He didn't look at the coiled-up mess close to his feet, but he continued staring at her as she hummed something tuneless and tossed her head around. She stopped abruptly, threw her head back and rolled her eyes so that only the whites showed. Then she gasped, jerked her head forward, stared straight ahead into the distance, and exclaimed:

'I see worms, worms and more worms. I see big worms, little worms, long worms, short worms.'

We've got a right one here, Vicky thought.

'Yes, Yes. I know.' He said tetchily.

'You know?' Asked the crone, quickly exiting from her trance.

'Yes,' said Vicky boldly, sure that she was a fraud. 'Just down the road, we've got fields and fields of them - long ones, short ones, big ones, small ones, fat ones – even dead ones. Millions of worms! Somebody must have told you.'

Offended by both his tone and his insinuation, Elvira gave him a look of contempt. She cleared her throat with a hacking sound and ejected a greenish projectile of something glutinous which travelled along a high trajectory before landing with pinpoint accuracy into the middle of the fire some distance away. When the globule of glue hit the fire, it writhed and hissed like a living thing that had been wounded and feeling pain and, as if it had bled petrol into the fire, it caused the flames to leap up. As the fire raged, Vicky cowered, and Elvira squawked like a demented hen. The flames dropped suddenly, and so did the temperature in the hut, but not enough to explain why Vicky was shaking and his teeth were rattling like a bag full of bones.

'My... my mistress wants to know when they will go away, the worms, I... I mean.' He managed to stammer.

The crone spat near his feet, more like normal saliva this time but still greenish and slimy. He did not move.

'Oh, so you want to know now...,' she said, as she rearranged the entrails by pushing them with a stick and changing their pattern before humming and going into another trance. Then she whispered, 'They will eat all that is hers. Yes, I can see it clearly. They will eat everything. Then they will come for her. They will feed on her flesh, then on her bones...'

Before she could finish, Vicky hastily dug into his pocket, pulled out some coins that had become warm and damp, and paid her. He dashed out of the hut and leapt into the trap; he got hold of the reins and turned the horse around, but just as he was about to move off, the horse reared up and whinnied. Standing in front of it with her arms outstretched in a howling wind, was Elvira. Vicky's blood ran cold. She was shouting something, but he couldn't hear her above the noise of the horse. She raised her opened right hand with fingers splayed and she stilled the horse. Then he heard her say: 'You forgot these.'

In her left hand, she was holding a pair of shoes.

When he got home, he reported to his Mistress that the crone had known about the worms, and he suggested that she must have heard about them through the grapevine. He left out the rest of her prophecy and the details of the night's proceedings.

The next day, Queenie sent for Tom.

'You can go ahead and flood the fields, Mr. Oliver, if you

have to. We will lose the crop and a lot of money, which is why I have to talk to you about making economies.'

As the fortunes of Albion plummeted, Queenie wondered where Daado was. She had sent many messages to him by means other than Vicky, who had grown shaky and unreliable. She had wanted to know if he had cast the spell, and, if so, why it wasn't working. But the *obeah- man* had ignored her. Yet, night after night, she could hear the drums and sense him in her sleep, rifling through her clothes, slamming into her repeatedly and leaving her ravaged. She had fulfilled her side of the bargain and he had not because the infestation was getting worse. She was at a loss about what to do. One thing she knew she couldn't do was to seek redress through the courts for breach of contract.

Prosecution: *Could you tell the court what your occupation is, Mr. Daado?*

Daado: *Obeah-man*

Prosecution: *Could you explain what that is?*

Daado: *I practise magic and make things happen in the old traditions of Vodoun.*

Prosecution: And what is this 'Vodoun.'

Daado: Those who don't know call it 'Voodoo' or 'Black Magic', but it is much more than that - far, far more. Let me give you a history…

Prosecution: *Ahem…That will not be necessary, Mr.*

Daado, I think the court understands that you are talking about a kind of Mumbo Jumbo that is used to terrify the slaves. What was the nature of your contract with the plaintiff?

Daado: Mumbo Jumbo? Mumbo Jumbo?

Prosecution: Answer the question, please.

Daado: *She gave me land, a lot of money and sex for me to get rid of the worms in her fields. Mumbo Jumbo, indeed!*

Prosecution: *And did you get rid of the worms?*

Daado: *I tried. I really tried, Sir. I cast spells - it's what we qualified obeah-men do, Sir.*

Prosecution: *Have your spells ever worked, Mr. Daado?*

Daado: *Yes, Sir. Many times.*

Prosecution: *Can you give us an example.*

Daado: *Yes, Sir. The same lady asked me to get rid of her husband in exchange for sex.*

Prosecution: *How?*

Daado: *By casting a spell, Sir; it's what we obeah-men do, Sir.*

Prosecution: *Yes, Yes. And did this spell of yours work?*

Daado: *Well, Sir, I don't want to boast, but her husband **is** dead.*

Prosecution: *And how do know that the husband's death was caused by your spell?*

Daado: *It was I who called forth Damballah, the Vodoun serpent God. Eyewitnesses claimed that a snake, ten feet tall with fangs as long as cutlass blades, had startled his horse, causing it to rear up and throw him upon the ground. He died from the injuries caused by my spell - not so long after.*

Prosecution: *And why do you think your spell worked on her husband and not on the worms?*

Daado: *Maybe men are like dogs, Sir, and their hearing is attuned to the obeah-man's spell.*
Whereas, with worms ... but this is only speculation, Sir.

One morning, after Tom Oliver had overseen the flooding of the fields, he paid a visit to the stables.
'Morning John.'
'Morning, Massa Tom.'
'I have just come from the Great House, where the Queen gave me some bad news.'
'Yessah, Massa Tom.'
Tom cleared his throat. 'You know that the crop is dead, and things are bad.'
'Yessah, Massa Tom.'
'Well...I don't know how to say this. Queenie has decided to sell Blackie and some of the other horses.'
John looked at Tom, his face devoid of emotion.

'I'm sorry, John. I tried, but there was nothing I could do. Of course, you will continue working here with the other horses.'

John swallowed and nodded.

After Tom had left, he sat down. He couldn't believe that she would think of selling Blackie as if he was a piece of common property that could be exchanged for money. She had not visited the stables since she inherited the Plantation, because she didn't need horses and all instructions came from Tom. John was grateful for this because he knew she didn't like him and he had no wish to see her on a day to day basis - or at any time, come to that, because of the brutal way in which she was treating the slaves. But now it was different; now it was an attack on Blackie and, therefore, an attack on him, and he couldn't just sit and let it happen without doing something. So, he decided to pay her a visit.

As he approached the gates, he wondered if the guard would let him in. Even though he was groom to the Queen's horses and the hero of the King's Cup, he had not been summoned, which was the normal way for all workers to secure entry to the Great House. When he arrived, though, there was no guard and the gates were wide open. He walked through with purpose and made his way along the avenue, the muscles in his jaw throbbing as if they were keeping time with his pumping heart and thumping feet. He did not notice how the canopies of the royal palms had been affected by a disease which had denuded their stems and left their branches looking like the spines and ribs of a human skeleton. He did not see the *Victoria Amazonicus* lilies sitting in ponds overrun by weeds, their flower stems rendered fruitless and stunted by an infestation of aphids, and their leaves lying all curled up as if in shame.

As he crossed the forecourt and approached the back door, his fists were balled and his breathing was like that of an angry bull which had been goaded by the lance of a picador; he was ready for any foolishness especially from that jumped-up little butler who thought he was better than anyone else. He pounded twice on the back door and waited for a few seconds. The door swung open to reveal someone who looked like Vicky; someone bedecked in white gloves and black jacket, but who was a quivering mess of diffidence and humility. John was taken aback when Vicky seemed to bow. But what shocked him most was when he said, 'Morning, *Tafe* John.'

The use of the word for 'uncle' from the language of the *Fon* people of the old country disarmed him. John's shoulders relaxed and he un-balled his fists. A smile played on his lips as he nodded in reply to Vicky's greeting.

Vicky asked, 'Are you here to see Maria, *Tafe*?'

'No, I want to see Queenie. But she didn't call me.'

'It's all right, *Tafe*. There are no rules now.'

Vicky escorted him up the stairs to the uppermost story, where Queenie spent most of her time in her rocking chair looking out onto the approach to the house. As they walked up, John noticed how run-down the place had become. All around, the paint of the walls lay peeling, with bits deposited on floors whose once highly polished surfaces were now worn through, leaving naked wood. As they passed the rows of windows on each floor, John noticed that they were clean but not as sparkling as before, and a few were hanging off their hinges. He wondered what had brought about this decay. He also thought about the change in the butler's attitude. Could this new sense of *camaraderie* have been forged by his realization that they were all victims of Queenie's callousness?

They reached the uppermost floor and when Vicky announced him, Queenie did not seem surprised; she had seen him approach.

'What do you want?' She asked gruffly.

'Massa Tom told me about the horses,' John said, his eyes focused on the shadow before him.

'Some are going to Pilgrim's Rest,' she said to the air.

John looked impassively at her. She had lost weight and didn't seem to pay much attention to how she dressed. Her cheeks had begun to lose their rosy roundness and her hair no longer sat upon her head all braided and glossy. Instead, it appeared to have been given the cursory treatment of a quick wash and brushback as if it were a nuisance. Her eyes, too, had become vacant, and there was no one living beyond them. She had become like the house.

'And Blackie?' He asked.

'Blackie too.'

'But I am the only person ...'

'Pilgrim's Rest wants him for breeding, and I need the money,' she said, cutting him off.

'I know about the crop, but you don't have to sell Blackie,' he said, with a plea in his voice.

'They will collect them later today,' she said, as if she hadn't heard him.

He ground his teeth as he looked at her sitting passively; rocking; laying down the law like the white Planters. He and Maria were free and were paid for their labour, so they had saved a bit and could move into the village and find other work. They had not decided to do this just yet, but it was something they had talked about doing whenever they left the Plantation. With Blackie gone, he felt he had nothing to lose.

'But why are you doing this?' He asked.

Silence. Only Rocking.

'Blackie is King Henry. He is Albion,' John exclaimed.

'He is just an animal,' she said firmly.

'You are selling out Albion.'

She said nothing. She rocked. And rocked. And infuriated him.

'You're paying for the way you have been treating the slaves,' he said, as he waded into deeper waters.

'It's none of your business,' she said evenly.

'How can you forget what it is like to be a slave?' He demanded.

She stopped rocking. She looked at him with contempt. 'Forget? Forget? Of course, I can't forget, Amadi!'

The use of his birth name threw him. Then the pieces began to fall into place.

'I remember!' She continued. 'I remember since the time I was captured. I remember every night when those men came into the pens and took me away and returned me, all violated and bloody. I remember every time I lay in the fields and looked up at the sky as the overseers panted and grunted on top of me. And I kept thinking of how I could get something out of it.'

John stood rooted to the spot.

'Nana?' He asked, his voice barely a whisper.

'No. Not Nana. Elizabeth! Queen of Albion! Nana died in the pens on the shore, in the fields and in King Henry's bed, many, many times. I recognised you the first time I saw you. Your features haven't changed. But there was - there is – nothing. Nothing at all. And even if I had felt anything, I wasn't going to allow sentiment and blood interfere with my plans.'

'What plans? You were a slave just like me.'

'That's where you are different. You accepted your

enslavement. I made it work for me. I used it to get what I wanted. And I wanted Albion! I knew that McKay lost his temper easily, especially when he was drunk. I had seen him with other women in the fields, the way he would savage them. So, when he tried to jump me, I kicked him in the balls. He lost his temper and he beat me up. It was worth it; I knew Henry would take pity on me. I knew he was soft, and he would just melt when I looked at him with my wounded eyes. I had heard that his wife was sickly and bedridden. He was like a ripe mango, soft, sweet, juicy and ready to be plucked and eaten.'

John's shoulders drooped as he listened. 'I can't believe someone can change like that,' he whispered.

'Change? I was never anything but just a little child.'

'But to plot and plan and use people like that?'

'And what did they do to me? Didn't they use me? Didn't King Henry use me? Didn't they use you? He wanted a nursemaid for his wife and a woman to warm his bed at night. She taught me English and I gave him what he couldn't get from her. I knew the power I had over him. All I had to do was to wait until she died.'

She went quiet and resumed her rocking. John stood looking at her.

'I am ashamed,' he mumbled.

She stopped rocking and slapped the arms of the chair.

'What are you ashamed of?' She rounded on him.

'Accepting your lot in life?'

'No, I am ashamed to tell anybody that you are my sister.'

'Your sister is dead. She died when they took her.'

'And Albion is dying because of you.'

'Leave now! And do not ever come back!' She ordered him. The she turned her back to him. And she rocked. And rocked.

John put his hat on, straws jutting out at every angle, and he left. He walked at a snail's pace, head stooped, dragging his leg as if it were a gangrened thing that had poisoned his entire being. He saw the overrun ponds; he looked up and noticed the ravaged palms; the blighted leaves of the lilies; the shrivelled flowers. And he felt at one with them.

He returned to the stables, but this time it felt strange. He felt like a stranger. He went from box to box and said goodbye to each horse that had been sold. When he came to Blackie, the horse whinnied as if it had known through the sixth sense which John knew all quadrupeds possessed. He rubbed Blackie's head and the horse nuzzled him.

'Now, boy,' he said. 'No more racing. You're free now.'

John's body juddered and he blubbered, and his tears flowed without inhibition.

He cried. He cried for Blackie. He cried for Philip. He cried for King Henry. He cried for himself, he cried for the memory of his little sister and he cried for being powerless. And he cried for all those times he should have cried but could not. Did not.

Every night, the drums beat with increased ferocity and, night after night, Daado came to Queenie in her sleep; night after night, she screamed and arched her back as he repeatedly drove into her, leaving her like a rag doll, unable to move the next day; unwilling to try. She had lost all interest in Albion and she had grown more and more distracted. She waited only for the night to descend. She waited for the drums. She waited for him. For him to come to her. For him to fill that vacuum in her life. And he did so, night after night, repeatedly thrusting his dagger into her as if he was avenging a wrong done to him.

And, one night, with each stab of his blade, he uttered with contempt, 'Elvira!'. 'Elvira!'

The next morning, when Maria went to wake Queenie, she found her naked and lifeless. Her head was buried in her pillows and her rear end was pointing upwards.

On the floor, all around the bed, were large muddy footprints, some of them caked, the others fresh.

Chapter Twelve

In England, the debate over slavery raged.

James Cropper, merchant, and philanthropist, wrote in a letter entitled, "Impolicy of Slavery":

"it had long been a matter of public notoriety, that the Slaves in the West Indies are degradingly driven, like cattle, by the whip at their labour, which, for nearly half the year lasts for one-half the night, as well as the whole day!"

Further, '*the slaves were held and dealt with as property, often branded with a hot iron, liable to be sold at the will of their master, compelled to work on the Sabbath for their own subsistence, and denied the advantages of religious instruction.*'

He argued that if the slaves in the West Indies were freed, they would not only produce more cane sugar and other tropical commodities but also consume much more of British manufactures.

Lord Howick, a Member of Parliament and Under Secretary for the Colonies, wrote in 1832 that the great problem to be solved was to draw up a plan for the emancipation of the slaves which would *"induce them when relieved from the fear of the driver and his whip, to undergo the regular and continuous labour which is indispensable in carrying on the production of sugar."*

Once it had become clear that the abolition of slavery in the West Indies was inevitable, panic began to grow among the Planters, and they speculated about what it would mean to their labour force.

'*Would the slaves vacate the land suddenly?*'

'*They have always fought against us. Why would they*

now stay and work for us?'
  'They might stay if we paid them.'
  'But, then again, they might just bugger off.'

While conjecture was rife and varied, it was this last insight that proved to be the most accurate. In what seemed like a gesture of two fingers thrust at their erstwhile masters, the former slaves left the Plantations in their droves and set up their own villages or they gravitated towards the towns, glad to see the back of the sugar cane fields and all that it had meant.

There ensued a fierce bidding war for labour which pushed up its price and unleashed a wave of ill-feeling among the Planters. Apart from the acrimony this caused, the rising cost of labour meant a shrinking of profits, which threatened the existence of the smaller Plantations. Some of the more reasoned voices argued that to avoid this, what was clearly needed was to find another source of labour. But what was also clear, was that any new sourcing of labour could not be done on the same basis as slavery. This system, which had existed for over two hundred years, had attracted the attention of free thinkers, philosophers, liberals and politicians around the world who had condemned it as 'heinous', 'abominable', 'odious', 'abhorrent' and 'loathsome'. Any new system, therefore, had to be based on free choice rather than forced enslavement, or, at least, so it ought to appear.

Attempts at recruiting from Portugal, Ireland, China and the Southern States of America had failed for one reason or another, and the Planters turned to India as the solution to their problems. John Gladstone, the father of future four-time British Prime Minister, William Ewart Gladstone, formed a partnership with John Moss, his friend and fellow absentee planter, and they hired labour recruiters to transport Indians from Calcutta. He wrote:

Dear Sirs, Liverpool, 4 January 1836

... We are therefore most desirous to obtain and introduce labourers from other quarters, and particularly from climates something similar in their nature. Our plantation labour in the field is very light; much of it, ..., is done by task-work, which for the day is usually completed by two o'clock in the afternoon, giving to the people all the rest of the day to themselves. They are furnished with comfortable dwellings and abundance of food; ... they have also occasionally rice, Indian corn, meal, ship's biscuits, and a regular supply of salt codfish, as well as the power of fishing for themselves in the trenches. ... Their houses are comfortable, and it may be fairly said they pass their time agreeably and happily. Marriages are encouraged, and when improper conduct on the part of the people takes place, there are public stipendiary magistrates who take cognizance of such, and judge between them and their employers. They have regular medical attendance whenever they are indisposed, at the expense of their employers. I have been particular in describing the present situation and occupation of our people, to which I ought to add, that their employment in the field is clearing the land with the hoe, and, where required, planting fresh canes. In the works a portion are occupied in making sugar, and in the distilleries, in which they relieve each other, which makes their labour light. It is of great importance to us to endeavour to provide a portion of other labourers ... independent of our negro population...,

John Gladstone.

Questions were asked about whether Gladstone knew that the above description of slave-life bore little resemblance to that described by James Cropper and Lord Howick but chose, nevertheless, to embellish it with falsehoods. Some challenged Gladstone's claim that the employment in the field consisted of *'clearing the land with the hoe and, where required, planting fresh canes.'* If this was so, they argued, who was it that did the back-breaking work of cutting, bundling, fetching, and hoisting the sugar cane stalks?

Whatever the case, a new source of cheap labour had to be found.

Chapter Thirteen
India

Eight and a half thousand miles away, in a field of nothing but parched and cracked ground, Valmiki sits on his haunches. He is crying. He has been doing this every day, for how long he cannot remember, but it has been for a very long time since the rain stopped falling and the sun in the sky assumed permanent dominion over the earth.

His appearance belies his age. He is fifteen, but he looks like forty. His hair, once an abundant crop of luxuriant black, is matted and streaked with dirt; and his body, while never robust, is skin drawn tight over bones. Below his bony buttocks are two spindly legs, which creak whenever he moves, no doubt grateful that they are not called upon to carry any greater burden.

Valmiki finds squatting to be the ideal posture for choking off the pangs of hunger that are gnawing away at his insides as if they are exploring every fault and seeking out every fissure. In order to satiate them, to stop the pain, he chews little lumps of dirt, and ferrets around dried cowpats for any seeds which might have escaped digestion by the four stomachs of the sacred animal.

But even shit is a rarity.

The continued drought has reduced the animals, like the people, to walking skeletons.

There is no grass, no cud for them to chew. There is nothing in their bowels for them to evacuate and no milk in their emaciated udders to expel. All around, in small plots of land, lies the evidence of the people's attempts to stem starvation before the drought descended. The parched shoots of the rice plants, the dried stems of okra, and the withered vines of pumpkin and squash, which once threaded their way all along the ground, fences and rickety trellises, now lie shrivelled like the moulted skins of serpents, drained of all substance and baked to a crisp by an unforgiving sun.

The rains, which the harbingers, soothsayers and augurs of North Western India had promised, have not materialised. Day after day, the people in the village look up into the clear blue sky hoping that by some miracle they would feel a cooling wind, witness a build-up of black cloud, see the silent benign flash of sheet lightning and hear the crack of thunder as malevolent forked lightning pierce and rupture the over-burdened rain clouds. Then they would feel and taste the first tentative drops of cool nourishing liquid as a prelude to being inundated by an ejaculation that would restore them, their animals, and the land to their previous fertility. Day after day, they look up, and hope and pray, but, day after day, they are convinced that their millions of gods and the heavens have deserted them.

In desperation, they decide to turn to the earth and mysticism for salvation. They had heard stories of The Holy Man. This Brahmin Priest, the holiest of castes, was an adept at coconut dowsing. He was blessed with the gift of being able to use a coconut to detect the presence of water, no matter how deep underground it may be lurking, heedless of the misery of those wretched souls who dwelled above. The Holy Man, some said, had a direct line to the gods. So, they scrape together every little thing of worth that they have and summon *The Holy Man*. And they wait.

The day comes. The whole village gathers in a large field. In the distance, they could hear a faint tinkling and the rhythmic beat of drums. It grows louder. They crane their necks and push each other out of the way to see what is happening. The musical procession comes into full view.

There are four men dressed in ankle-length gowns of bright red, one tweeting away on his flute, another two drumming away on their *dholak and chenda* and the fourth tinkling away on his *dhantal*. In the middle, before the villagers' eyes, in flesh and blood, is The Holy Man. He is all resplendent in flowing saffron-coloured robes and his complexion bears the colour and translucence of a perfectly ripe peach. They gasp.

A saviour is in their midst.

Children of all ages run; they fall; they get up again; they try to keep up with the procession. Even the adults are enthralled by the image of this tall imposing mystic whose measured strides aided by a six-foot-long staff, seem to devour the very ground from which he is expected to draw forth water.

Like all *Brahmins,* he carries himself with an air of detached superiority as he looks down the length of his long *Aryan* nose at these peasants who do not deserve to be in his exalted presence. They whisper, and they are immediately silenced by the acolytes whose venerable leader stands with arms outstretched, the one holding his staff, the other a peeled coconut. Like Moses about to part the Red Sea, he stares at the ground, then in disdain at the people for the paltry sums they have paid for his services. He commands them to be quiet, and there is an immediate hush.

With the coconut lying horizontally on his palm, The Holy Man circles the field. He traverses from east to west, then from north to south - all the time concentrating and muttering something incomprehensible.

'Sanskrit', someone whispers, and those within hearing gasp in wonderment.

Valmiki and the haggard village people look on with an air of expectancy. They hold their breaths, afraid to breathe out in case the mirage evaporates. The discovery of water would slake their thirst, lubricate their parched mouths and throats, and would nurture the soil that had turned to powder through years of overplanting and drought. Perhaps they could eke out just one more crop of rice or vegetables to feed their starving families, and grass to feed their cows.

Beyond this, they dare not hope.

After much to-ing and fro-ing and mumbling and grumbling by The Holy Man, the coconut in his hand shudders and shimmies, then it defies gravity by standing bolt upright. Its straight fibrous hairs bristle as if it has stuck a finger in a power socket, and its three piggy-like little eyes are wide open and staring fixedly at the ground as if they are penetrating the depth and darkness of the earth's soul, looking for water.

There are gasps of bewilderment from the throng, who are immediately silenced by the acolytes as though any noise in the presence of their leader is an irreverence that would contaminate this act of divine inspiration. As they wait in anticipation for some utterance from The Holy Man, the men, women, and children stand with open mouths, many miraculously producing streams of spittle from glands that had long since lost the art of salivation.

The Holy Man stops dramatically and closes his eyes as if he is thanking one of the multitudes of Hindu Gods for answering his prayers. Then he opens his eyes, stares into the distance, and commands the villagers: 'Dig! Dig! Dig!'

And they dig. How they dig! Like dogs reacting to a Pavlovian signal, those weakened, emaciated, wretched victims of geography dig and dig. With sticks, cups, spoons, and fingers, the nails of which had been chewed down to their base as a substitute for food, they dig.

Soon the landscape is pockmarked with holes, from which not a single drop of water has issued. There are mounds of dirt heaped around the mouths of the holes, as if a labour of industrious moles had been at work, but they are dry and powdery and do not bear the remotest trace of dampness.

The people are too shocked to voice their dissatisfaction. They are too enfeebled to demand their money back. They are too exhausted to give chase. They could only look on in stupefied silence as the Holy Man and his orchestra scurry away with their money in such a haste that the coconut falls to the ground and cracks open releasing a trickle of water. Those who see it before it is quickly absorbed by the earth, lick their lips.

All around the land, in Bihar, Bengal, Uttar Pradesh and Southern India, the hungry crawled. Devoid of sustenance and robbed of the means of providing it, they scavenged and scrounged to stay alive. And everywhere, the vultures circled – at temples, at bazaars, at wells and in towns – anywhere towards which the hungry and thirsty gravitated in search of food. Sensing the people's hopelessness, these preying *arkatis,* the recruiters of cheap labour, swooped and wove their spell with their smooth tongues and glib patter.

They intoned seductively: *Trust in me… trust in me… I can take you to a land of milk and honey. You will never be hungry again. Freedom … Food and Money… After five years you can return, rich and independent.'*

And their victims fell under their hypnotic spell.

Valmiki often left his village in search of food and as he walked and walked towards the town, he foraged, only to discover that whatever might have been there, had long been taken by the hordes of others who had passed before him. Often, he would end up at the big temple in the town, where he would sit for hours listening to the Pandit reciting passages from the holy books to an audience like himself - an audience that had nowhere to go and nothing to do. Like most of them, Valmiki did this, not out of curiosity, a thirst for knowledge or religious fervour, but because he knew that at the end of the torture the multitude was always fed.

He had lost both his parents through smallpox and had learnt that as a street child, he could only survive by using his wits. He was quick at absorbing information and he listened and learnt by heart all the prayers and the intonation of each incantation said or sung by the Pandit. These he would recite on his long journey into town and on his way back towards his village. He did not know what they meant, but it helped to dull the pains he felt when walking. One day, as he approached the outskirts of the town after his long journey, he saw a group of people around a well; they were shouting, pushing each other and swearing. As he was thirsty, he joined the melee but when he finally reached the well, there was no water - only a faint dampness around the bucket, barely enough for him to rub on his cracked lips to remind him of what a real drink was like. As the crowd dispersed in different directions, he stood there unsure of what to do next, the overgrown long nail of his left big toe scratching his right calf.

'Are you looking for a job, my friend?' Came the dulcet tone.

Valmiki looked around and saw a man in his thirties; he

was dressed in a white long-sleeved shirt which was buttoned up to his neck. The creases, which ran along from shoulder to wrist, were as sharp as a sliver of bamboo, and his clean khaki trousers had been freshly pressed and kept in place by a broad black belt over a budding paunch. In his hand, he grasped a battered old briefcase, which somehow gave him an air of importance. He was about a foot taller than Valmiki, who stared up in fascination at the man's clipped pencil moustache, which began to twitch and dance as he spoke again.

'My name is E.J. Badri,' he said. 'Imagine,' he continued, bending towards Valmiki with the thumb and index finger of each hand joined to imitate a screen. 'Imagine,' he said again, slowly moving his hands apart as if to reveal an unfolding picture. 'Imagine a place where there is plentiful water, food, fruit trees, and grass as far as your eyes can see. A place where you can get a lot of money for doing easy work.' He held his hands in the air as if to give Valmiki time to digest the possibilities. 'Imagine,' whispered Badri seductively.

Valmiki stared and swallowed. The mention of water and food, set against the image described by Badri, stirred distant memories. He searched for words to articulate the many questions going through his mind, but before he could speak, E.J. Badri said:

'Come, come, I can see that you are hungry and thirsty. There is plenty of time for questions, but you must eat and drink first. Don't you want to do that?'

Valmiki nodded and nodded, despite the question being rhetorical.

'And your clothes! Well, we must get you new ones, mustn't we?' The enticer trilled.

Stupefied by this possible upturn in his fortunes, Valmiki allowed himself to be propelled by the man's firm hold of his elbow, all the time listening to the constant chatter that promised halcyon days ahead.

They came to a building, a kind of depot, from which came the sound of people and plates, and the smell of food that wafted through the air. Valmiki inhaled and salivated. Badri showed him to a room where he could wash his hands. He went in, but before washing, he cupped his hands and scooped up three double handfuls of water and lapped them up in quick succession.

'Easy now, easy, my young friend. You don't want to choke, said Badri. 'Come, sit down here and make yourself comfortable.'

Valmiki did as he was bid and sat at a long table in a space created by two other skeletons who had made themselves smaller.

Food was brought - first the rice and roti, followed by the vegetables and dhal. And he, like the others, ate and ate, oblivious to all around them. There was no conversation, only a single-minded concentration on the task at hand as if it were an Olympic event in which they were representing their country, and which they had to win as a matter of national pride.

When he had had enough, Valmiki leant back, closed his eyes, and tried to remember the last time that he had been so close to attaining nirvana. He recalled that it was when the daughter of a rich local farmer was getting married. He was about eight, and he and his friends had gone along, uninvited, and they had sat in the section of the tent reserved for untouchables, beggars and vagrants - an appeasement to the gods by the host in exchange for their blessings - and they had eaten and asked for more.

His reminiscence was interrupted by the noise of trays

being plonked under his nose. He opened his eyes and beheld a panoply of sweetmeats of different shapes, sizes and colours laid out on the table. A few minutes earlier, after he had scooped up the last bit of dhal-rice-and-roti with his fingers and put the mix into his mouth, licking his fingers as though his years of starvation had taught him that nothing, nothing at all, must be wasted, he had felt that he couldn't eat another grain. But now, looking at the display set before him, he wondered how he could resist such a kaleidoscope of colours and the promise of obscene amounts of sugar so typical of Indian confectionery, and which lay so invitingly in front of him. He set about them as if he was going for a second gold medal; a second orgasm.

Badri, who had been overseeing the other eaters, came over to him and asked if he wanted anything more to eat, to which he shook his head as he washed down his meal with a sip of water. Badri then led him to a large room. Here an attendant looked him up and down before reaching up to a shelf and taking down a pair of white trousers and a white long- sleeved shirt, which he handed to him, pointing him in the direction of a screened-off room.

Valmiki went behind the screen and closed his eyes as he sniffed at the clean clothes before trying them on; then he returned, looking all sheepish and timid.

Badri clapped and said: 'Perfect. Perfect,' even though Valmiki's shirt drooped over his shoulders and the cuffs overlapped his fingers. The trousers, too, fell straight from his waist, past his hips and dragged upon the floor. Valmiki tripped a few times as he walked and Badri stopped him, bent down, and hitched up one of the trouser legs. He looked at Valmiki's naked dirt-stained foot, and said to the attendant, 'Shoes!'

The attendant came over and appraised Valmiki's exposed foot - not for the aesthetics - but to gauge its size.

He nodded, then he went to the back of the room and returned shortly after with a pair of white canvas sneakers, which he gave to Valmiki to try on. Valmiki was thrilled at the sight of the pristine footwear and the smell of the fresh rubber. It had been many years since he had worn anything on his feet, and he wasn't sure how they would feel. He sat down and tried them on, then he stood up and walked unsteadily up and down, smiling all the time.

'Perfect! Perfect!' Badri cried, but Valmiki kept tripping over the generous cuffs of his trousers which overlapped his sneakers and dragged along the floor, gathering black dust as they did so.

'Not a problem,' said Badri, as he bent down again, this time rolling up the cuffs to a point just below Valmiki's shins, just to make sure. He stood back, arms akimbo, and appraised Valmiki.

'Perfect! Perfect!' He said, and while this temporary alteration to Valmiki's sartorial appearance meant that he was unlikely to trip over, it did make him look a bit like a man who was expecting a flood.

Badri then showed him into a washroom with buckets of water, bars of soap and lots of towels which were hanging on nails. He spent some time there washing off the years of dirt that had accumulated on the surface of his skin and which had, no doubt, blocked every pore in his body. As he rubbed the transparent soap on to his body, the whiteness of the suds quickly turned into a mucky brown scum, which he washed off. He soaped his head, then he poured a calabash full of water over it, using his fingers to untangle the matted mass and licking some of the foamy streams as they descended past his mouth. After a while, he emerged, fresh and sweet-smelling; his hair was washed and combed; he was dressed in new clothes; and his feet were shod in a pair of white shoes - all of this, and a full belly!

He couldn't stop smiling.

Badri told him that if he agreed to go to the West Indies to work, he could continue to eat and drink at the depot and receive medical attention until the depot's doctor declared him fit to travel.

Valmiki reflected upon his state of life before Badri. The constant scrimmaging with others for a drop of water, the dog-like daily scavenging for food, the pangs of hunger, the sleeping wherever night befell him – in short, the nothingness of his life – and he didn't have to think long before nodding his head several times. Thereafter, he stayed at the depot where he slept and ate, and where he was treated for his scurvy caused by years of malnutrition.

In the weeks that followed, Valmiki slowly started to change. His chest and arms began to fill out thus tightening the Indian cotton of his shirt and taking up the sag around his shoulders and cuffs. Nor was this bloom restricted to his torso; it made its way down to his hips and buttocks where it began to reclaim the slack from his trouser legs, eventually rendering the folding up of his cuffs unnecessary. As his anaemia receded, so too did his eyes begin to show some colour and life, and his skin, previously dry, flaky, and blotched in places, began to take on a moistened glow. He was subjected to regular medical examinations and was vaccinated to ensure that he was free from the threat of the most prevalent diseases.

When Badri adjudged the time to be right, he took Valmiki before a magistrate whose job it was to ascertain that the potential emigrant was disease-free and had agreed to leave voluntarily. There had been many cases in which unscrupulous agents and doctors had conspired to pass recruits off as fit when they were not. This had resulted in many deaths before the workers had even set foot on the Plantations, and met with protest from the Planters, who had invested large sums of money. Neither had it escaped the attention of human rights watchers around the world, who cautioned that more care was needed in the recruitment process if another era of human degradation was to be avoided.

'Do you agree to go to the West Indies to work as an indentured labourer for five years?' The magistrate asked Valmiki.

'Yes,' replied Valmiki, just as Badri had coached him. 'And do you know where the West Indies are?'

'Yes,' he replied.

'How old are you?

'Twenty years old,' he lied.

'And where were you born?'

'Bihar.'

After each answer the magistrate wrote or ticked something on a form. He was still writing when he asked the next question:

'And what caste are you?'

In coaching him for his appearance before the magistrate, Badri had not prepared him for this question. After all, every Indian knew their place in the caste system and never questioned it. In fact, the basement position in the hierarchy of Castes, which people like Valmiki occupied – the *Dalit, Chamar* or *untouchable* - was so drummed into them every minute of their lives by the demeaning and humiliating way in which they were treated by others, meant that a response should have been automatic. But Valmiki bit his lip and hesitated.

'What *caste* are you?' The magistrate repeated, putting his pen down and looking at Valmiki. He emphasised the word as if speaking to a half-wit who was wasting his precious time.

In front of Valmiki's eyes flashed the image of The Holy Man, the imposing figure of the coconut diviner in his saffron robes.

'Brahmin,' he lied again.

The magistrate stamped, signed, and issued him with an emigrant certificate, and everyone was happy. Badri would get his commission, the far-flung Plantations would get their cheap labour, and the British, having done the right thing by abolishing slavery, would be seen to be acting with respect for Indian human rights. Above all, Valmiki, the untouchable, would be able to get a job in 'West India'.

'Perfect! Perfect!' Badri clapped. And Valmiki beamed.

Badri encouraged Valmiki to attend the Temple every day so that he could listen and learn from the Pandit. He had viewed Valmiki's lie about being a *Brahmin* as a coup, and even though he had had nothing to do with it, he saw some of the glory as being his, because it was he who had discovered Valmiki. It was he who had approached the forlorn and unkempt vagrant at the town's dried out well, and now Valmiki had become his mission. The latter had been taught to read and write by his mother, who was a schoolteacher, but since her death, these skills had shrunk from the lack of use and the need to survive. However, under Badri's tutelage and Valmiki's own hunger to learn, they revived gradually.

Badri's enthusiasm knew no limits. He searched around and found a dog-eared copy of The Vedas - a collection of hymns, poems, prayers, and mythological accounts of the

Vedic religion, written by the Aryans in Sanskrit but translated into everyday Hindi for the benefit of the non-scholastic, non-*Brahmin* classes. And, from somewhere obscure, in what he alluded to as an instance of divine guidance, Badri produced a copy of *Ramayana*, an epic poem of 24,000 verses of philosophy and ethics, which tells about the life of Rama, his banishment from his father's kingdom, his travels and travails, and his eventual return to be king.

The *Ramayana* was written by a scholar called Valmiki.

After months of seasoning at the depot, Valmiki, like the other emigres, was given medical clearance by the depot's doctor and he was therefore ready to travel. They were all given packages of food, extra footwear and clothing for the journey to Calcutta. They were prime assets for whom the Planters were paying well so they had to be nourished and kept healthy for the long tedious journey ahead.

Badri was sad to see Valmiki go. He added a second pair of plimsolls and a few saffron coloured robes along with an extra pair of trousers and a red cap. Moved by this, Valmiki thanked him, and when he tried to return the Vedas and the Ramayana, Badri said,

'No, no, Valmiki, you keep them,' adding with a knowing wink of a tear-filled eye, 'they are meant only for Brahmin scholars.'

Chapter Fourteen

Aboard the ship, there were people drawn from all sections of Indian society who had signed on for different reasons. Most, like Valmiki, were escaping starvation and unemployment; some were getting away from increasing violence and some were fleeing from justice. There were also those who were getting away from over-attentive wives or brutal husbands, and there were also some families - parents and children. One thing they all had in common, though, was that they were going to a place where the opportunities were endless, so they had been led to believe. There were also those who had been kidnapped and forced aboard the ship. These were kept in slave-like conditions in the hold with the hatches battened down, and they were only let out on deck after the ship had left port. At the end of their journey, these were absorbed into the immigrant workforce by rapacious Planters and their agents, notwithstanding the absence of proper documentation.

As word spread that Valmiki was a *Brahmin,* people treated him with reverence. He was regularly greeted with the *Namaste* by those of inferior castes - the Kshatriyas (warriors), Vaishyas (skilled traders, merchants), and Shudras (unskilled workers) - which he returned as an act of humility. Most of the passengers, however, were untouchables who kept a respectful distance from the *Brahmin*. With the memory of The Holy Man in his mind, Valmiki practised walking with his back straight and holding his head high, always clearing his throat as if he was contemplating some higher truth. There were times, too, when he would open the worn Vedas and read and chant as he had seen the Pandit do at the temple, which all added to the respect with which he was held by his companions. On one occasion a fat man approached him and humbly asked if he might talk to him, to which Valmiki nodded.

'I am Manoj from Bihar, Sahib. I am married and I am having four children, Sahib. One day, I was sitting on the bank of a stream fishing so that I could feed my family and I was attacked by two or three men – I can't say how many. Sahib, they put a bag over my head and hit me hard with something. I can still feel the lump on my head, here, just here.'

Manoj bent his head and rubbed a spot. He seemed to be inviting Valmiki to do the same for verification, but Valmiki resisted, as *Brahmins* never indulged in such acts of familiarity with those of lower castes. However, he pulled a sympathetic face and invited the man to continue.

'When I woke up, I was in a dark place and couldn't hear anything but loud noises and people whispering next to me. I asked them where we were and what had happened, and they all had similar stories. One man was walking along a path and one was sleeping when they were attacked and hit over the head, Sahib. One was even squatting in the bush answering a call of nature when he was captured. But, to cut a long story short, Sahib' (and Valmiki was glad for his consideration) 'it was only when the hold was open, and the light flooded in and we saw the sky moving that we realised that we were in a ship and going somewhere. Do you know where we are going, Sahib?'

'We are going to West India to work,' said Valmiki with authority.

'Where is West India, Sahib?'

'West India is the other side of East India,' Valmiki said, again with authority. Manoj nodded in understanding.

'But how long would it take, Sahib, and how long are we going to be away, Sahib? I have a little baby and my family depends on me to feed them.'

Valmiki felt genuinely sorry for the man and explained that he too was a bit in the dark, but that they were going to a place where they could work and get a good life and that they could return after five years. The man shrugged his shoulders in resignation and, thereafter, he stuck close to Valmiki, who did not mind.

What he did mind, though, was the five foot five, stocky, one-eyed man who kept sidling up to him and calling him 'Pandit'.

'I am not a Pandit,' retorted Valmiki.

'But all *Brahmins* are Pandits,' the man replied.

'All Pandits are Brahmins, but not all Brahmins are Pandits,' Valmiki said haughtily, as he turned and walked away from the man, leaving him to ponder this assertion.

The harping-on about him being a Brahmin had made Valmiki uncomfortable; it was as if the man was prodding him, teasing him; it was as if the man knew something or knew him. But, how could he? Valmiki asked himself. They had never met before because if they had, he wouldn't have forgotten him. He therefore concluded that it was his own guilt that was making him over-sensitive. In any case, he did not like the man. It was not because he was short of an eye; nor was it the slowness of the other eyelid to open and close, often stopping halfway, which gave him a snake-like appearance whenever he blinked. No, there was something else about him that gave Valmiki goosebumps and made him shudder. It was as though the man could see everything, despite his affliction. Valmiki had heard that senses tended to compensate for any weaknesses, either in themselves or in other senses. Perhaps this was true, and the man had a third, an all-seeing eye in addition to his good eye and the partially closed socket. Even though Valmiki made sure he kept his distance, the ever-present reptile always gave him a wave and a slow lazy wink.

'You know that man, Sahib?' Asked Manoj, his companion from Bihar.

'No. I don't. But I don't like him.'

'Sahib, I know who he is,' Manoj whispered.

'Who is he?' Asked Valmiki.

'Not now, Sahib; he is watching,' Manoj said, eyes staring uncomfortably at the ground.

Valmiki stole a glance and saw the man scowling at Manoj and drawing a finger across his throat.

Later, when they were alone, Manoj said to Valmiki:

'Sahib, I am very afraid.'

'But why? I know he looks evil, but he can't do anything to us if we avoid him.'

'But, Sahib, he is a dangerous Dacoit called Bagoutie. He is wanted for robbery and murder. His pictures are all over Bengal. I saw them when I went to visit my cousin.'

'No wonder,' said Valmiki. 'I feel as though there are insects crawling all over me whenever I look at him.'

'He is evil, Sahib. Everybody is afraid of him.'

'Well, let's keep far from him; that way he can't hurt us.' Valmiki said.

As the journey dragged on into weeks, then months, some sought enlightenment from the learned man and asked him how far West India was from where they had left. Others sought to discover from him if it was true that West India was a land of plenty, as Badri and the other *arkatis* had said. When it became clear that the sage had no idea and just wished to be left alone, their respect seemed to dissipate. This process was accelerated by vomit, that great leveller of men. The conditions on the ship were like those on the Black slave ships where diseases like dysentery and cholera were prevalent and claimed many lives. Even though he had grown in strength and had been immunized against most common diseases, Valmiki had no defence against the effects caused by the ship being constantly buffeted and beaten about by high winds and violent waves as it crossed the black waters. He was violently sea-sick during most of the journey, regularly spewing his guts out and groaning in discomfort. Sometimes, when the griping in his stomach became too much, he doubled up and swore in the kind of language that would have damned a real *Brahmin's* soul. Many of his shipmates also fell ill and many of those who had been passed fit to travel when they had been in no condition to do so, died, unable to resist the ravages of the sea.

The journey lasted three months, and those who had survived were distributed to various Plantations where they were allocated to different gangs to start working. There was no time for them to regain their strength or to adapt to their new environment; there was no period of assimilation or seasoning for the newcomers because there was a premium on labour and the Planters were anxious to see a quick return on their investment.

Valmiki was grateful for one thing, though. He saw Bagoutie being put into a cart whose horses were pointed in the opposite direction to his. As the cart began to move, Bagoutie looked directly at him and their eyes made three. The bandit grinned, winked, and waved to him as his cart moved off. Valmiki stared at his retreating form, thankful that each turn of the cart's wheels made him smaller and smaller until he vanished. He shuddered as he thought about Manoj, his kidnapped boat companion from Bihar, who had mysteriously disappeared during the latter part of the journey.

Valmiki's cart rolled off towards Plantation Albion and as the journey progressed, it became clear to him that they were not in India, West or otherwise. Here the rulers were all white, and most of the people were *habshis* - black, but not in the way of the dark-skinned South Indians. They were physically different, too, in that their hair was curly and grew close to their heads, and their lips were fuller. They also spoke a language which was foreign to his ears. The climate, too, was more humid than the one to which he had been accustomed. And the food! Well! He had never eaten anything so bland and stodgy as that which he had been given upon arrival.

Soon, he came to realise that all Badri's promises were false. The accommodation at Albion was nothing like he had described back in Calcutta. Instead, he was billeted in an unlit range-type room, and he had to sleep on the mud floor using whatever cloth he could find to put between himself and the cold hard ground. There were also frequent visits from brown rats which disturbed him whenever they nibbled his toes.

He worked as a cane-cutter for most of his first year and he was slotted into the base of a hierarchical system on the Plantation where the white planters issued orders through an overseer, who passed them down to a 'driver', a type of foreman, who relayed them down to the workers.

The wages were as stipulated in his contract, but he found on many occasions that the overseer had made deductions for 'incompletion' of work. When he tried to complain to the driver, he was told that the deductions were legal. He had also heard, but not experienced it himself, that some overseers demanded money from the workers every week and that if they refused to pay up, they were chastised. There were also occasions when he saw workers being whipped in the field for nothing less than stopping for a drink of water. The freedom, which Badri had so extolled, was non-existent.

While all this fell far short of the promises made to him, at least he was earning money and he was able to eat. The uninspiring food he had been given when he had first arrived was replaced by rations of split peas, rice and vegetables, which he soon learnt to concoct into something more palatable and satisfying to his Indian palate. The work was hard and dangerous, but at least it was done in fields where things grew, where animal and insect life abounded, unlike what he had known.

'Grass, as far as the eye could see', Badri had boasted, and this was the most accurate of his promises. Everywhere, no matter how far, and in whatever direction he looked, there were unending fields of green razor-like leaves topping off the sucrose-filled multi-jointed stalks of the sugar-producing plant which rose to eight feet or more into the sky.

As he neared the end of his first year, Valmiki could not believe his luck when he was made *Sardar,* a leader of men How this came about was due to a mixture of good management practice and luck. But, above all, it owed much to his own duplicity.

After the Queenie era, Albion had passed into the hands of the Consortium and Tom Oliver had been appointed Administrative Manager. He knew that while the immigrant labour force would function like the slaves, there was no place for violence in the new order. When he was told that one of his overseers, a man called Jacobs, was in the habit of using a whip and demanding money from the workers, he decided to visit the fields to see what he could discover. He found nothing to substantiate the allegation on that occasion, but he did notice something strange about the deferential way in which the other cane-cutters were behaving towards one in their ranks - a tallish, dark-haired man of fair complexion, who had a rather regal bearing. He asked the driver for the latter's name and work number and when he returned to his office, he fished out the man's disembarkation papers. As he sat at his desk going through Valmiki's papers, his eyes widened when he saw the word *'Brahmin'* under the heading 'caste.' He drew in a breath. This was as rare as hen's teeth. He, like all Planters and Managers, had been made aware of the nature of the Indian workforce - the caste system, the taboos, the dietary peculiarities and the holiness of the cow. Previous shipments of Indians had been made up mainly of the labouring *Shudras* and the untouchable *Dalits*. There had been a few *Vaishyas* (farmers), caused by crop failures and droughts, but Oliver had never encountered a *Brahmin,* the apogee of the Indian caste system, the caste of priests and scholars, the caste that all others held as superior. He knew that what was needed in the new order of things, with the whole world watching on, was not overseers with bullwhips and cats-o-nine-tails, but coercion of a subtle type; and he had also learnt that there was no better coercive implement than the Hindu caste system.

He sent for Valmiki.

As Valmiki could speak little English, Oliver called in another Indian who had arrived in the colony some years earlier and who had picked up enough English to act as a translator. The translator was a *Dalit,* an untouchable, called Parhab Singh. He was a five-foot-tall man of dark complexion who wore wire-framed glasses, which kept sliding down along his nose as he spoke, and which he kept pushing back up. Having been told by Oliver that he was going to translate for a *Brahmin,* Parhab observed the protocol of the Hindu caste system by bowing, keeping a respectful distance, and never looking Valmiki in the eyes. Oliver looked on in fascination at the two figures in front of him, one proud and erect, the other stooped in humility. He had never seen the Hindu caste system in full flow.

Oliver to Parhab: Ask him why he signed up.

Parhab: Sahib, he said that he and his parents are never getting along, so he is leaving home and trying to make a life for himself, but the drought came and there is no food for eating.

As Parhab spoke, his head bobbled like an Einstein doll, but Oliver knew that this did not signify anything negative; it was merely a characteristic of the way Indians spoke and was, therefore, an integral part of their language.

Oliver: Ask him how he learnt your language if he is a *Brahmin.*

Parhab: He says he is being a scholar and has learned many different dialects, Sahib.

Oliver: Tell him that I want him to work as a *Sardar* in the cane cutting gangs; he will be paid better than the workers.

Parhab: He said that he is being most humbled by your esteemed generosity, Sahib. And, Sahib, it is a good idea because I, Parab, and all the other Indians will be doing what he is telling them.

Oliver: Where did *you* learn such big words, Parhab?

Parhab: I am listening always when the English is being spoken, Sahib.

Oliver: Ok, from now on, you will translate between him and the overseers so that there is no misunderstanding.

Parhab: Okey dokey, Sahib.

Valmiki worked as Sardar of cane-cutting gangs made up mainly of Indians and a sprinkling of former black slaves, who were now paid for their labour. The language was a problem when dealing with them, but he got by with Parhab's help and, in the fullness of time, he began to pick up bits and pieces of the curious creole mix without Parhab's embellishments. He became respected by the workers for his fairness and he often interceded on their behalf with Oliver when their pay was stopped for one spurious reason or other by some bloody-minded overseer or other.

Valmiki knew about the cruelty and extortionate activities of overseer Jacobs towards the workers, but as Jacobs was white and part of the 'plantocracy', management was not likely to listen to allegations made against one of their own by a *coolie,* like himself. So, he waited until one day when Jacobs, with overnight liquor still coursing through his system, beat a worker and drew blood. Valmiki took the worker to the sick house, where he was patched up, but this meant that he and the worker had missed hours of work for which their pay was docked as 'incompletion of task'. Valmiki went to see Oliver to explain why he and the worker could not complete their tasks. The doctor attested to the cause of the man's injuries ('deep lacerations caused by a whip, perhaps a cat-o-nine-tails, applied with considerable force,') and this, together with Valmiki's and the worker's evidence, provided enough evidence for Oliver to dismiss Jacobs.

Valmiki grew in confidence and often made representation to management on matters extraneous to cane-cutting activities and outside his own remit.

'Sahib,' he said to Oliver one day, 'have you visited the sick house recently?'

'No, Sardar. Why?'

'Pardon me, Sahib. It is not clean. It is stink and disgusting.'

Oliver duly visited the sick-house and wrote to the chairman of the Consortium:

'The sick house is filthy. The people are crowded into one ward and lie on the floor, often in soiled and bloody clothing. This can only lead to death, disability and increased costs.

I do not need to remind you of the recent scandal at Plantation Bellevue, where the sick house was described by the magistrates as wretched and filthy and the patients had no mattresses to lie on but had to improvise by putting their bundled clothes under their heads as pillows. For these infringements, the estate manager and the doctor were fined heavily.

I have spoken to Doc Munro about why he hadn't reported it. He said he had done so 'till the cows come home' to Stanley Howard, the welfare officer for coolies. I have spoken to Howard and warned him to function or else he will be dismissed.

In order to avoid sanctions from the authorities and to restore the dignity with which these people should be treated, I have authorised immediate improvements. I will report in full on this issue at our next meeting.'

Oliver knew that all expenditure had to be justified by the contribution it would make to profits. On its own, workers' welfare was not a primary consideration for the Consortium.

Iniquities were still rife in the Plantation system. The workforce was confined to their own estate and needed to have a 'pass' if they wished to go walkabout or to visit someone they had bonded with on the ship, but who lived on another Plantation. Because the Indians were easily identified by their skin colour and dress, they were frequently stopped by law enforcement officers and questioned as to their reason for being away from their Plantations. This system ensured that workers behaved well, as that was the only way in which they would be given a pass. It also ensured that troublemakers did not hear about better conditions that obtained elsewhere and so agitate for the same on their Plantation. Protests about the deprivation of their freedom, their lack of recourse to justice, sharp practices and poor working conditions still took the form of strikes, go-slows, malingering in the sick houses and, sometimes, violence against overseers and managers. However, the punishment was less brutal than during slavery, not least because the iniquitous plantation system was under scrutiny by the British and Indian authorities back home. Dismemberment and death were outlawed under the new system of indenture, though some workers who tried to abscond were chained to a post and whipped when caught.

There were also some subtle shifts in language, such as the gradual substitution of the term 'sugar estates' for 'Plantation', because of the latter's association with the iniquities of slavery.

All this led some to question whether the importation of the new workforce was such a good idea. At a monthly meeting of Planters, one Planter declared:

'These fucking coolies are no different from the fucking darkies! And we're not even allowed to touch them!'

'Perhaps we made a mistake by bringing them,' said another.

'How else could we have survived?' Asked another. 'At least they are more docile than the blacks.'

'Don't be fooled by all that smiling and head shaking,' said yet another.

'Saw some Indian soldiers who had captured one of ours,' said Humphreys, a retired Sergeant Major-turned-Planter. 'They smiled and nodded pleasantly, they did, before decapitating the poor bugger!'

'And Tom,' said Robert Watford of Waterloo, addressing Oliver. 'What's this I hear about you dismissing Jacobs?'

'It was a long time coming,' said Oliver.

'Why? What did he do?'

'He was skimming off the workers' wages.'

'That's hardly a crime!' Sgt Major Humphreys said.

Oliver ignored him. 'The last straw came when he thrashed one of them for stopping to drink water.'

'Why didn't you give him a warning?' Asked Watford.

'We've been down this road before, Bob. He was warned on many occasions for coming to work stinking of booze, beating the workers, and groping the women in the fields. He treated them like slaves.'

'But that's what they are, man!' Said Humphreys.

'That kind of loose talk isn't helpful,' said Watford.

Humphreys ignored him. 'And what's wrong with grabbing the odd milk jug, eh!' He demanded, looking around the room for approval. 'We've all done it in our time.'

Silence.

'If you ask me, Oliver, you're going soft. Spare the rod and all that!' Said Humphreys.

Oliver said nothing, but he thought about his retirement in a few years' time as something to look forward to.

Chapter Fifteen

Valmiki worked hard and saved hard and at the end of his indenture, he signed on for another five-year term. He did not wish to return to India, not at that moment. Famine was still widespread, and violence was raging, and while there was much wrong with being where he was, it was better than starvation. In any event, he had not saved enough for a return passage home, what with the docking of wages and other sharp practices. If he served another five years, he would be able to save more and be given a free passage. He was now twenty in real years, but twenty-five in contrived ones. Whichever it was, he was in the spring of his life and naturally, his thoughts turned to marriage.

Even though the female population on the Plantation had grown since he came, he hadn't found any woman he could marry. The problem was that he had gone to elaborate lengths to establish his *Brahmin* credentials and, while this had served him well in other aspects of his life, it had restricted his choice in matrimonial partners because a *Brahmin* did not marry outside his religion or below his caste. He had seen a beauty in the weeding gang once but, upon enquiry, she turned out to be a Muslim. There were other sightings of nubile womanhood, but he discovered, sadly, that because they were of other castes, he was prohibited from marrying them. In his experience, there were some marriages across other castes, albeit only a small number, but the *Brahmin* tectonic plates never shifted, not for love nor for money. In the Hindu religion, it was a law, immutable, like those of Physics, that *Brahmin* must marry *Brahmin*.

'Oh, Sahib, what a hurting of the head, this is,' said Parhab, when Valmiki mentioned his desire to find a suitable woman to marry.

'You mustn't tell anyone here, Parhab. It must be a secret,' cautioned Valmiki.

'Oh, Sahib, Parhab will be keeping the secret. You can trust me. I will ask Sahib Tom for a pass and will visit my friends at Plantation Waterloo on Sunday. It is not very far. I am finding out if they know any beautiful Brahmin lady who is wanting to marry a most honourable Brahmin Sardar.'

'But don't tell Sahib Tom why you are going to Waterloo. Just say you are visiting your friends.'

'Okey dokey, Sahib.'

When Parhab met Oliver, he said, 'I am going to visit my friends at Waterloo.'

'Oh, good. I hope you have a good time,' said Oliver, as he signed the pass.

'Thank you, Sahib, thank you.' Then he lowered his voice to a whisper. 'I am also going to be finding out about a *Brahmin* with a daughter for marrying Sahib Valmiki.'

'Oh? I didn't know he was looking.'

'Oh, yes, Sahib. And I am helping.'

'Well, I hope you find your needle in a haystack.'

'Sahib?'

'Never mind, Parhab. Good luck.'

The next afternoon, as Tom Oliver was riding out, he saw Parhab sitting under a tamarind tree smoking a cigarette. He hailed out:

'Relaxing?' Said Tom.

'No, no, Sahib. I am Parhab Singh,' he said, jumping up.

'Quite; quite so, Parhab. Did you find a *Brahmin* for Sardar Valmiki?'

'Oh, no, Sahib. I am not finding anybody yet. But my friend is thinking that he is knowing somebody at Bellevue. He will be finding out and telling me soon.'

Valmiki was disappointed when Parhab gave him the news, but he was still hopeful. He had thought through his plans. After he had completed ten years, he could get a piece of land on which he could build a house and plant a few crops, as there was no way that he and his wife would stay in the range housing where he lived.

The wattle-and-daub walls were paper thin and everything people did could be heard. His next-door neighbours, Pillay and his wife, were South Indians who often quarrelled before making love. He could hear every word, every expletive, and the sound of every slap, which marked their foreplay. Soon after, would come the woman's low moaning, soft and barely audible at first, then developing into the whine of a distant police siren which grew louder and louder until it reached crescendo with her commanding Pillay, at the top of her voice, in Tamil, to do something to her; to do something to her; to do something to her. Valmiki needed no translation. After hearing the performance a few times, he had come to know the score by heart and somewhere between crescendo and climax, he would put his fingers in his ears to deaden the noise.

Some mornings, when he went out to the barrels to wash, he saw a rather bashful Pillay, head bowed, trying to hide his black eye and scratched face.

After some time, and as if in atonement for its parents' sexual activity, baby Pillay was born. Valmiki was relieved - at last, he would be given some respite - but he could not believe that such a little thing could cry so. He had encountered babies in passing, and they would cry and then stop when pacified, but in the range house where Valmiki was a captive audience, baby Pillay would go on crying and screaming for hours before falling asleep. Only then was Valmiki able to drift off, sometimes to dream, sometimes to fantasise.

The baby's crying had replaced the noises of its parents for about a month or so but then the hostility between them resumed, with all that it heralded. What was worse, was that the baby's crying now ran consecutively to the parents' lovemaking and served merely as a prelude to what followed. The next morning, through his blood-shot eyes, Valmiki sometimes saw a different Mrs. Pillay on the stoop, cooing, and suckling the contented baby from her engorged breasts. He had heard that some people could have two contrasting personalities, but this was the first time he had witnessed it. As he looked at her, he told himself that he should not be fooled by this maternal side of her, as things would change when the night came. He couldn't continue to live here - being deprived of his sleep night after night and having to go to work feeling all befuddled and ratty - and he certainly had no intention of exposing his wife to such vulgarities. Besides, there was his own growing status to think about and he shouldn't be party to his workers' intimacies.

He reassured himself that it would be all right when he and his wife were in their own house, where their baby would have its own room and he could get a decent night's sleep. In any event, the matter was out of his hands. He had been feeling the urge for too long - for far too long had there been a restless lion roaming around in his nether region, desperately seeking a way out of its confinement.

When his ten years were up, Valmiki was given a piece of Crown Land upon which he set about building a wooden house complete with a veranda at the front, and stairs at both back and front. The house was built on stilts, a common architectural practice in the West Indies, which served to avoid flooding and curious reptiles. With the help of Parhab and his friends, the frame of the house soon went up. They worked each Sunday without pay until the structure was fleshed out and only the painting was left. Parhab suggested a range of primary colours but Valmiki had always abhorred anything too gaudy. For the outside walls he chose white, and for the interior, he opted for cream. These were the kind of understated colours he imagined a good *Brahmin* girl would like. As a concession to Parhab for his help, he agreed to paint the corrugated zinc roof in a bright green. Parhab was pleased that his friend had listened to him.

And that is what their relationship had become; one of friendship. Valmiki had come to like and respect Parhab and had felt that while it was alright to dupe everyone else in a bid to survive, it was morally wrong to do so to a loyal friend. But contrite though he was, there was no way in which he was going to reveal anything about his history as things had gone too far for that, and he could ill-afford complications. Instead, he said to Parhab:

'You must stop bowing and treating me like a superior, and you must look at me when you speak to me.'

Moved by this act of humility, Parhab instinctively stooped and tried to touch his friend's feet in respect.

'No, no. No more of that,' Valmiki said.

Parhab raised his eyes and looked at him for the first time. And Parhab wept.

Valmiki looked at this simple man. He had been born into the same lowly caste as he had, but he did not need to pretend to be something other than himself in order to be good. He knew how lucky he was to have found such a kind and generous friend. For his own part, even though he sometimes felt a tinge of guilt, he thought that his deception was forgivable. He had adapted so well to his assumed persona that even he had sometimes found it difficult to tell who he really was, but he had used the position it had afforded him to do good things. Had he not read somewhere that deception practised in the cause of goodness was not itself averse to goodness? It was true that it had started out as an act of dishonesty, but had he not in ten years made amends by becoming a good leader who represented his more unfortunate brothers and sisters? Had he not used his influence to get better conditions for the workers in the sick house and in the fields? Above all, had he not read the Ramayana (trans.) and learnt some of the religious rituals like a good *Brahmin*? True, he was finding the Vedas heavy going - and the Mahabharata? Well, that would have to wait. But, *honestly, what more could God ask of anyone?*

As if to placate God and beg for his forgiveness, he invited Parhab and the men who had worked on the house to a *puja,* at which he said all the prayers, thanked the Gods for his good fortune and enjoined their blessings on his new house and all those present. He cooked the traditional seven curries for his guests, and they sat crossed legged and ate out of the waxed lily leaves that grew in abundance in the nearby canals. Soon after, he erected a quintet of colourful *jhandi* flags on bamboo poles in his yard, each representing a Hindu deity - red for Hanuman, black for Sanichar, yellow for Lord Krishna, white for Sarasvati and the blue for Shiva.

And so, Albion's first Brahmin house was born.

Chapter Sixteen

After abolition, most of the slaves had left the plantations and established little villages along the coast where they turned their hands to a variety of activities. Some became artisans and worked for the sugar estates on a piece-work basis, some farmed small plots and sold their produce at the market, and some remained in the employment of the sugar estates to work as paid labourers, mainly in the factory and workshops, but also in the fields. Others gravitated towards the city where they did a variety of jobs.

John and Maria had left the sugar estate sometime just before abolition and lived in a village not far away. After Blackie had been sold, John had gone to see Tom Oliver and asked to be moved to another job.

'I love the horses, Massa Tom, but it isn't the same working at the stables without Philip and Blackie. I see them every time I turn around.'

'I understand, John; I can put you to work with the blacksmith if you want.'

From the archives of his memory came the smell of singeing flesh, and his face contorted involuntarily.

'The blacksmith now does all the farrier work since old Elias died.' Tom said.

John didn't know what a farrier was, but he knew that Elias used to shoe the horses.

'So, I'll still be working with horses?' Asked John.

'You'll still be working with horses, but you'll be doing many other things.' Oliver reassured him.

John agreed to work with the blacksmith, and he remained there perfecting his skills until he and Maria moved into the village where, having bought a second-hand forge, an anvil and tools from the sugar estate, he set himself up as the village blacksmith. Maria stayed at home and raised their three children. She did the laundry for civil servants, teachers and even overseers from the estate - fetching, washing, starching, ironing and delivering the finished items.

They had also bought a cart and donkey so that John could transport his materials whenever he had to travel to a job. He was helped by their eldest child, David, who was seventeen, while the two girls - fourteen and twelve - attended school in another village, not far away.

Neither Maria nor John ever mentioned Queenie, but it would have been surprising if such a force had passed quietly into oblivion, given her many sins against her own people. Instead, her spectral form was often invoked by parents to bring their disobedient children into line.

'If you don't behave,' they would say, 'the Black Witch of Albion will come for you.' Queenie had passed into a legend which told of a time past when the great Albion was ruled by a black woman, who consorted with the white Planters and other evil forces to continue the enslavement of her own people.

John and Maria were grateful that no one living knew of John's relationship to her, except Tom Oliver, and he had more reason than most to put her at the back of his mind.

Throughout the sugar belt, there was little contact between the former black slaves and the new Indian workforce. Indeed, because they looked different, dressed differently, spoke a different language, ate different food, and lived in different ghettos, they looked upon each other with suspicion. Even those blacks who continued to work on the sugar estate came in to do just that; they did their job and returned home to the villages.

The absence of social interaction between the two groups suited the Planters and was even encouraged by them. The pass laws, in addition to keeping the Indians confined to their Plantation and insulated from troublemakers at other Plantations, also served to separate them from the blacks so that the latter could not pass on what they knew of the iniquities and sharp practices of the Planters. Thus, by cocooning the Indians on the sugar estates, the Planters hoped that they could avoid or minimise any corrupting influence that the former slaves might exert on their new, docile, malleable, and religious *coolie* workforce.

But this isolation could not prevent unrest, as certain excesses continued. At Plantation Bellevue, there was an armed insurrection by men and women, black and Indian, because of the rape of an Indian woman in the field by an overseer. Overseers were pulled off their mules and beaten up, and fields were set on fire prematurely, causing damage to property and profits. At Waterloo, where there was widespread estoppel of wages for the smallest reasons, the disturbances were so severe that management had to make a show of sacrificing one of their offending overseers by sacking him in order to placate the protesters. But they were all in cahoots and the sacked overseer resurfaced at another Plantation, un-chastened and unrepentant.

The feeling of injustice was further aggravated by the fact that visiting magistrates, who were supposed to be impartial, were viewed as part of the establishment because whenever they visited, they stayed at the Great House and enjoyed the hospitality of the Planters. Judgements by the magistrates invariably went in favour of their hosts and against the workers.

In general, Albion continued to have better labour

relations than most Plantations because of Tom Oliver, but this did not mean that it was immune to agitation.

One day, Oliver received a message from the senior overseer that trouble was brewing, and he was needed urgently in the cultivation because the workers had gone on strike, so he hastened on horseback to the scene.

The day was dry and there was a crisp feel to it. The sun was at nine o'clock and its rays were already beating down upon the earth, telegraphing their intemperate intentions. There were no clouds in the sky to break the dome of blue and the fields of cane below had been burnt ready for harvesting. On the dam, the cane carts were all lined up like a funeral cortege, their oxen standing still in harness, chewing, and waiting. A pall of sucrose hung heavily in the air.

It was a perfect day for cutting cane.

When Oliver arrived, though, he saw no frenzied activity like that which typifies cane cutting. Instead, what he saw was the overseers walking up and down, unsure of what to do. All over the fields, in total silence, *coolies* were squatting like a sea of doves, moving only occasionally to swat a fly or squash a blood-filled mosquito. On the ground, all neatly laid out by each man's side, were their food carriers, cutlasses, and head pads, upon which they carried the bundles to the carts. Oliver took in the scene before dismounting and speaking to the senior overseer.

'What's the matter, Clive?' He addressed a tall, fair-haired, freckled-faced man.

'Don't know, Tom. Nobody's talking. Not a word. We asked what was wrong, but they just kept studying the ground. It's eerie.'

'You can say that again! Never seen anything like it in all my years. Any threat of violence?' Asked Tom.

'Not openly, but you never know with these *coolies*. Is today some special Indian religious day, like the Jewish Sabbath?' Clive asked.

'Don't think so. Valmiki would have said. Were there any incidents - any whipping, hitting; anything like that?'

'No. You know we don't use whips, Tom,' said Clive, his eyes darting somewhere to the left, over Oliver's shoulder.

'I hope not. Which field is Valmiki in?'

Clive pointed to a field some distance away. Oliver nodded, mounted his horse, and rode off.

When he arrived at the field, he saw Valmiki squatting a little distance from his men and chewing on a blade of grass. He dismounted and crossed over the trench, balancing on the narrow coconut tree trunk which served as a bridge between the dam and the field.

'Good morning, Valmiki.'

'Good morning, Sahib,' Valmiki replied, quickly standing.

'What's the problem? Why aren't the men working?'

'Sahib, the men want to have an extra water break, because they get too thirsty.'

'Did you ask the overseers?'

'Oh, Sahib, many times. But they just say, "work on", Sahib.'

'I see. And do you think the men should have an extra break?"

'Yes, Sahib. I think the men should get an extra water break.'

'Okay, tell them I agree, but they must get back to work

now.'

'That is very good, Sahib,' replied Valmiki, and he turned to walk towards his men.

'And, Valmiki…,' said Oliver.

'Yes, Sahib?'

'In future, if there is a problem, you must tell me.'

'But what about the overseers, Sahib?'

'You must speak to Sahib Clive first, and if nothing happens, then you come to see me.'

'I understand Sahib. And Sahib?'

'Yes, Valmiki.'

'Please, Sahib, no deductions.'

'Okay. No deductions this time, but you must tell your people that they can't just stop working when they feel like it.'

'Ok, Sahib, I will tell them. And thank you, Sahib.'

Valmiki shouted something in Hindi to the first field of labourers and this was relayed through to the other fields in many different dialects. Within minutes, the fields were transformed into a beehive. The worker bees were buzzing again and laughing and talking as they went about their business, chopping and bundling, chopping and bundling; then loading. Some overseers scowled, others relaxed, and Valmiki's reputation climbed up a notch or two.

The next morning, Oliver had a meeting with all his managers and overseers before they set out to work.

'Yesterday was not a good day,' he said. 'We lost a lot of time and sugar.'

'But what are we supposed to do in future if the *coolies* down tools?' Asked a young overseer.

'You try to find out why,' Oliver replied.

'But how could we when they wouldn't say a word?'

'Do you think they did it for no reason? This was brewing

for some time; it wasn't just some spontaneous act of cussedness. I understand that they had been asking for an extra water break. Is that true?'

'Yes, they did ask me a few times,' said Clive.

'And what did you say?'

'I told them that they had enough breaks as it was,' replied Clive.

'It's not up to individual overseers, senior or not, to make such judgements. You need to pass it on to me so that I can take an overview and factor-in costs. We can't afford industrial action; it costs too much. Look at what's happening at some of the other plantations. Do you want that here?'

'So, we just give in to their demands?' Asked Clive.

'No, that's not what I am saying. I will look at the merits before deciding, but I don't want to be put on the spot by having to make snap decisions to stave off a crisis. I told the *Sardar* to raise everything with you and that you will talk to me. Our production deadlines are too tight to allow for stoppages which can be avoided by early action.'

'You're the boss,' replied Clive.

'Yes, I am. And in all my years doing this job, I have learnt that you'll catch more flies with honey than with vinegar.'

The meeting ended with some of the men frowning and scratching their heads. Others, who seemed to have understood what Oliver had meant, began chatting informally.

'You should have seen it!' Said an overseer. 'All these *coolies* just squatting there, like they were having a shit… saying nothing… just looking at the ground.'

'They were menacing,' said a fresh-faced overseer. 'I was really scared.'

'At least, we knew where we were with the slaves. They just walked out or used violence,' said another.

'It was the silence… no conversation, no discussion… just a silence full of menace. The rattlesnake at least rattles before it strikes.'

'And did you see how they had their cutlass and things neatly laid out on the ground beside themselves like they were preparing to commit *hara-kiri*?'

'Their hands were never far from their weapons.'

'Och, mon,' said Scottie, the oldest overseer, who had seen service in the British army in India and who had been sitting quietly in a corner. 'What you saw yesterday was a demonstration of mental and psychological power.'

'It was as effective as violence, though,' said Clive.

'Just so. Believe me, some of those *coolies* could have skinned and filleted you in no time if they had wanted to. But they prefer to get into your head,' he said, tapping his temple with the knuckle of his forefinger, which gave out a dull knocking sound like the popping sound made by pulling a finger out of the mouth. 'Which do you think is easier to deal with - someone who is threatening you with a cutlass, or someone who is squatting quietly, saying nothing, and doing nothing but drilling into your mind with his own?'

Scottie donned his sun helmet, picked up his riding crop and left.

His question hung in the air like the thick black smoke of a burning sugarcane field.

Chapter Seventeen

The banging was incessant, and it seemed as if it was coming from some distance away.

Valmiki stirred, then opened his eyes as he realised that it was his front door that was being battered. *What now?* He had just drifted off into a deep sleep and had been transported to a distant world where he had been cavorting with nymphs in various stages of undress. He swung his legs off his bed and became aware of a protuberance straining against the flimsy material of his shorts. He got up, grabbed his trousers and shouted as he was putting them on: 'Coming! Coming!'

He unbolted the door and saw an excited Parhab.

'Sahib! Sahib! Sorry for the disturbing but I am receiving a message from my friend at Waterloo.'

It took a few minutes for Valmiki to understand what he was going on about.

'He is knowing somebody who is knowing a Brahmin with daughters at Highbury Estate. Four daughters, Sahib, four!'

With sleep evaporating, Valmiki realised that this was the best news he had heard in a long time. After the previous disappointment, he had begun to wonder whether he would ever find someone to marry without having to lose face or exposing his secret.

'Four, Sahib! Four!' Shouted the irrepressible Parhab.

'I only want one,' he said. 'When can we go and see?'

'I am going to send a message to him.'

'Make the arrangements for any Sunday. Highbury is far

away, so we will have to start out early in the morning.'

'We, Sahib?' Asked Parhab, holding his breath. 'Of course. You will go with me, no?'

'Yes, Sahib. Of course. Thank you, Sahib,' said Parhab, as he fought the temptation to touch Valmiki's feet.

Valmiki returned to bed, but he couldn't sleep for some time. His fantasy was one step away from becoming reality. When he finally drifted off, his sleep was fitful. He was haunted by melodramatic Indian music with beautiful wraithlike sylphs dancing and swirling. He was now cavorting with fully clad, coy beauties, their silky forms teasing, enticing, seducing, only hinting at what might be his if only he could catch them as they flitted about on hills, on snowy slopes, around trees, on carpets of multi-coloured flowers and along river banks which sandwiched placid waters. Lust had given way to romance but when he woke up, there was no tumescence in his shorts, just an imbecilic smile on his face and a feeling of being on top of the world.

When Parhab told him that the arrangements for visiting the Brahmin family had been made, Valmiki congratulated him.

'Four daughters, eh? You've done well, man.'

'But, Sahib, which one will you choose?'

'I wouldn't know until I see them. But I will choose the most beautiful one, my friend. The most beautiful one.'

It was a Sunday, and they were fishing in a little stream at the back of Valmiki's house. The sun was midway in the skies and Parhab was busy disentangling a piece of weed that had sneered his hook.

'But, Sahib, they are being Brahmin,' Parhab replied as he bit and pulled on the weed.

'I know, Parhab. That's just what I want.'

'No, no, Sahib. You don't understand.' He spat out the

weed and said, 'You cannot see their faces before you are deciding.'

'Why not?' Asked a puzzled Valmiki.

'Oh, Sahib, how could you forget? They are Brahmins.'

'So?' Valmiki looked puzzled.

Then Parhab's meaning dawned upon him. In his excitement, he had forgotten that it was the custom among Brahmins for a suitor to discuss marriage with the woman's parents or guardian without her being in evidence. If he agreed to a marriage, he did so sight unseen. Thereafter, the woman was in purdah until the marriage, when it was too late for either of them to do anything about it.

Shit! Shit! Shit! Valmiki *thought. What if she looks like a camel? What if she is mentally unstable? And still worse, what if she is a mentally unstable camel?*

Parhab saw the change in Valmiki's face and tried to cheer him up. 'Don't worry, Sahib, all Brahmin women are beautiful.'

Valmiki was overcome by a feeling of gloom which lasted for the whole of that day and well into the next week. He wondered if he might have overplayed his hand and that his whole deception was about to unravel. Pretending to be a Brahmin had served him well up to then. It had conferred upon him a status to which he could never have aspired as an untouchable, and he was highly respected by both management and workers on the sugar estate. Now, because he was a Brahmin, he was faced with having to marry someone whose face he could not see. This realisation caused his spirits to lose their buoyancy.

A week later, when Parhab told him that a meeting had been arranged with the *Brahmin* family, he told himself that things would work out. He did a mental audit of his life, of how he had come from nothing to something, purely by chance and his own inventiveness, and he assured himself that the same convergence of circumstances will favour him in his new venture. Therefore, it was with some measure of zeal that he set about making the arrangements.

'It will take us two hours to go and two to come back, so we must start out at six in the morning, the latest seven.'

'Not if we are walking, Sahib.'

Walking? To Highbury? No. We will travel in style. Do you know anyone in the village with a donkey and cart?'

'Yes, Sahib. Blacksmith John is having one.'

'Well, go down to the village and tell him we want him for Sunday. Get a reasonable price... what else... clothes? Let me see... saffron robe? Dhoti... Hmm. No, no. Shirt and trousers and hat. Yes, hat. Definitely. And passes! Mustn't forget the passes.'

When Valmiki went to ask Oliver for the passes, he told him the truth.

'Well, this comes as a real surprise!' said Oliver. 'I didn't know you were looking for a wife.'

'Oh, yes, Sahib,' Parhab has been helping me.'

'Oh, jolly good. Good man, Parhab.'

'He is a very good friend, Sahib.'

'Well, good luck and have a safe journey.'

When Valmiki returned with the passes, Parhab asked: 'Did Sahib Tom say anything, Sahib?'

'He was surprised. He said he didn't know I was looking for a wife.'

Parhab's shoulders relaxed and he silently exhaled, 'Oh, goody. Surprise is always good,' he said.

On Sunday morning at six, when John's son, David, arrived at Valmiki's house, the sun was up but there was still dew on the leaves and a slight chill in the morning air. David was sitting aboard a sturdy cart which was made of polished purple-heart wood, unlike the ones that were commonly seen. There was a detachable canopy, which offered protection from both sun and rain and which could be removed when the cart was used to transport materials. Even the donkey looked a class above those in daily evidence. It was brown, taller, and sleeker, a testament to its fine Spanish heritage.

When Parhab appeared, he was grinning widely; he was dressed in a pair of white trousers with razor-sharp creases and a blue shirt. His hair, doused with coconut oil, was slicked back and it glistened in the sun as if it was in competition with his buffed brown shoes and pearly white teeth. When he saw Valmiki, he said:

'Oh, Sahib, you are looking like a filim star.'

Valmiki blushed and said, without thinking, 'You, too, Parhab. Perhaps we could fix you up with one of the sisters.'

'Oh, Sahib, how could you be saying that? You know that can't happen,' Parhab replied, his head bowed.

The journey was quicker than expected because David kept the donkey going at a steady trot. All along the coast, there were villages at different stages of growth, mostly populated by black people. There were a few Indian villages but not as many. David called out the names as they drove along. This of itself was of little interest, but it helped to pass the time.

Eventually, he announced, 'Plantation Highbury,' and Valmiki became tense and anxious. Parhab described to David the kind of house they were looking for and they all craned their necks and scanned the horizon.

'There!' David said. 'Over there!'

The building that David was pointing at stood on stilts; it was two storeys high with a tower that reached into the sky.

It was three times the size of Valmiki's house and had been newly painted. It was surrounded by a white picket fence, and between the house and the fence, in the front of the yard, there were five tall bamboo poles standing like sentinels upon which triangular *jhandi* flags had been hoisted. As they drew closer, Valmiki saw that each flag was stained with an image purporting to be that of the god whom the flag represented. At the end of each flag, there was a knot in which there was a coin, not just an offering to the god, but a practical way in which to keep the flag from fluttering in the wind and distorting the godly image, which, the truth be told, had already been falsified by man's imagination.

As David pulled on the donkey's reins, a gentle breeze wafted the smell of burning incense towards them. Valmiki's heart sank a little, and then a little more, when he saw a portly, clean-shaven man in his early fifties standing at the foot of the front stairs, dressed in a white dhoti and kurta with a yellow scarf draped loosely around his neck. His wire-rimmed glasses and wooden sandals completed this embodiment of *Brahminism* and filled Valmiki with apprehension and a fleeting wish that he could be somewhere else.

David brought the donkey to a standstill and Valmiki jumped off and walked towards the gate, his head held high and his stride measured, hiding the turbulence within his stomach.

Parhab followed at a respectful six feet behind, head bowed, as David tethered the donkey and cart. They exchanged *Namaste* and the host introduced himself as 'Pandit Shukla'.

At the bottom of the house, which was concreted over, there was a table and four chairs, and a hammock which was tied between two of the stilts. Valmiki recognised it as an Amerindian hammock, woven in cotton by the women of the Wapishana tribe, one of the Indigenous tribes of the country. These were far superior to the common hammocks made of jute bags and were owned only by the rich. In his nervousness, he allowed his mind to wander for a moment. He had never seen an Amerindian, as they lived deep in the interior of the country close to nature and they seldom ventured out into the coastal areas. He had only seen pictures of them, half-naked in loin cloth spearing fish in a river, but he just could not understand why they were called Amerindians; they looked nothing like Indians – if anything, they looked more like Chinese.

'And who is this?' Shukla asked Valmiki, as he looked at Parhab.

'Oh, I'm sorry. This is my friend, Parhab Singh.'

Shukla raised his eyebrows almost imperceptibly, and he indicated that Parhab and David should sit and wait at the bottom of the house while Valmiki accompanied him upstairs, a generous interpretation of which arrangement might suggest that it had more to do with Valmiki being the suitor, than with the caste and race of the other men.

Once inside the house, Shukla showed Valmiki to an upholstered armchair which was covered with a plastic sheet. Valmiki lowered himself into the chair and sank into the plush cushion as the plastic scrunched in protest under him. Shukla sat on a straight-backed chair about four feet opposite Valmiki, which meant that he was sitting a foot higher than Valmiki, a classic stage-setting for the matter at hand. Some distance away from the scene of the impending interrogation sat a rather large, veiled, and bejewelled woman who covered most of the plastic of the settee. She remained quiet as the two men made small talk.

'Imported from England. Chesterfield, you know,' said

Shukla, pointing to the suite of chairs. 'I bought it through the Estate Manager,' he boasted.

'Oh, it's very nice and comfortable,' replied Valmiki, trying to steady the tremor in his voice.

'He is my friend, you know. The Estate Manager.'

Impressed, Valmiki nodded. 'You have a nice big house,' he said, and added, 'and that hammock downstairs - it's Wapishana, isn't it?'

It was Shukla's turn to be impressed. 'Not many people know that. The Estate Manager, who is my friend, has many contacts, you know. Wapishana hammocks are very rare and expensive.'

'The tower storey looks magnificent,' Valmiki said.

'You can see as far as the City from up there. I will show you later.'

Valmiki had the distinct feeling that his being shown the view from the tower depended on whether the impending negotiations were successful.

He said, more to himself than to Shukla, 'You have done very well.'

'Oh, you haven't seen anything yet!' Enthused Shukla. 'At the back, I have ten acres of land under rice and another two under coconut. It hasn't been easy, mind you. I came on the *Hesperus,* you know. I was the first Brahmin to set foot in this country and I was the only one in the whole country for a long time. But how things have changed!' He said ruefully, and he made some reference to them allowing any Tom, Dick and Harry into the country, a remark which eluded Valmiki.

'What about you?' Shukla asked.

Valmiki said that he had arrived much later and had worked at Albion as a 'Sardar'. He knew that the mention of Albion always impressed those from other sugar estates.

He said he had built a modest house with three average sized rooms, but that he was in the process of clearing up two acres of land for growing rice, which he intended to do on a larger scale when he left the sugar estate - an idea which sprung to mind in some kind of a vain attempt to match the braggart's firepower.

Shukla re-joined: 'I also have a large dry-goods shop in the village; I employ three people, you know.'

Valmiki appeared doubly impressed and, unable to match this boast, he just smiled and nodded.

Shukla introduced the elephant in the room as his wife, whom he ordered to fetch drinks. As she dutifully got up and waddled towards the kitchen, Valmiki's heart plunged. She returned a few minutes later with two painted glasses of lemonade on a tray, her bangles jingling ostentatiously and the ice in the glasses tinkling with her every footfall, reminding Valmiki of the sounds made by the orchestra of the Holy Man. He took a glass and thanked her as a picture bubble of Shukla riding an elephant, all turbaned and resplendent like a Maharajah, came into his head. The bubble burst as Shukla's voice brought him back to reality.

'So, you are interested in marrying one of my daughters, eh?' He said.

'Oh yes, Sir,' Valmiki replied. 'I understand you have four daughters.'

'Yes. Sati, Shanta, Sona and Savitri. But only two are available – Sati and Shanta. The other two are 13 and 12 and are at the *Brahmacharya Hindi School*.'

Thus, with one sweep, had Valmiki's choice been reduced by fifty percent. *What if one was a camel and the other mental … or what if both …?* The feeling of dread returned, only now he had to factor in the genes of the gargantuan mother who was waiting in the wings and trying to make herself as inconspicuous as her ample dimensions

179

would allow. He sipped his drink and put a finger in his glass to stir the ice, looking on with fascination at the transparent lumps swirling around in the liquid.

'Is it the first time you're seeing ice?' Asked Shukla. Embarrassed, Valmiki nodded.

'I get it from my friend, the Estate Manager, and he gets it from the depot in the city. Not many people have seen ice.'

Valmiki nodded again.

A short silence ensued, then he blurted out, 'Can I see them?'

Shukla looked at him, his eyebrows raised, this time in question.

'Your...Your two daughters, I mean,' Valmiki stuttered.

Shukla gasped and gave him a look which suggested that being a Brahmin, he should know better.

Realising his *faux pas,* Valmiki said, 'I'm sorry, Sir. I don't know what came over me.'

'That's all right. Every *Brahmin* man would like to see who they are marrying. But the rules are the rules.'

Valmiki changed tack.

'How old are your daughters, Sir?'

'Sati is twenty and Shanta is eighteen. Both went to the *Brahmacharya* School, you know.'

Still uneasy, Valmiki rummaged around his gene pool, searching, searching with growing exasperation for something that would get him out of this quicksand into which he had fallen, and which was slowly sucking him down towards the base of the armchair. Scrunching. Scrunching. At last, he located it, the crooked gene which had led him in the first place to lie to the magistrate about being a *Brahmin.*

'I am thinking of building a *mandir.*' He said.

'Excellent! Excellent!' Clamoured Shukla, as he

regarded Valmiki in a new, a more respectful, light. 'What made you think of doing that?'

'Well, there are no *mandirs* at Albion.'

'What? No *mandirs* at Albion? I can't believe it! Where do the good Hindus worship, then?'

'In their homes and in the fields, and in makeshift shrines in their gardens - if they have one.'

'And if not?'

'In the open – anywhere.'

'That is not good enough! Thundered Shukla. 'For worship, Hindus must have a *mandir* with a real Pandit. Hinduism is not a religion that should be hidden and practised in secret or in the open spaces where people and animals defecate! It is a communal religion,' said Shukla with authority.

'I agree, Sir. That's why I thought of it,' said Valmiki softly, trying to affect an air of cool.

'Tell me more. How far have you gone?' Shukla said, leaning forward.

'Oh, not very far, but I have discussed it with the Manager, and he thinks it is a good idea. He thinks the estate might be able to give me a piece of land,' he lied.

'That's wonderful. A real *Brahmin* leader! And at Albion no less!' Enthused Shukla, and he turned to the settee, and said, 'Wife! Bring Sati here!'

Mrs. Shukla got up and trundled along a passage which Valmiki suspected led to the bedrooms. Trundle, bump trundle bump. Like a *stalag* guard keeping a close eye on her prisoner, she came out a few minutes later jingling, jingling with her eldest daughter walking close behind her. Valmiki craned his neck trying to see beyond Mrs. Shukla, but the width of the woman, like a sightscreen at a cricket ground, obscured the entire passage. Only when she entered the sitting room and sat down, was he able to see

Sati, whose face was unveiled. She was attractive. She was demurely dressed in a sari, beneath which Valmiki could detect a voluptuous body, which excited him. However, as he gazed at the swell of her breasts, he noted a sturdiness in her build, especially around the shoulders, which made him wonder whether her mother might have looked like her at that age. His heart dislodged itself and plunged into the pit of his stomach, where it lay smouldering. He nodded a thank you, and she left. He swallowed.

He was now into Hobson's territory.

'Bring Shanta!' Commanded Shukla.

Mrs Shukla, who had lowered herself into her settee while the viewing was going on, levered herself up with difficulty; she stood breathing heavily, then jingled her way slowly towards the passage, giving Valmiki the distinct impression as she pitched and rolled, that she was grateful that only two of her daughters were eligible for marriage.

A few moments later, she returned, more ponderously and less watchful, but still obscuring Valmiki's view.

When Shanta came into sight, Valmiki's heart leapt from the floor of his stomach, spiralled all the way upwards through his gullet and nearly popped out of his mouth. Like her sister, she wore a sari, but hers was wound so tightly around her body that the drooling Valmiki could not take his eyes off her. Her shiny black hair fell to her waist and her dusky eyes danced mischievously as she teased him like a kitten toying with a mouse. He had seen her naked in his fantasy and he knew that she was the one. She was no camel, and who cared if she was mental! She mesmerised him; she enchanted him; she enthralled him. He stared at her, his mouth agape.

Her full lips slightly parted, she stared back at his bronze skin and black hair, his sculpted jawline and his straight nose, whose sharpness was toned down by a kindness in his brown eyes. She let her eyes drop to his chest, where his well-honed pectorals strained against his shirt. She kept them there for a little while before slowly dropping them to his abdomen, where men in his line of work did not accumulate any fat. Valmiki looked at her. The sleeping lion had begun to stir.

Shukla, who had been watching this *pas-de-deux,* shifted uncomfortably in his chair and cleared his throat.

Shanta's eyes quickly darted back upwards, and she said to Valmiki that it was nice meeting him. She turned and walked back to the passageway, slowly, deliberately, it seemed to Valmiki. Like the moving windscreen wipers of a motor car, his eyes followed the rhythmic sway of her ample hips, lingering, until she disappeared.

'Which one?' Shukla asked.

Valmiki swallowed and hesitated, not because he was in any doubt about the answer, but because he had not fully recovered from Shanta. He tried to strike a pose by crossing his legs before answering Shukla, but after a few attempts, he gave up trying as there was now an impediment which made it difficult for him to achieve any air of nonchalance.

'Shanta.'

'I was hoping it would be Sati. She is the eldest and it is only right that she should marry first.'

'I know, I know, Sir. But I am sure. I have often dreamt of someone like Shanta.'

'But Sati is as beautiful as her mother was when she was twenty.'

'I have no doubt, Sir. But my mind is made up.'

'Okay. I will consent - but on one condition.'

'What is that, Sir?'

'You must build that *mandir* at Albion.'

He promised that he would. He would have promised anything just then. And, as if to seal the deal, they feasted, he upstairs with the family, and his two companions, downstairs. After eating, Shukla took him up to the tower to show him the view. Valmiki was all agog as his host pointed out the steeple of the City's cathedral, which was thirty miles away. He thought to himself, *someday I will build a house with a tower higher than this.*

Chapter Eighteen

Two months later, Valmiki and Shanta got married in true Indian style – festive, loud, colourful and extravagant. There was one incident during the marriage ceremony, though, that threatened the harmonious relations which had developed between Valmiki and Shukla.

At the time when Shukla had consented to the marriage, he had proposed a dowry to which Valmiki, intoxicated by love, had nodded his assent without fully understanding. The truth was that he, being of a lowly untouchable caste, had no idea of what a dowry was. During the marriage ceremony, when Shukla pompously offered the dowry with his arms outstretched, one handful of coins of the highest denomination resting upon the palm of the other, Valmiki refused it by gently pushing Shukla's proffered hands away. That did not offend Shukla, as it was conventional for the groom to refuse the first offer and for the bride's father to increase the amount before the groom nodded his acceptance, thereby sealing the marriage. But when Valmiki refused three, then four times, each time gently pushing away Shukla's increasingly heavy hands, Shukla hissed through clenched teeth, 'Take the blasted money and don't piss me off!' To which Valmiki reacted by grabbing the money and apologising to the officiating Pandit, who pretended that he hadn't heard.

'Pa was really upset with you,' Shanta said after the wedding.

'I didn't know. It was embarrassing taking money in front of all the guests.'

'But it's the tradition.'

'Maybe. But it isn't right that he should pay me to marry you.'

'You are a funny kind of *Brahmin*,' Shanta replied.

Some months later, he raised the idea of the temple with Tom Oliver, not least because of Shukla's constant requests for a progress report.

Oliver said he wasn't sure whether it would be allowed. He was aware that the Church of England and the Roman Catholic Church had a duopoly over religion in the country and didn't know whether the encouraging of other religions was consistent with Colonial policy. However, when Valmiki pointed out that the Hindu religion was a pacifist one, and that by allowing the Indian workers to practise their religion, they might be better able to control any rebellious fervour in them, Oliver said he would recommend it to the Consortium.

Some members of the Consortium argued that by espousing such concepts as freedom and equality, the Christian religion had not best served their interests, and they questioned whether another religion, pacifist or not, might do any better. In fact, some argued, it might even compound their problems.

'But,' said Oliver, 'religion has been instrumental in controlling the workers because it has taught them that the meek shall inherit the earth and all that. This has caused fewer rebellions because they know that if they rebel in this life, they will get nothing after they die.'

He was surprised when Humphreys weighed in on his side. 'Yes, and, the Bible also teaches that it is easier for a poor man to enter the kingdom of heaven than it is for a rich man to pass through the eye of a needle.'

'Yes, that too,' mumbled Oliver.

To which Humphreys mused, 'Though, why any bastard - rich or otherwise - should want to pass through the eye of a needle, is beyond me.'

While some members believed that it was a good idea and others did not, the Consortium concluded that to allow another religion the same freedom as the other two would be to tempt fate. And not just any religion, but a pagan one with thirty-three million gods.

When Valmiki got the news, he held his head in his hands and moaned. Shanta, though, as positive as she always was, told him not to worry as it was only a temporary setback. She then began working feverishly with her father, who had used his contacts at Highbury estate (the estate manager being his friend) to produce statistics that showed that industrial disputes at that plantation had fallen by more than fifty percent after the first temple was built, and by seventy percent after the second.

Armed with these facts, Oliver went before the Consortium and argued that there could be no doubt that temples had had a calming influence on industrial relations at Highbury.

However, what clinched his argument was when he said:

'Hinduism is a religion that believes in reincarnation and the Hindus believe in *karma* - the belief that what you do in your present life will affect you, not only in this life, but also in future lives.'

'Sounds like you believe in all this jiggery-pokery, Oliver,' scoffed Humphreys.

'What is important is not what I believe, but what they believe.'

'So, tell us how this *karma* thing can help labour relations,' retorted Humphreys, his scepticism barely concealed.

'Well, it seems that after death, a person can be reborn as another person or as an animal.'

'Tosh!' Humphrey interjected.

'However,' Oliver continued, unruffled, 'how you've lived your life will determine what you come back as. Not only will your *karma* affect your re-birth, it will affect your future in this life.

'It doesn't make sense, man!' Replied Humphreys.

'Simply put,' said Tom, as if speaking to a child, 'if you behave badly in this life, burning property or killing people, you might get your comeuppance later in this life or you will return in your second life as someone or something despicable, like Attila the Hun or a snake.'

'Hocus-pocus!' Sneered Humphreys.

'They believe that if you behave like an ass in this life, you will return as an ass in the next,' Oliver replied calmly.

Despite Humphrey's protestations, the Consortium voted for the allocation of a parcel of land for this purpose, but they made it clear that no money would be given towards the building costs. When he heard this, Valmiki complained that it was one headache after another, but Shanta came up with the idea that they should appeal to all the Hindus in the area for contributions.

She and Parhab sent out flyers in Hindi and some common dialects, also translated into English, and soon money came pouring in.

Shanta took the lead in what she called, 'The Project' and divided it up into Three Phases - Phase One being the clearing of the land, Phase Two, the laying of the foundation, and Phase Three, the erecting of the superstructure. She then called a meeting of Hindus at her bottom house to appoint a committee to oversee the project, as she was clear in her mind that no one person should be responsible for disbursements. In all these activities, she had made it appear as if Valmiki was in charge and, for his part, he was happy to let his wife use her youthful energy, initiative and undoubted organising ability in his name.

The temple was a wooden structure built on top of a concrete base. It was painted white and yellow with streaks of green, and its many alcoves were graced by a number of blue marble statuettes of gods and goddesses - some with many arms, some with ruby red lips, some with cherubic faces and others with simian and elephantine features, which were all purchased from Shukla's emporium - at cost price, so he claimed.

The wrought iron work around the temple was fabricated by John and his son David. It was the first time that Valmiki had met John, and while David and a helper were building the fences and gates, Valmiki and John sat on a bench under a mango tree, drank green tea and chatted. It was also the first time that Valmiki had heard about what slavery was really like, not from little snippets gleaned from something that someone had heard or said, but from someone who had lived through enslavement - the non-payment for work; the beatings; the dismemberment; the hangings; and the rapes. Valmiki remarked that while there were cases of brutality at the present time, these were generally limited to the whip. There had been reports of two Indians who had run away and had drowned in a creek, but while rumour had it that they had been caught before being drowned, the investigating committee set up by the Governor had found nothing untoward. And sex, well, that was much more discreet, and rapes were less overt and were punished when discovered.

John even lifted his shirt and gave Valmiki a glimpse of the map on his back - once marked by ruts cut deep into his skin by a bullwhip but now full of welts like one vast loaf of plaited bread. Valmiki tried to understand how people could have done this to other people, but he was a fish trying to understand a frog's description of a walk on dry land.

Later that night, as he and Shanta sat on the veranda, he told her about John's experiences.

'No wonder he never smiles,' she said.

'He said that the only time he was ever happy was when he became disabled and was put to look after the horses. There was a special horse, which he really loved, and he was never the same after they sold him.'

'Is he married?'

'Oh yes, he has three children.'

'And isn't he happy with them?'

'Yes. But I think he meant after all the brutality in his other jobs, it was the one with the horse that brought him happiness.'

'Poor man,' said Shanta.

'He was like me before I met you,' said Valmiki.

Chapter Nineteen

Valmiki had been suspicious of Shukla's insistence that he must build a *mandir* at Albion, but he really couldn't figure out why. True, Shukla was a Brahmin, but why would the promise to build a *mandir* persuade him to breach the convention of *purdah* and let a suitor see his daughters' faces before marriage? He, being a Pandit and all. It just didn't make sense. Not that Valmiki had regretted it. He could not be happier being married to Shanta. His gambit had paid off, and he was grateful that he was able to see and choose his prospective wife before marriage and not been confronted by any surprises on his wedding night.

Still, this Shukla thing was a bit of a mystery.

Enlightenment came one night when he and Shanta were discussing what VIPs they should invite to the opening of the *mandir*. The list included the local headmaster, the district administrator, the estate's midwives and doctor and Tom Oliver.

As Valmiki looked at the galaxy of stars on his list, he said, 'You know, I will need some Pandit clothes – a new dhoti and kurta, a yellow scarf and some wooden sandals. We can buy some from your father's shop.'

'I was meaning to talk to you about that, Val,' Shanta replied.

'Oh, I know the old fox overcharges us,' he said, smiling.

'No, that's not what I mean. I mean that he should be the Pandit who opens the *mandir*.'

A silence ensued. *So that was the plan after all!* He thought. *I will build the mandir, and he will get the honour of opening it. Cunning bastard!* But, more worryingly, was Shanta's apparent disloyalty to him. It was the first time that

191

she had appeared to be taking sides.

He looked at her, wounded.

'I think Pa should be the Pandit,' she looked at him and repeated firmly.

'Why?'

'Well...to be a Pandit you must have a *guru* to teach you.'

This came as news to him. He had never really delved too deeply into the finer points of the religion's practices. He had got by in life here by being, well, the one-eyed man in the country of the blind. He had learnt the rituals and prayers by heart over the years and had hoped that here, at Albion, where there were no Brahmins, he would be able to muddle through. After all, most of his congregation were illiterate and wouldn't have the faintest idea whether what he was reading was what had been written in the good books.

'But I can do it,' he said.

'I know you can,' she replied. 'But what would happen if, not tomorrow or the day after, but in years to come, it was discovered that you were an imposter? That you were marrying and burying people and doing *pujas* when you were not a true Pandit? That you were, as Sri Babbajee used to quote from the Bible, "a wolf in sheep's clothing," – an imposter.'

'Who is Sri Babbajee?'

'He was a teacher at the *Brahmacharya* school.'

'Why was a teacher from a Hindu school quoting from the Bible?'

'Man, what stupid question are you asking me when we are talking about something serious? Would you like people to think that you are an imposter?'

'Of course not. I wouldn't want people to think that I am an imposter!' He said, as if the very thought was preposterous.

'Do you know the shame you would bring upon us – upon our children? The Pandit of Albion can become a very important man. *You* can become a very important man, so we must do it right. We don't want people to think that you're dishonest and pretending to be something you aren't.'

Valmiki bit his bottom lip, then said, 'I've never thought about it like that.'

'This doesn't mean that Pa will take over. He has his own *mandir* and business at Highbury. After the opening, he will come a few times and you will learn from him. Then you will take over.'

'You are right of course. Tell your father that we would be humbled if he would do the opening. And tell him about this *guru* thing,' he said, holding her hand. 'I don't know what I would do without you.'

She squeezed his hand.

As he led her towards the bedroom, he said, 'You know those children you were talking about...

The children came in rapid succession. For the next three years, Shanta was pregnant with barely a three-month respite between each child. The first was a girl named Devi. The second was a girl called Indira and the third was a girl, Radha. Valmiki greeted each pregnancy with eager anticipation that it would yield a son, and he was good at hiding his disappointment each time a daughter popped out. Shukla was ecstatic about the third girl, exclaiming:

'You are just like me! I know my fourth grandchild will be another girl!'

Sensing Valmiki's disappointment, Shanta said, 'Don't mind Pa. He would like a grandson, but he just can't resist making you feel miserable.'

'Stupid old goat,' mumbled Valmiki.

When he announced the birth of the third child to Parhab, the latter said, 'You are a lucky man, Sahib!'

'Lucky!' He snorted. 'Why?'

'You are knowing that in Hindu philosophy the birth of three daughters or sons, one after the other, is being a great blessing, Sahib?'

Valmiki had not heard of this. He had read the main texts of the religion but had never come across anything resembling this. He knew that Indians were a superstitious lot and they could have come up with this saw way back in the distant past in order to console people like himself who believed that a man had not established his manhood unless he had fathered a son. Parhab himself had got married and had fathered two sons and, perhaps, he was hoping for a daughter. If he had another son, he could pretend that he was blessed. Either this, or he was trying to make him feel better, as always. Valmiki felt that no matter how caring and sensitive daughters were, they could not carry on the family name or do manual work – and there was the matter of dowry. Three daughters meant three dowries, and it seemed to him that he would have to work all his life to pay for wedding ceremonies and dowries.

No, what Parhab had said about the luck of having three of a kind, bore less of a resemblance to Hindu philosophy than to the rules of Poker.

He was sure of one thing, though. He didn't want to try for a son just in case he became too lucky and got a fourth daughter. He would stick at three. As his daughters grew, he was to reflect on the wisdom of this decision. All three had taken after Shanta. They had inherited her beauty, her grace and her intelligence. On balance, the probability was that a fourth child would have been another girl, in which case she might not have been as fortunate as the others and might have inherited her grandmother's genes instead.

Shanta had agreed with Valmiki that it was perhaps prudent to stop at three. As her child-bearing years receded, she turned her attention to avenues of commerce. The population in the country was growing rapidly and the Indians, with their proclivity for big families, soon equalled the number of Africans. Food was at a premium, and anybody with spare capacity of land devoted it to rearing livestock or growing cash crops.

'You remember when you asked Pa to marry me, you told him that you were clearing two acres of land for rice?' She asked Valmiki.

He scratched his face and smiled sheepishly. 'I only did that because he was boasting about his land.'

'I know, I know. But I think we should look into it.'

'I'm not sure ...,' he said hesitantly.

'Pa has been selling his rice for years and he is thinking of buying more land.'

'That doesn't mean I should do it.'

'You don't have to if you don't want to,' she said. 'But you must think about the future – after you stop working on the sugar estate.'

'I agree. But I'm not sure about rice. Rice farming needs land, and land needs money.'

'We could buy a few acres to start with,' said Shanta.

'And where are we going to get that kind of money from? I have to save up for dowries.'

'We could borrow from Pa,' she suggested.

'What? I must have no pride now?' He said, aghast.

'Pride won't pay for the girls' dowries.'

'So, I must go and beg the old goat?'

'That old goat could lend us cheaper than anybody else.'
'You mean at cost price?'

Later that night, as he was rocking in the hammock, he thought about what she had said .Even though he had not really discussed it with her, he had already been thinking about what the future held for him in a sugar industry that was changing rapidly. Factories had already begun to experiment with better and more efficient ways of extracting and clarifying the sugarcane juice by using steam and equipment that was more scientifically engineered. And there was talk, only talk - that one day, machines would replace men in the harvesting of the sugar cane - that, one day, field workers would no longer have to inhale the poisonous gases produced by burning the cane, and that, one day, men would not have to slash, bundle, hoick and hoist. One day, then, technology would reduce the numbers of workers in the fields. It was only speculation. He had heard Tom Oliver say that people had laughed at the idea of non-natural flight before the Chinese invented the kite.

However, it was not because of how the industry might change in the future that occupied his thoughts. He knew that changes would always happen, that knowledge and technology would always push things on, and that people would always adapt.

No, there was something more immediate and practical that was weighing heavily on Valmiki's mind. As the sugar estates employed most of the country's workforce, each estate's weekly payroll was substantial and was always going to be a target for robbers. There had already been a spate of payroll robberies at many sugar estates, but the style and methods used had been largely amateurish and primitive.

However, throughout the world, the development of better communications had spread the exploits of such robbers as the James gang in America and Ned Kelly in Australia, and had led to greater boldness and a growing degree of inventiveness in the way that the local banditry went about their business. Previously, they had used cutlasses and knives and large numbers of bodies to engulf the payroll detail, but they were now increasingly using shotguns, which resulted in fatalities. In one case, the robbers had placed a canoe across the road so that the horse-drawn vehicle transporting the money to the pay office had to stop. A gang of masked men with muskets descended upon them from the cane fields, seized the cash, and escaped the way they had come, leaving two security guards dead. Since then, whenever the Plantations were on the payroll run, they would scan the path ahead for obstacles placed in the middle of the road and take evasive action, which proved successful in foiling the robbers on some occasions.

In a more recent robbery, as the payroll was making its way along its route, the security guards spotted an alligator by the side of the road. This was not unusual, as alligators were often seen emerging from one waterway and crossing the road to get to another. The detail slowed to allow the animal to go about its business. As they got closer, they realised that it was not travelling under its own power but that there was a rope tied to its neck and that it was being pulled across by a group of masked men who were hiding in the cane fields. Naturally, it was an imposition which the animal resented and one from which it tried to free itself. As it struggled, it lashed out with its long sharp tail, causing the horses to rear up and upturn the carriage containing the money. The horses carrying the security outriders also reared up before bolting with their passengers who clung on tightly to their necks so that they wouldn't be dumped upon the ground near the reptile. Thereafter, it was easy for the thieves to seize the money boxes and disappear through the fields.

There had been some cases, too, where the bandits had waited for the money to be deposited in the safe at the offices before launching an attack. This version of thievery endangered not just the armed personnel guarding the money, but also ordinary workers who happened to be in the vicinity. In a few instances, some of them had been killed.

Insurance companies insisted that the sugar estates should double up on payroll security and that they should pay for former policemen to perform this function. While this was an added cost to the estates, it was nothing compared to the risk posed to their payroll and the lives of staff by the greed of the robbers.

The bold attacks were the talk of the country, but it was not until the third attack at another sugar estate that people began whispering about the robbers in something approaching respect. In a daring daylight grab, the bandits had descended upon the payroll out of thin air. A stand-off ensued, and after two hours, a policeman had been shot dead, but not a single robber had been injured, killed or captured. In defence of his men's seeming ineffectiveness, a police spokesman claimed that the masked leader had been shot twice in the chest, but he had managed to flee somehow. This fuelled all types of speculation, mostly bordering on the occult. The way the bandits seemed to appear out of nowhere and the invincibility of their leader had convinced the superstitious that they were phantoms, as must have been the seven-foot-long alligator of the earlier raid. *For, who had ever seen or heard of a man being shot twice in his chest and escaping, or, indeed, of an animal of that species growing to such enormous proportions?*

'Sahib, do you believe that these bandits are ghosts?' Parhab asked Valmiki.

Valmiki replied 'No Parhab, I don't. Not really.'

'I am being afraid, Sahib,' said Parhab.

'Ghosts and phantoms don't steal money and shoot guns, Parhab.'

'Maybe, Sahib, but I hope they catch them before they attack Albion.'

'They won't attack us. We have the best security police in the country.'

'And the most money, too, Sahib.'

The adventures of the ghostly gang were on everyone's lips. Adults talked about their escapades in whispers and children fantasised about the spectral gang, as if they were heroes. Despite the brave face he had put on to allay Parhab's fears, Valmiki was deeply worried that the size of Albion's weekly payroll made it an attractive target which the robbers might find hard to resist. What was worse, if they chose to attack the offices, he might be caught up in the crossfire. The nature of his job had changed, and he spent more time around the offices, filling in forms, attending meetings and representing workers' grievances and, while such activities allowed him to escape working in the sun, being around where the payroll was stored overnight was fraught with danger.

One night, as he was in the *mandir* making sure that all was in readiness for the next day's prayers and singing, he heard a voice:

'Well, well, Pandit, it's been a long time.'

He froze.

'Turn around slowly,' said the voice, which hadn't lost any of its menace. 'I have a gun.'

Valmiki swallowed and turned slowly around.

There, laughing and winking with his one sluggish good eye, was Bagoutie, the Dacoit wanted in Bengal for murder, the one who had travelled on the boat with Valmiki. Except for his eyes, his appearance was different. He was much stockier than when Valmiki had last seen him, and he had grown a moustache, but he was still recognisable because of the aura of evil which he exuded. It was undiminished, and it still had the potency of being able to send a chill down Valmiki's spine.

'What are you doing here?' Valmiki asked, his voice trembling.

'Oh, I was just in the neighbourhood and thought I would visit my old friend, the Pandit. And you can't deny that you are a Pandit now.'

'What do you want?'

'Ah, come, come, Pandit. Is that any way to greet an old friend?'

'I am not your friend. I have never been.'

'I don't think you should be too choosy about your friends, Pandit. Seeing as how they might know a thing or two about you.'

Valmiki pretended that he wasn't shaken: 'I don't know what you are talking about,' he said.

'Come now, Pandit. You don't really think I was kidnapped and put on that boat, do you? I, Bagoutie? Wanted by the whole State of Bengal for murder and other crimes? I, Bagoutie, the most dangerous Dacoit in history, kidnapped? By whom? No, no. You see, Pandit, I have a cousin called Badri, an *arkati*. I'm sure you know him. He made it possible for me to get on the boat – to escape the Police. I saw him with you before we boarded, and I asked him what was so special about you that he was fussing over you like a mother hen. He didn't want to tell me, but he caved in and blabbed after I told him that I would deal with him and his family if he didn't tell me.'

'What do you want?' Valmiki said, almost in a whisper.

'Now, that's more like it. No need to be unfriendly, Pandit.'

'Did you kill Manoj, the Bihari, on the boat?' Valmiki asked.

'No. Not really. I just helped the fat fool over the side. He did the rest. Talked too much.'

Valmiki shook his head. 'You are a murderer.'

'We are all one thing or another, Pandit,' Bagoutie said. And, consistent with this philosophical turn which the discourse had taken, he postulated the question, 'Is it better to be a murderer than a leader who encourages his flock to accept their circumstances without protesting. Baa! Baa! Black sheep, have you any sugar? Yes, Massa; Yes, Massa; three bags full.'

'Did you come here to insult me?'

'No, but it's no wonder the Estate management gave you land to build your *mandir*, Pandit! Your religion keeps the workers under control. You are doing the Estate Management's work for them.'

'Why are you here? What do you want?'

'They want you to be good little boys and girls and serve them because it's your fate – your *karma*.'

Valmiki said nothing.

'I do want something from you, Pandit,' said Bagoutie. 'And what is that? Money? You want money from me?'

'Ha! Ha! You make me laugh, Pandit. I know you're not poor. You have come a far way, from a starving *chamar* from Bihar to Pandit of Albion; a leading figure in the community; and married to a very beautiful woman from a prominent Highbury Brahmin family. You have done very well for yourself I must say. But I don't want your cash, Pandit. I am after bigger fish.'

'What bigger fish?'

'The Albion payroll.' Bagoutie's eyelid descended slowly in a wink.

'What? You?'

'Yes, me. Didn't you guess?'

'At first, I wondered… I thought… But I should have known that the Bengal tiger does not change its stripes.'

'The Bengal Tiger! Oh, that's very clever, my friend, and funny, too.'

'But they said a policeman had shot you twice in the chest.'

'He had, Pandit; so, he had.'

'Then you should be dead. What happened?'

'Perhaps I am a phantom, as they say.'

'I don't believe in phantoms and ghosts,' said Valmiki.

'But the people do. They see me as the re-incarnation of Robin Hood. A hero. Someone who is paying the Plantations back for what they have done to them; paying them back for sucking their blood.' Bagoutie spat his words out and waved his gun about. 'Every time I strike, I have the people behind me. They don't know who we are; all they know is that we are hurting those who have hurt them for so long. Everybody, black and Indian, celebrate when we strike. That's why they have conferred supernatural powers upon me and my gang. They don't want us to die.'

'You are no Robin hood. You just steal for yourself. You are a wolf in sheep's clothing,' Valmiki said, almost sneering.

'A what?'

'Nothing. Just something Sri Babbajee used to say.'

'Who is Sri Babbajee?'

'Never mind. What about the big alligator?'

Bagoutie threw his head back and guffawed. 'I have never seen an animal grow so quickly and to such a length. When we caught him, he was just three feet long.' He stretched his arms out to measure three feet, but Valmiki kept his eyes on the end of the tape measure that was holding the gun. Bagoutie continued, 'That animal has grown with every re-telling of the tale, till he has become a seven-foot spectral monster! Who knows to what length he will grow with the passage of time? Twenty? Thirty feet? I am surprised that zoologists from all over the world have not tried to contact me.'

'But that doesn't explain why you didn't die.'

'Oh, you are such an inquisitive man, Pandit,' replied Bagoutie. 'But, as you're my friend, I will show you.'

He put his gun down on a bench, within easy reach, then he unbuttoned his shirt and pulled out a crude sheet of iron, which had been hammered very thinly and shaped to fit his torso. There were three holes along either side, through which lengths of coarse cord were looped so that they could be pulled and tied around his back to keep it in place. In the centre of the metal sheet just a bit to the left, around the area of the heart, there were two indentations. He put his two fingers in the indentations and caressed them.

'See? Bulletproof. That's why they call me Ned Kelly.'

'Who is Ned Kelly?'

'Never mind, Pandit. What I need is information about next week's payroll. It's the end of the crop, so bonuses will be paid. This is the mother of all payrolls. This is my retirement fund. After this, I am finished. Back to India.'

'But I don't know anything about the payroll...'

'Maybe not. But I know you can find out. I know you have contacts in the office. And, make no mistake, Pandit, I know where you live.'

The movement of Valmiki's Adam's apple was barely noticeable, but Bagoutie hastily added,

'Oh, no, I won't kill you. No, no! That will be too easy, Pandit. Much more fun if I told everybody your secret.'

'What do you want to know?' asked Valmiki.

'I want to know the date and time of the payroll, the route they'll be taking and how many policemen will be guarding it.'

'I will try…'

'No, don't try, Pandit. Triers don't get medals. Only winners. I will send you a message before Sunday to tell you where to meet me. You will have one hour. And Pandit…'

'What?'

'Don't be a hero,' Bagoutie said, as the shutter of his eye slowly descended and stopped halfway. He snatched up his gun and disappeared into the night like the shadow of a wind.

Valmiki steadied himself and sat down on the bench. He couldn't believe that after all this time, this aspect of the past should come back to haunt him. He had forgotten about this man who had reappeared, more deadly and more menacing than before, because he had information that could destroy him. He could forgive Badri for giving his secret away as nobody could resist this criminal without dire consequences. Now, he was threatening to unravel his whole life unless he did what he wanted. He couldn't see how he could betray Tom Oliver, a good and kind manager, and all the people who depended on the sugar estate, directly and indirectly, for their living. If there was a solution to this problem, he couldn't see it. The more he thought about it, the more impossible it seemed, and this was one problem that couldn't be halved because it couldn't be shared, not even with Shanta. He decided that he would sleep on it.

When he went home that night, he poured himself four fingers of rum, then he lay in the hammock and pondered. Shanta had seen him pour out the drink, but she had said nothing. It was not something that he did often, and he did it only when he was under pressure. She let him be as it seemed that he had something on his mind, and she knew that he would tell her when he was ready – if he needed to. After some time, he fell asleep in the hammock.

He awoke next morning in a confused state, none the wiser about what he was going to do. He went to work that morning and spent the day thinking hard about what he should do. That night saw no change.

Another four fingers of rum; another restless night in the hammock.

When he woke up the next morning, he seemed more relaxed. Sometime during the night, without really being conscious about it, he had come to a decision.

That night, close to midnight, a white man approached the back entrance of the temple where he was let in by Valmiki.

'Thank you for coming, Sahib,' Valmiki whispered in the darkness.

'I received your note from Parhab. It said urgent and most important, but why all the secrecy? Couldn't you have met me in the Office?'

'No, Sahib. It would have been too dangerous.'

'Well, I'm here. What's so important, Valmiki?' Asked Oliver.

Valmiki told Oliver about Bagoutie.

'He said he will harm my family if I don't give him

information about the payroll.'

'But all payroll arrangements are secret. Only the bookkeeper and I know,' declared Oliver.

'Is it the same on other estates, Sahib?'

'Yes. It is an agreed procedure. Even Security is only told at the very last moment to avoid any leaks.'

'It can't be such a secret, Sahib, if the bandits managed to rob the other estates.'

'Hmm. That's true.'

'He said he knew I had contacts. I have come to you because I didn't know what else to do.'

'You did the right thing, Sardar. But why did he pick you? Do you know him?'

'Sahib, we were passengers on the same boat when we came from India all those years ago. Another man told me that he was a Dacoit, a bandit, wanted for robbery and murder in Bengal. The other man disappeared during the journey and when I asked the bandit, he admitted that it was he who had thrown the other man overboard.'

'My God! What are we dealing with? Is this the first time he has contacted you?'

'Yes, Sahib. I didn't talk much to him on the boat because he scared me, and I was glad when he was sent to another estate. He's a very dangerous man.'

Oliver sensed Valmiki's distress. 'Ok, Valmiki, when and where are you meeting him?'

'He said he would contact me an hour before and tell me where to meet him.'

'We could set a trap – if we knew the time.'

'But we don't know, Sahib, and if it is here in the temple again, I wouldn't want any bloodshed.'

'Of course. Ok. Leave it to me. I will have to talk with a few people.'

'Sahib, the man had a gun, and he appeared from

nowhere and disappeared the same way.'

'Ok. Don't speak about this to anyone. I've got to work out a few things and I'll let you know.'

'And, Sahib,' Valmiki persisted, 'the reason he wasn't killed when they shot him was that he had an iron plate under his shirt. He said that people call him Ned Kelly.'

'Oh, he did, did he? Well, it didn't do Ned Kelly much good. I will come into the field in a day or two and give you the information, but we will pretend that we are talking about work matters.'

'Sahib, who is Ned Kelly?'

'Oh, that? He was an Australian bandit. Used a breastplate too, but they caught him and hanged him.'

'You will make a good Indian, Sahib,' Valmiki said, as he let Oliver out.

Neither man smiled.

After he had left, Valmiki sat down and wondered if he had done the right thing, but he kept telling himself that he had had no choice. In any case, who could he trust if not Tom Oliver?

Two days passed before Oliver and the senior overseer, Clive, dismounted from their horses, crossed over on the coconut trunk bridge, and went into the fields. When he approached Valmiki's field, he told Clive to go and inspect the plants in the adjoining field.

'Everything all right, Sardar?' He hailed out loudly to Valmiki. And Valmiki shouted back, 'Yes, Sahib. Only one problem.'

Oliver bent down and pulled up a young cane plant. He studied it, then broke the stem in two and examined the insides. Satisfied that there was no sign of infection, he threw it away.

'What's the problem?' He said, walking towards Valmiki.

'Sahib, one of my men has something wrong with his foot and he can't work.'

'Has he been to the sick house?' Oliver asked.

'Not yet, Sahib.'

'Call him over.'

The man hobbled over, and Oliver stooped to examine him. 'Looks like an abscess. He can't work like this. Tell him to go to the sick house for treatment. Oh, and he should get a letter from the doctor, which he should give to Sahib Clive.'

'Oh, thank you, Sahib,' Valmiki said. Then he spoke to the man in dialect, gesturing and giving him directions, before the man limped away. If the man was accosted and questioned by Bagoutie's men, there would be nothing suspicious to report.

What followed then was a mastery of silent theatre. Valmiki and Oliver were out of earshot of the other workers, and anyone looking on would have believed that the two were talking about agriculture. Hand gestures, shaking and nodding of heads and digging toes into the earth to test for moisture, accompanied the words:

'Payroll next Thursday at six p.m. We'll take the back route to the factory. Two carts and four guards, all with shotguns.'

'Two carts?' Asked Valmiki.

'Big payroll,' replied Oliver.

The pointing and gesturing continued, then Oliver said goodbye to Valmiki in semaphore.

They were both satisfied that no onlooker would think that what had just taken place was anything other than a routine discussion between employer and employee.

Chapter Twenty

After he had seen Valmiki at the temple, Oliver had wasted no time in contacting Consortium HQ in the City, where a meeting with the Police Chief and the Governor's Deputy had been hurriedly arranged. The planning of how to rid the country of its 'Public Enemy Number One', as the Police Chief called Bagoutie, and save the country's economy at the same time, was clearly of great importance.

In the Police Chief's office, the three men sat down, and Oliver laid out a map of the sugar estate on a table. He traced the normal route of the payroll detail, which was lined on both sides by sugarcane fields, but he suggested that they should break with practice and take the back route to the factory instead.

'That route passes through open land for the greater part and there are very few trees or bushes for about a quarter of a mile, so that anybody approaching could be easily seen.'

'What if they attacked in the open land?' Asked Chief Isaacs.

'That is most unlikely as they appear to depend on the cane fields for cover and surprise,' said Oliver.

'Good thinking. Criminals do not vary their M.O. Where do you think the attack will take place, then?' Asked Chief Isaacs.

'Here. The point of attack is more than likely to be here,' Oliver said, jabbing a well- manicured finger at two parallel lines on the map. 'Here, at the bridge, where the road narrows and the fields start. There are cane fields on either side, allowing both easy ingress and egress.'

'Hmm,' said Chief Isaacs.

'I figure the robbers will see this as the most advantageous point of attack,' continued Oliver. 'They won't attack much further in because that would be too close to the factory and people. What do you think?' He asked, looking at the Police Chief.

'Hmm,' said Chief Isaacs. 'It seems a good assessment, and we will have the advantage because we'll be ready for the attack at the bridge, armed with the new rifles.'

'I agree. The bandits will lack the element of surprise because they don't know what we know,' said Oliver.

'How many carts do you normally use for transporting the payroll?' Asked the Chief.

'One cart with a driver and the two guards, and two outriders on horseback.'

'I believe the week in question is a bonus week so there is a lot more money to transport. Isn't that so?'

'Yes, but it doesn't need more than the one cart; just more money boxes,' said Oliver.

'And the six extra policemen? Where are we going to put them?'

'Six!' exclaimed Oliver. 'I was thinking of the regular four. Six more? The bandits are bound to suspect something if they see so many policemen.'

'That's as may be, Mr. Oliver,' said the Deputy Governor. 'We must get this man and his gang at all cost. He has been wreaking havoc among the estates and he can't be allowed to get away with it. If what your man said is true, and this bandit is a Dacoit who is wanted for murder in India, then I don't think he will ever stop, even if he says that Albion is his last payday.'

'What I'm suggesting is ten guards in two carts,' said Chief Isaacs. 'Two and the driver visible in the first cart, and two and the driver visible in the second cart with six hidden in the second, covered by a tarpaulin. The robbers' greed will lead them to believe that both carts contain money, but they won't suspect that the second one is the Trojan horse. What do you say Mr. Oliver?'

Oliver bit his bottom lip. 'And outriders? I think they are important if the robbers aren't to suspect anything.'

'Yes, that's a good point. Ok. No more than the two outriders. They will be the men most exposed and I can't afford to lose any more of them.' Chief Isaacs scratched out the old numbers and wrote the new ones above. 'So, that will be two guards visible in each cart, two outriders and four concealed in the second cart.

'I think it just might work, Mr. Isaacs,' said Oliver. 'But we must aim to approach the bridge at about six in the evening.'

'Why is that?'

'Most of the workers would have gone home by then, out of harm's way. The factory will be manned by a skeleton crew. And it would still be light,' said Oliver.

'That's fine,' said Chief Isaacs.

As Oliver gathered up his things and pushed back his chair to stand up, the Deputy Governor said, 'We feel that catching this bandit is top priority.'

'I agree, Sir,' replied Oliver.

'Oh, one other thing before you go, Mr. Oliver,' said Chief Isaacs, as he took the map from Oliver's hand and spread it out again on the table: 'What's this structure here, overlooking the factory?' He asked, stubbing a nicotine-stained index figure on the map.

'Just a look-out tower we use for spotting any potential factory saboteurs. Why?'

'I want Corporal Murphy installed there.'

'What, as a look-out?'

'No. Murphy is my best marksman.'

'Really, Chief, isn't that going a little too far?'

'Not if you remember that two bullets to the chest failed to kill the leader the last time because of his iron plate. In the end, we might have to go for a shot to the head,' Isaacs said, as he lit up a cigar. 'And we mustn't miss. Phantom or no phantom. Ned Kelly or no Ned Kelly.'

On Saturday night, a messenger told Valmiki that he was needed at the temple in an hour's time. He hurried over and busied himself while he waited.

'Well done, Pandit,' came the now familiar voice. 'My friends reported that you kept our meeting a secret. Turn around. What news have you got for me?'

'Next Thursday at six p.m. - along the back route leading to the factory.'

'Excellent, Pandit. I knew you could do it. And how many guards?'

'Six.'

'With guns?'

'With shotguns,' Valmiki said.

'How many carts?'

'Two.'

'Why so many?' Bagoutie asked suspiciously.

'Crop bonuses. Biggest payroll ever. They need more than one cart to carry the money.'

'Ah, Pandit, you don't know how happy that makes me. You are a true friend.'

'Why do you keep saying that? I am only doing this because you have threatened me and my family. Not because we are friends!'

'You know, Pandit, I think that the fates have linked us together and that one day, we will both be famous.'

'Yes, you as a bandit and me as a traitor,' said Valmiki with his head bent.

'I think they will write a book and make a film about us. I can see it now.' Bagoutie said as he peered into the distance.

'You're talking nonsense', said Valmiki, sucking his teeth.

'No, seriously, Pandit.' And Bagoutie stared into the distance as if he was reading something that had been written. 'I can see it now: *"The Pandit and the Bandit."* Not in our lifetime, of course, and maybe they will get that kid Charles Chaplin to star.

'You *are* crazy.'

'Perhaps, Pandit. But soon I will be rich, and if you value your life, you will act like Charles Chaplin and shut your mouth. Do you understand? Not a word about me to anyone. Remember, I see everything. That's how I knew that fool on the boat had told you about me. So, no heroics, Pandit. Ghosts haunt people. Do you understand?'

'Yes. I understand.'

'Oh, and one other thing. Your secret is safe, so long as I pull this off. But if I suspect, if I get just a whiff that you have not been straight with me...'

'I have told you the truth.'

'Good. Good. Well, this is goodbye, Pandit. I will see you in India.'

And Bagoutie, whom Valmiki had begun to think of as his nemesis, disappeared. For good, he hoped.

Chapter Twenty-One

Thursday had been a dry and sunny day, but by the time the payroll carts turned into the back route and made their way towards the factory, the azure of the sky had given way to the amber aura of a large sinking sun. On the open land, a few sheep grazed; a couple of blackbirds dotted the sky and occasionally swooped down to pluck an insect from the grass; and crickets and grasshoppers chirped and hopped about from blade to blade, oblivious to the danger from above. The horses snorted occasionally, and their chains jangled as they pulled their burden – the first one laden with men and money, the second with men. The only other noises that could be heard were the creaking of the cartwheels and the crowing of a cock which appeared to have lost its sense of time.

The carts approached the bridge slowly, solemnly, like a funeral procession. As the walls of sugar cane got closer, the drivers and outriders tensed their muscles, gripped their reins tightly despite their sweaty hands, and looked all around with apprehension. They restrained their horses to a slow walk and the soft thud of the animals' hooves marked out a rhythm of heightened expectation.

Suddenly, the peace was shattered by a loud explosion which fragmented the wooden bridge and sent splinters, like matchwood, flying in all directions. The horses spooked, whinnied, and reared up, but the drivers held on to the reins and steadied them. Through the fog of thick smoke and the stink of gunpowder, twelve phantoms, all heavily armed and masked, leapt from out of the cane fields and attacked the train.

In the opening salvo, one outrider was wounded in the shoulder and two bandits were shot dead, but the other bandits kept coming with single-minded intent. It was only when the cover of the second carriage was jettisoned and the other policemen emerged with rifles blazing, that the bandits hesitated and appeared confused. They tried to run back into the fields so that they could make good their escape, but they were felled one after the other by the policemen's more sophisticated weaponry. Bagoutie, the shortest and squattest of the attackers, kept barking instructions to his men. He was shot twice in the body, but he appeared unharmed as he sprinted to the edge of the fields, within a short step to safety. As he reached and parted the green curtains, he looked back, but he couldn't react to the split-second explosion from the look-out tower, which propelled a single shot from Murphy's gun and sent it winding through the air, landing with a splat and drilling a hole into Bagoutie's skull thereby performing a pre-frontal lobotomy, which didn't just alter the bandit's behaviour but ended it.

Bagoutie fell and lay on the ground, unmoving. The head of the security detail, closely followed by the other policemen, hurried over to the prostrate body, and kicked his gun out of his reach before booting him with some force to make sure he wasn't feigning death. Satisfied that the ringleader was dead, he ripped off his mask. They all gasped. Bagoutie's bad eye was open and empty and his good one was open half-way in a squint. His third eye, the all-seeing one he had often boasted about, was a neat red circle in the middle of his forehead.

Later that night, Parhab woke Valmiki up.
'Sahib! Sahib! Good news! They caught the phantom.'
Valmiki feigned ignorance. 'What phantom?'

'The robber, Sahib. They caught the robber and all his men.'

'Where? Who caught them?'

'Sahib, the gang tried to rob the estate payroll at the factory bridge, and they had a shoot-out with security.'

'Did anybody die?' Valmiki asked.

'Some, Sahib, but I don't know how many; and they captured some.'

Valmiki supposed it was good news to the extent that the robberies would stop. But what if Bagoutie had been one of those that had been taken prisoner? His secret was not safe as long as the bandit was alive and, what's more, he would know that Valmiki had sold him out. This was not good news.

Just then, Tom Oliver rode up to Valmiki's gate and Valmiki left Parhab on the veranda and went down to meet him.

'Good evening, Sardar. Sorry to disturb you so late,' said Oliver as he dismounted.

'Oh, no Sahib.'

'Have you heard the good news?'

'Perhab was just telling me, Sahib.'

'Yes, thanks to you, we were able to stop the robbery.'

'Were many killed, Sahib?' Valmiki asked, as he tried to keep the anxiety out of his voice.

'We had a few injuries, but nothing too serious.'

'And the robbers, Sahib?'

'Oh, we got most of them all right.'

'And Bagoutie, the leader?'

'Oh, we got him too, 'said Oliver.

After a few seconds, and to clear up this ambiguity, Valmiki asked, 'Is... is he alive, Sahib?'

'Alive? Good God, no! He was shot in the head!'

'Oh, Sahib, I am so glad to hear that. He can't harm people anymore.'

'Thanks to you, Sardar. Look, I must go now, but I would like you to come by the office in the morning. Take the day off.'

'Thank you, Sahib.'

Valmiki tried to climb the stairs but found that he was shaking like a leaf in a strong wind. He steadied himself, inhaled deeply and managed to get to the veranda, where he sat down next to Parhab.

'Are you all right, Sahib? You look like you are seeing a ghost, Sahib.'

'Fetch the rum and two glasses, Parhab.'

When Parhab returned, Valmiki poured out two generous amounts and gave one to him.

'The phantom is dead.' He said.

After Parhab had left, Valmiki remained on the veranda. He was feeling much lighter and relaxed, but he kept thinking what a close-run thing it had been.

Shanta came out on to the veranda.

'Is everything all right, Val? I heard voices.'

'It was just Parhab. He came to tell me that there was an attempted robbery of the payroll, but security shot and killed the robbers.'

'Who was it? The same phantom?'

'Yes, the same phantom of flesh and blood.' A few minutes silence elapsed before he said, 'I think it's a good idea, you know.'

'What is?'

'This idea of yours.'

'Which idea?' She asked, not wishing to anticipate him.

'I've been thinking about the future, about after I leave

the sugar estate. About your idea of planting rice.'

'It was only a suggestion … if you don't want …,' her voice trailed off.

'No, No. It's a good idea, and I'm serious about leaving the sugar estate.'

'Are you sure? Is it anything to do with the robbery?'

'Not really. I've been thinking about it for a while, and I believe it's time to move on. There's some good land at the back, which we can buy.'

'How much will it cost?'

'I will have to find out.'

'And where will we get the money from?' She asked. 'You said we could borrow it from your father.'

She nodded and said nothing.

They borrowed the money from Shukla and bought five acres of land that had been previously used for hosting a variety of weeds, scrub, bush and trees and upon which stray animals grazed. Shukla visited often and advised them, and, with the help of Parhab and some neighbours, they worked on the land at nights and on Sundays. They pulled up weeds, dug drains and rogued out plant roots and tree stumps until the land lay free of vegetation; then they erected a fence all around it to keep out stray animals. Finally, after six months, the land was ready to be planted.

Valmiki stood and surveyed the next phase of his life. He reflected on his days of nothingness in Bihar, his chance encounter with Badri, the boat journey into the unknown and the incident with Bagoutie. And he wiped his eyes.

What no one knew was that the day after the attempted robbery, he had been to see Tom Oliver as arranged. Oliver had told him that the Consortium was very grateful that he had tipped them off about the robbery and wanted to give him a reward. Before Oliver could tell him what the reward was, and instead of asking, Valmiki said:

'Please, Sahib, I don't want anybody to know that I helped.'

'But I don't understand…'

'Oh, Sahib, even though that man is dead, I am still afraid of his shadow. Perhaps he has left other men who might suspect that I was responsible for his death. Any reward would only confirm it.'

'But they don't have to know. It will be a secret'

'Sahib, you thought that the payroll information was a secret, yet the sugar estates were robbed.'

'But this will be a secret between us and HQ.'

'There are no secrets among people in the sugar estates. You must know that by now, Sahib.'

'But there must be some way in which we can express our thanks, man.'

'Sahib, you have done too much already. You gave us that land to build the *mandir* so that we could practise our religion. And, Sahib, you have always treated us with respect, which is the greatest reward any man could wish for. But nobody must ever know about my part in this. I beg you. I haven't even told Shanta.'

Valmiki thanked Oliver and left. Oliver stood looking out of his office window at the upright figure of the Sardar retreating through the gates; he stroked his chin and shook his head.

Chapter Twenty-Two

When Shukla came to see the land, he said to Valmiki, 'You've done an excellent job!'
'We couldn't have done it without your help and advice,' Valmiki replied humbly.
Shanta smiled to herself.

They planted the rice, and it grew; and it was harvested, milled, and sold at a profit. Realizing that this was the way forward, Valmiki left the sugar estate and took his old friend Parhab with him, making him the foreman of his rice operations. After the second crop, he and Shanta were able to pay back their debt to Shukla and, thereafter, to manage their own financial affairs.

Their daughters went to primary school in the village. The first two, even though they were clever, ended their formal education there. They were destined to follow the tradition of Indian women of the time by getting married and procreating, thus perpetuating the species. For Valmiki, their dowries were not going to be a problem.

What was going to be a problem, though, was his youngest daughter, Radha.

One day, a black man in a white drill suit rode up to Valmiki's house on a large-framed Raleigh bike. He was wearing black shoes and white socks, and a white sun helmet which was perched upon his head with chin straps in place. He dismounted, undid his bicycle clips, and introduced himself to Valmiki as Edgar Williams, headmaster of Radha's primary school.

Valmiki invited him upstairs, and after they had exchanged pleasantries, he asked, 'How can I help you, headmaster?'

'I thought I would pay you a visit because I am worried about Radha.' Valmiki and Shanta exchanged glances.

Williams continued, 'I know Devi and Indra did not continue studying after primary school and I am concerned that the same might happen to Radha.'

'But in Indian culture girls go to primary school only,' said Valmiki.

'I know, Mr. Valmiki, but she is an exceptional student. She is the top of her class.'

He had never thought about it, but it struck Valmiki that the juxtaposition of 'Mr.' before his only name meant that people believed that he might have another name - a first name. He had only ever had one name which had served him well, until Shanta went to register Devi's birth. There, when she was asked for 'father's name', she had said 'Valmiki', so Devi's surname became Valmiki, the same as the other girls. If 'Valmiki' was the surname of his daughters, he mused, then, technically, he was Valmiki Valmiki. However, while it was nice to have two great names, he didn't think it was normal - and it certainly didn't seem reasonable for one person to have two of the same names. It was something he must remember to discuss with Shanta.

'I think she should go on to high school,' said Williams. 'Neither I nor my sisters did, Mr. Williams.' Shanta said.

'But things are changing, Mrs. Valmiki. There are greater opportunities for girls today. Radha could take the scholarship exams, and if she passes, she could win a scholarship to one of the best secondary schools in the capital.'

'She likes books, that girl; she is always reading,' said Valmiki with pride.

'That's a good thing,' said Williams. 'She is an intelligent child and she could go very far.'

'I don't know...,' said Valmiki.

'Can we discuss it and give you our answer later, Mr. Williams?' Said Shanta.

'Of course, Mrs. Valmiki. And if you need to talk to me, please send a message or come to the school.'

While it was tacitly assumed that Radha, like her sisters, would follow the Indian woman's pre-destined path, the visit from her headmaster raised new questions.

'What is this scholarship thing?' asked Valmiki.

'It means we don't have to pay for fees and books at high school.'

This appealed to him, but he furrowed his brow. 'What did Mr. Williams mean by *in the capital*?'

'Well,' explained Shanta, 'the best high schools are in the city. If she gets a scholarship she could go to King's High School. It is the best in the country, but the fees are high.'

'You mean she must travel to study in the city?'

'It's not very far, and we could buy a bicycle for her.'

'I don't know. This means she must ride on the road. It's too dangerous.'

'But many people do it. Mrs. Singh's son does it every day.'

'He's a boy.'

'We should think about it,' said Shanta.

'Why can't she be like other girls? Her head is always buried in a book.'

'She is like me. But when I was growing up, our parents didn't think beyond marriage.'

'That's the Indian way,' said Valmiki, 'and I am glad.'

'But it doesn't have to be. Our world was different. Why shouldn't women be educated?'

Valmiki held his head and muttered something about

222

having a headache. 'We will discuss it with your father when he comes,' he said, sure that Shukla would agree with him, seeing as how he had raised four daughters none of whom had progressed beyond primary school.

Shukla's reply, though, hardly helped his headache.

'I agree,' he said. 'Times have changed, and now Indian children are going on to high school and further. If Radha is clever enough, we should give her the opportunity. Who knows? Maybe before I close my eyes, I might even get a grandchild who is a doctor!'

Valmiki groaned and held his head. He loved all his children, but he was closest to Radha. Of the three, she was most like Shanta - playful, wilful at times, and fond. There were times when he would be sitting deep in thought and she would sidle up to him and rub his balding pate, something that his other daughters would never do. It was not an act of cheek, merely one of fondness - the kind of overt expression of affection that was the preserve of wives and daddy's pets. He would often take her on bicycle rides whenever he visited Parhab and his family in the next village, she, sitting on a cushion on the crossbar while he pedalled away.

While she was not easily cowed into obedience, she could best be described as assertive rather than insubordinate and it was a trait that Valmiki loved. But it was one that would later cause him much grief.

Chapter Twenty-three

Shukla visited often to mentor Valmiki on matters religious. On one such visit, Valmiki took him on a tour of his rice fields. Looking at the vast expanse of green, Shukla said:

'Best decision you've ever made.'

'I have to thank Shanta for that,' said Valmiki. 'And I'm thinking of expanding,'

'Hmm…That's a good idea, but there is an even better one.'

'What's that?' Asked Valmiki.

'Coconuts,' said Shukla.

'Coconuts?' Asked Valmiki, not sure if Shukla was being serious.

'Yes, man. The simple coconut.'

'But why? You can't do much with it, except drink the water and make oil.'

'You can use the fibre to stuff mattresses; they are even using it to make matting for cricket pitches and doormats. The coconut oil that we Indians use so liberally on our heads can be used for making face cream, for cooking, and used as a lubricant. And after extracting the oil from the copra, the residue can be used for feeding animals. You can even use the shell for fuel and to make buttons. And don't forget that the spines of the branches could be bundled and tied together, and what have you got? Hey presto, a broom! The coconut is versatile – you can use it for anything. We import many of these things, so it would make sense to produce them locally. Besides, it does not take much labour to grow coconut. It's versatile, I tell you. It can be used for anything!'

Except for finding water underground, Valmiki thought wryly.

Not wishing to dampen the old man's enthusiasm, he said, 'It sounds like a good idea. How many acres have you got?'

'Ten, but I've got a bit of a problem right now.'

'What's that?'

'The bastard who owns the land next to mine is claiming that four acres of mine belong to him.'

'Why?'

'Because he is a Muslim. That's why. No other reason. You know how they hate Hindus.'

'But don't you have the deeds?'

'Of course. But Abdul claims that it's a forgery.'

'Can he prove it?'

'Of course not. It was his grandfather, a man called Tallim Black Jacket, who had sold it to me.'

'That's a funny name.'

'You think so? His brother was called Honey-bee Bottle. Don't look at me. They said Tallim had only one jacket, which was white when he bought it; but because he lived in it and never ever washed it, it turned black through the accumulated dirt.'

'So, what are you going to do?'

'Nothing. He is claiming that the old man was crazy when he sold me the land. Says he's going to take me to court.'

'But won't he have to prove it?'

'Of course! But he can't. As far as I know, Black Jacket never went near a doctor, nor did he spend time in the madhouse, so it can't be proved. And Black Jacket's habit of talking to himself doesn't prove madness.'

'Maybe the court would get a doctor to examine him.'

'That would be a miracle. Mad bastard's been dead for

five years!'

'Well, you've got nothing to worry about.'

'I know. But his grandsons and his sons keep throwing all kinds of rubbish on to my farm, just to let me know how they feel. It's annoying, and they're doing it out of spite. Frigging beefeaters.'

'Coconuts, eh?' mused Valmiki.

'Yes, man. It's a most versatile fruit. It's a good insurance in case the rice crop ever fails.'

'I will think about it. But right now, we are thinking of getting the two girls married.'

'Have you found anyone yet?'

'No, not yet. Shanta has been looking.'

'Don't worry. I know some good *Brahmin* families. I will find out,' said Shukla.

'Coconuts, eh?' Said Valmiki.

'Yes, man. I swear that is the way forward.'

'There is some good land at the back of the village,' said Valmiki.

'Just make sure it's not owned by beefeaters. Do you have many in this village?'

'Many what?' Asked Valmiki, his thoughts far away.

'Beefeaters. Muslims.'

'A few, but they're all right.'

'All right? They'll never be all right. Don't trust them. Mark my words, they will soon want to build a mosque.'

Valmiki said nothing.

When he returned home, he said to Shanta: 'Why does your father hate Muslims so much?'

'Because he is a Hindu.'

'And that's an answer?'

'It's the best answer I can give.'

'I can't understand why he thinks they shouldn't be allowed to build a mosque.'

'Did you ask him?'

'No. He's got a problem with one of them, so I didn't want to upset him more.'

'Does a cat need a reason to fight with a dog? It's the same with Hindus and Muslims,' Shanta said.

'Your father thinks there is something wrong with them wanting to build a mosque. I don't see why they shouldn't be able to worship as they like.'

'I agree. It's not a competition. They have their god and we have ours. In fact, why should Hindus be worried about Muslims? They have one God, but we have millions.'

'I agree,' said Valmiki.

Valmiki knew that the Hindus and Muslims had brought their many prejudices to their adopted country, but he felt sad that it had to be so. After all, there was only one difference between the two religions: for the Hindu, the cow was sacred; for the Muslim, it was food.

And nobody knew better than he what a man will eat when he is starving.

A few moments of silence passed before he said to Shanta:

'What I didn't tell your father is that driver Ahmad and teacher Khan came to see me about helping them to build a mosque.'

'You didn't tell me either,' Shanta said.

'Oh, I'm sorry; it must have slipped me.'

'Don't worry. What kind of help did they want?'

'Just to lend them the plough team and some men to help them clear the land at the back. What do you think?'

'Why are you asking me when you've already agreed?' Said Shanta.

'What makes you think I've agreed?'

'I don't know my husband?'

'Well, as the Pandit of Albion and a rice farmer, I

suppose I am a kind of leader in the community and I must help. But you mustn't tell your father, or he'll never talk to me again.'

'Of course, I won't,' said Shanta.

Valmiki helped the Muslims level the designated ground, and, soon, The Albion Mosque, complete with minaret from which the muezzin could call the faithful to prayer, was penetrating the skyline. It was a rather imposing structure which added colour to the village. However, on one of his visits, Shukla went wild with rage when he saw it.

'There should be a law against such sacrilege,' he ranted. 'The good people of Albion should tear it down.'

'But, Pa, they have the same right to worship as everybody,' Shanta said.

'Not like us! My friend, the Manager of Highbury, would never condone such a thing and he would find ways of preventing it. These Muslims should know their place,' he concluded, his uncontrollable anger spraying saliva in all directions.

Valmiki looked at Shanta; her head was bent in embarrassment.

Later, after he had left, Valmiki said, 'I hope to God he never finds out that I helped them.'

'I wouldn't worry; I think you did the right thing. Besides, who's going to tell him?' Shanta replied.

'I told him that I was thinking of expanding the rice cultivation, but he suggested that I should think of going into coconuts.'

'Coconuts?'

Valmiki repeated Shukla's praise for the versatility of the coconut.

Shanta seemed impressed, but said, 'I was thinking that perhaps we could open a general store in the village.'

'You mean like your father's?'

'Yes. But not as big.'

'And who will run it? You are already busy doing so many other things.'

'Devi and Indra could run it. They could do with the extra money.'

'Hmm…,' he said. 'A general store, eh.'

'Nothing too big, of course,' Shanta said, as she saw him nibbling at the bait.

'Might be a good idea. There is only one around here, and they don't sell a wide range of things. You should look into it,' he said to Shanta.

It didn't surprise him when she said that she had already done so. She produced a book with pages and pages of numbers relating to the shop which she had in mind. He left it all up to her, and within a few months, there was a new emporium in the village, 'Shanta's Store', which was being talked about far and wide.

Shukla came to visit and expressed his disappointment that they had not consulted him, but Shanta explained that she had done it quickly because she wanted to help her two daughters - and she also wished to surprise him. This seemed to placate him somewhat and when she told him that she had designed it like his in Highbury, he grunted and allowed a half smile to cross his lips.

This fragile peace, though, was short-lived. Two things were responsible for this.

As Pandit of the Hindu temple and a rice farmer who had strong connections to the sugar estate, Valmiki was highly respected. It was therefore only natural that when the local emerging village politicians were looking for someone of influence to join them, they would turn to him. A group of them had approached him. Their invitation was shrouded in flattery about the high regard in which they held him and of how he had done so much to put the village on the map.

Valmiki listened patiently and said that he was honoured but that he was very busy and was beginning to feel his age. They didn't inquire about how old he was or told him that he looked too young to be complaining of ageing. Flattery, even in those days, had its limits. Nevertheless, he told them that he would be willing to lend his name and influence for anything they saw fit.

When Shanta proudly told Shukla, the old man raised his voice. 'What the hell does your husband think he is doing?'

Taken aback, Shanta said she couldn't see what all the fuss was about.

'Fuss? Fuss? I'll tell you what the fuss is all about! Who are these councillors? Tell me!' He fumed and spat.

'Just local leaders, like the Headmaster, the Sanitary Inspector, the Surveyor, and Mr Simpson, the builder.'

'Exactly!' Shukla roared. 'Exactly! All *habshis!*'

When Shanta pointed out they were not all black and that Mr Ahmad, the driver and local businessman, was also a Councillor, Shukla screamed.

'Four *habshis* and a *beefeater!* Hasn't your husband any shame? Doesn't he realize that he is a *Brahmin* and is superior to these people? Doesn't he realize that one *Brahmin* is worth a hundred *habshis* and beefeaters?'

As they walked towards the store, he kept up an incessant tirade about the country going to the dogs and about how *habshis, beefeaters,* and Valmiki, had no shame. Shanta ignored him; she was sure he would mellow when he saw the store. She pointed it out to him in the distance and he grunted; he wasn't talking to her. When they entered the store and he was greeted by his two granddaughters, Devi and Indra, he began to melt a bit. As Shanta showed him around, his grunts increased in length and frequency, which signalled that they would soon be converted into conversation.

That is, until Teacher Khan entered.

'Good afternoon, Mrs. Valmiki. What a beautiful store you have built!' He enthused.
'Thank you, Teacher Khan.'
Shukla moved to the end of the counter, farthest from Khan.
'I am sure you'll get a lot of support from the local community,' Khan said.
'I hope so, teacher Khan,' she said, eyeing her father working himself up into a state of rage in the corner.
'And from us too. We are eternally grateful for the help Mr. Valmiki gave us in building our Mosque,' Khan said, as he left the shop. And a good thing too, as there is no telling what would have happened had he tarried a second longer.
As it was, Shukla's collar size seemed to be shrinking and strangling him in the corner.
As he grew progressively redder, he fought for words and, finally, he managed to utter them.
Never had his granddaughters heard such obscenities and, what was worse, they were issuing from their grandfather's mouth. Much of it, too, was directed at their father, and they just couldn't understand why.

Chapter Twenty-Four

John had grown old and weary. His hands had become gnarled and he could only walk with the help of a stick because of the arthritis in his knees. His son David had taken over the business, but John sometimes accompanied him when he had to travel to a job, especially if they had to provide farrier services at a racetrack. 'The fresh air will do me good,' he would say, but Maria knew that this was an excuse as he had neither lost his love of horses nor all the memories which he had stored up during the time he had worked with them. Much to his children's boredom, he often regaled them with tales of how he had ridden Blackie to victory all those years ago and of how he had upset the Planters. Maria would listen but say nothing as she knew that there was a part of his heart to which she had no access.

He had become a devout Christian and was given to quoting passages from the Bible - sometimes for no reason, but always, to his children's annoyance. They would look at their mother for help, but Maria would shake her head as if to say that the meaning of his utterance had escaped her too. Sometimes she would say, 'Don't pay attention to him; he is old.'

Once, while he and David were travelling on their donkey cart to a race meeting, they passed Indian villages with *jhandi* flags, and black villages without, and John said to David:

'How things have changed. When I was a slave, there were no villages. All this land was either wasteland or covered in sugar cane. It was only when we left the sugar estate that little villages started to spring up all over. There were no Indians and no flags. Now, look at how many different villages there are. Also, we were never allowed to go into a racecourse on race day, you know. Weeks before, yes, but only because we had to cut the grass, clear the weeds and stones from the track and repair and paint the fences and stands. Things are so different now.'

'We still can't go into the stands, Papa,' David reminded him.

'But we can still watch from the ground.'

'Only because we're providing a service.'

'It is an improvement, though' John said.

'But it should never have happened,' David said.

'What should never have happened?'

'Slavery.'

'The Lord has his plans for all of us, son.'

'Papa, you can't believe that it was the Lord's will for you to be made a slave.'

'Things are changing, son. Look at the Indians. Do you think it was much different, for them? They left their country and came here and met hardship too.'

'But they weren't kidnapped and forced to come.'

'No. Not all of them; but things were bad in their own country, so they didn't have a choice. That is a kind of forcing – if you don't have a choice.'

'But they weren't brutalised like you were.'

'And we should be thankful; two wrongs don't make a right. Life was hard for them too. Now we are all living in this country and building our new home.'

'But, Pa...'

'Things change, David,' continued John. 'You must have faith. You must believe that it is God's way. Sometimes, young people catch that piece of cotton floating in the wind and you blow it off your hand for fun, just to see how it floats. That's a seed, a spore, and it will land somewhere, take root, and grow. Maybe it was God's plan to blow us all to this country, so that we could build a New Jerusalem.'

Knowing that there was not much point arguing with his father, David changed the subject.

'So, you think we might see a black jockey today, then?' He asked.

'Things haven't changed that much,' said John. 'I only got away with it because of King Henry, God rest his soul. It was only because of him that the other Planters didn't kill me. No, I don't think we will see a black jockey.'

What they did see, though, was a black horse.

During the parade, the horse had lost a shoe and his groom had brought him over for David to replace it. John's attention had been fixed elsewhere, but when he heard the horse whinny, he was immediately transported back to his days at the stables.

'Let me do that, David,' John said, as he struggled to get off the cart.

'No, Papa, it's all right. You sit down.'

'I want to do it,' John said gruffly and grabbed the tools from David's hands. David had never seen him so insistent - indeed, so animated. He could hardly walk, much yet shoe a horse. David looked at the groom, rolled his eyes upwards, and stepped aside.

John picked up the horse's forefoot and set to work. He tested the sole for any tenderness and, once he was satisfied that the horse was sound, he replaced the shoe and nailed it into place. David looked on, surprised at the dexterity that his father displayed despite his arthritic hands and lack of recent practice. It was as if he had been transported to another time, back to when he was younger.

As he bent over and worked, the horse playfully nuzzled him and almost threw him off balance. John smiled in a way that David hadn't ever seen him do.

'What's his name?' John asked the groom.

'Purple Lightning.'

'Do you know who his father was?'

'Yes,' replied the groom proudly, 'Black Lightning.

'Well,' replied John, as he used the rasp on the nails. 'Purple Lightning's line goes all the way back to a horse called 'The Black Thunderbolt.'

'How do you know?'

'I rode him when we won the King's Cup many years ago.'

'But ...' the groom started to say.

'It's a long story, and the bugle has sounded,' John said smiling. 'You must hurry.'

As the groom led the horse away, John looked at the horse wistfully. The horse looked back at him, neighed, and tossed his head about.

'He will win,' John shouted to the groom. And he did.

The journey back was quiet. John wore a contented smile throughout, and David, sensing that he was reminiscing, did not disturb him with idle chatter. When they got home, he told Maria and his sisters about everything that had happened. He was amazed, he said, at how alive and sprightly his father had become during the time he was shoeing the horse. Maria looked indulgently at John who was somewhere else.

The next day, John was found dead in his bed, with a smile on his face.

Maria told Tom Oliver that she had not seen him smile since the day they took Blackie away.

Chapter Twenty-Five

Pushed by Head Teacher Williams, Radha had secured a scholarship to the best girls' secondary school in the country and, thereafter, a scholarship to study Social Anthropology.

'What's that?' Asked Shukla when Shanta told him. 'Something to do with human societies and cultures,' she replied.

'I think Society is a lot of nonsense. What matters is money and status.'

'And what about people?' Asked Shanta.

'Oh, people do matter, but only those who have money and status. She should have become a doctor, instead.'

'She didn't want to,' said Shanta.

Valmiki, who was sitting nearby doing some calculations on paper, smiled occasionally. He knew to stay out of such discussions between father and daughter. Besides, the old man stood no chance against Shanta when it came to the defence of her daughters.

'I know you are disappointed, Pa, but it was her decision.'

'You two have spoilt her. Since when do children make decisions?'

'Radha is an adult, 'Shanta said.

'Why couldn't she become a lawyer then?'

'She said she doesn't believe in playing a game with people's lives.'

'But she could make a lot of money.'

'You mean like Mr. Narine, who tells his innocent clients to plead guilty, and he would beg the judge for a shorter sentence?'

'What's wrong with that? It's the British system.'

'Then she should play cricket.' Shanta sneered. 'Besides, she is happy with what she is doing.

'It's time she got married,' Said Shukla, changing tack. 'I could find a good *Brahmin* boy, just like I did for Devi and Indra.'

'Things have changed, Pa. She will decide when she is ready.'

'All this education is filling their heads with a lot of nonsense. She will end up an old maid, just like Mr. Mishra's daughter,' scoffed Shukla.

'That girl is only twenty-two, and Radha is twenty-one,' Shanta railed at him.

'It would have been nice to be able to tell people that my grand-daughter was a doctor or a lawyer. I am ashamed to tell people that she is a... I can't even pronounce this other thing.'

'What? Social Anthropologist? So-shal-an-tro-pol-o-gist,' said Shanta, giggling.

Shukla was not amused. Nor was he when he saw Radha's notes and decided to sneak a peek:

All along the coast, there is evidence of the diaspora of Africans and Indians caused by sugar. Villages, some of just blacks, some of just Indians, and very few of both, dot the landscape. Slaves, first imported and treated as chattels, had gained their freedom by pressures from outside and by their own resistance and had left the fetters of the Plantations and set up their own villages. Attempts by the 'plantocracy' at importing labour from elsewhere had failed, and it is possible that the former slaves might have been able to hold the Planters to ransom by demanding wages more consistent with the laws of supply and demand had a new source not been found. But inventive as they ever were, the Planters, by means both fair and foul, succeeded in luring the much-besieged Indians to fill the vacuum.

The Indians, through no fault of their own, came - first as a trickle, then as a flood - and they had to endure conditions like those of slavery with the promise of freedom after five years, of which few could take advantage. They therefore remained and became part of the tapestry of the West Indies. However, there was little intermingling, which suited the Planters, as compartmentalising them allowed easy control and made them unable to forge any kind of unity.

This situation breathes resentment by the former slaves towards the newcomers who, by the mere act of coming, had undermined their bargaining power. This is not helped by the Indians, who boast that they are 'indentured', which, in their minds, is a state superior to slavery.

The situation lends itself to exploitation by future politicians who might widen the fissures in trying to gain power, thereby creating a society characterised more by cleavage rather than by consensus.

'What nonsense!' Shukla thought.

Radha had always been the scholastic type, a bookworm who showed little interest in anything but her studies and the agitation for better working conditions for people on the sugar estates. The only close friend she had was Ravi, Parhab's older son, who was about her age and a driver on the sugar estate. He and Radha were very close, and they would often meet and chat for hours about world and local politics.

It was therefore natural that Shanta should feel all excited when Radha told her that she had met someone with whom she was in love. She later confessed to Valmiki that, prior to this admission, she had worried about Radha, about whether she would ever marry or whether there was something, you know, wrong with her. The relief at hearing this news led her to conclude that the object of Radha's affections was the only boy to whom she had ever been close.

'Ravi is a nice mannerly boy, and your father would be very happy because he and Uncle Parhab are like brothers.'

'But Ma...'

'I know you are worried about the caste difference, but it wouldn't matter to your father – or me. Your grandfather might have something to say, but I will deal with him.' Shanta said, running out of breath.

'But Ma, I am not talking about Ravi. Ravi is like a brother to me.'

'Then who... who are you talking about?'

'I met him at the Central Library when I was doing my research. I have been meeting him there every week.'

'Who is he? Who are his parents? Do we know them?'

'No. He grew up with his grandmother. They live in Bellevue.'

'How old is he?'

'Omar? Omar is twenty-five.'

'Omar? You mean he is a Muslim?'

'Yes, Ma. Didn't I say?'

'Oh my God!' Shanta cried.

'What's wrong, Ma?'

'You've been too busy with your head in your books to know what's been going on around you. Your father and grandfather are *Brahmins,* and Pandits too! Do you know

239

what that means?'

Radha looked confused.

'Well, I'll tell you what it means. They - not your father so much – but your grandfather and most *Brahmins*, think that everybody is inferior to them, except the Whites. And when it comes to Muslims, your grandfather thinks they are the lowest form of life, on the same level as the untouchables!'

'Ma, this is all nonsense. How can one person be superior to another?' Radha said. 'And what if I said I was in love with a black man?'

'Oh, God. In their eyes what is worse than a Muslim or untouchable, is the black man. The first two are Indians of a kind, but the last is a completely different race.'

'I can't understand this. If Pa was an untouchable and you were in love with him, would you still marry him?'

'Now? Now I know him and love him, but at the time when your Grandfather was trying to marry us off, nobody but a *Brahmin* was good enough. If I had said I was in love with a Muslim, untouchable or black, your grandfather might have killed me, the man, and then himself. That's how things were; you had to do what your father said.'

'But that was how things were a long time ago...'

'Some things never change.' Said Shanta.

'How do you think Pa would react?' Radha asked.

'He wouldn't be happy with anyone except a *Brahmin*. He would bawl for a week or two and ask God what he had done to deserve this. It's not about him, but about how he thinks people will judge him. I mean, what with him being a Pandit and allowing his daughter to marry a Muslim!'

'And Grandpa?'

'Oh, he would never talk to us again.'

'Well, I think this is all stupid. Why should there be all this fuss over having a relationship with someone of a different religion or race?'

'I wish I lived in your world, but the one I grew up in is unforgiving.'

'I will not give up Omar, Ma.'

'Don't say anything to anyone – not even your sisters. I will talk to your father tonight.

What is he...Omar...like?'

'Oh, Ma. He is wonderful! He is clever and gentle, and he is studying to be a biologist. He believes that most of the problems in the world are caused by greed and organised religion, and I agree with him.'

'That's an interesting point of view.'

'And he believes that we should care for our planet, of all the plants and animals in it. He says that people would not think of destroying the house they live in, but they are willing to destroy the house in which we all live. Don't you think that is clever?'

Shanta regarded Radha's enthusiasm. 'Yes, I have never thought about it like that. He seems like a nice person.'

'Do you really think so, Ma?

'Yes, darling. It's a pity he is a Muslim!'

Radha looked up, her mouth opening.

Then they both laughed.

Later that evening, after Valmiki had had his dinner and was on the veranda swinging in his hammock, Shanta joined him. They spoke about many mundane things such as, the weather, rice prices, disquiet on the sugar estate, of their dog, *Kalika*, which was due to give birth soon, and about how many pups she might have and what they will do with them all.

'Parhab wants a bull,' Valmiki said. 'He says Jaggernath is getting old.'

'And Pa wants one of each for his estate Manager friend,' said Shanta.

The Wapishana creaked as Valmiki swung. 'Dry day tomorrow, many stars in the sky,' he said, looking up.

After a few beats, Shanta said, 'Val, don't you think it's time Radha got married?'

The Wapishana stopped creaking and came to a standstill.

'I never really thought about it before,' he said, scratching his head. 'She is still young, and she is different from the others. She wants to be a career girl.'

'But even career girls get married.'

'I suppose so. But she is only eighteen,' he said.

'No. She is twenty-one. Where have you been? You men!'

'Twenty-one? How time flies! Yes, I suppose it's time we started thinking of finding someone for her. Why not ask your father? He knows people. Not many *Brahmins* around here.'

'That's what I wanted to talk to you about. She has met someone she likes.'

'Our Radha? But she never leaves the house.'

'She goes to the library every week to do her work.'

'But you don't meet men at a library. I… I mean. Who is he?'

'He is called Omar.'

'Oh, my God! Lower your voice.'

'She really likes him. He is studying to be a biologist.'

'I don't care. He is a Muslim! What would your father say? You know how he hates Muslims. It will kill him!'

'I know, but Radha is my child and I love her.'

'So, do I, but why can't she find a *Brahmin* boy!' Valmiki held his head in his hands. 'Oh, God! What have I done to deserve this?' And his shoulders started to quiver as a low moan began to issue from deep within his chest; then he began to sob.

In the weeks that followed, the atmosphere in the house was funereal.

On most days, Valmiki left the house early and returned only late at night, which was unusual for him. After dinner, which was eaten in silence, he retired with his glass of rum to the Wapishana hammock, for which he had shunned the marital bed. On the days when he returned early or stayed at home, he was surly and non-communicative and whenever Shanta asked him a question, he grunted, which had become his preferred mode of communication. Shanta let him be as much as possible, except when she judged that it was essential to speak to him or get a decision about something or other.

Radha stayed in her room, as she realised that what her father was going through was a catharsis that was necessary before he could deal with this problem which was causing him so much unhappiness. She had learnt this from the Psychology 1 module she had done at University, and knew it was a process that couldn't be hurried.

Even the dog, *Kalika*, felt the atmosphere. Whenever Valmiki approached, she scurried away as best she could, dragging her distended body, full of bloated teats and unborn pups, all along the floor. Not much later, either precipitated by the stress or because she had reached full term, *Kalika* gave birth to a litter of seven pups. Shanta and

Radha fussed with the little ones and examined them closely to see what gender they were. Shanta was in the process of determining how the pups would be distributed, when Valmiki's voice startled her:

'Don't forget your father wants a male and a female.'

Shanta did not visibly react; she continued: 'This little fat boy for Uncle Parhab. This little girlie for the midwife; you, good little *Brahmin* boy and you good little B*rahmin* girl for grandfather's friend, the Estate Manager ...'

That night, after Valmiki had eaten his dinner on the veranda, Shanta joined him. The hammock was in a rhythmic swing.

'We have to talk,' she said to him. 'Radha is unhappy.'

The hammock slowed down, then stopped. Valmiki looked at her and said, 'How do you think I feel? I am Pandit of Albion. How do you think it would look if my daughter gets married to a Muslim?'

'I understand that Val, but do you think people go around with their caste or religion stamped on their foreheads? Things are changing. My hair is going grey and for you, a full head of black hair is a distant memory. Radha did not grow up in our world and she can't understand what this is all about. Now she is upset because she feels she has hurt you.'

He bent his head. 'I am the one that has hurt her, and I am sorry. I am her father and should have acted like it, instead of taking everything as a personal insult.'

'You should go to her, Val.'

He left Shanta and went into the house. When he returned, he was hugging Radha and they were both tearful.

Shanta said, 'So, no plant-watering tomorrow?' And

they laughed, wiped their faces, and talked.

'Darling,' Valmiki said to Radha, 'I have always taught you that there is no problem that is too difficult to solve. I must confess, though, that this one of the hardest I have ever come across.'

'Never mind, man,' said Shanta, 'we'll think of something.'

'But I don't understand why it is so difficult,' Radha said.

Valmiki continued, 'I have been behaving like a mule. All I could think about is how people would look at me, rather than how happy my daughter could be. In the past two weeks or so, I haven't heard you laugh, and that has depressed me, but I didn't realise that I had caused it. I am very sorry.'

'You mean you agree to my marriage to Omar, Pa?' Radha asked.

'I'm not saying that.' Then he turned to Shanta and said, 'Have you met this person?'

'No, not yet.'

'Then I think you should meet him first.'

'Should we invite him home?'

'No, no. Not here where people can see. Meet him somewhere away – maybe at the library - and don't discuss this with anybody.'

Three days later, when Valmiki returned home, Shanta said to him, 'I went with Radha to meet her friend at the library.'

'What is he like?'

'Oh, he's very nice and mannerly and he seems clever. If I had a son, I would have liked him to be like Omar. He and Radha are very much in love and she won't give him up. So, we will have to think of something.'

'I can imagine how she feels. If someone had asked me

to give you up all those years ago, they would have had to kill me.'

She bent her head and smiled.

After dinner that night, he said to Radha,

'Is … ah …this boy… Omar…religious?'

'I don't think so, Pa. He said his parents died when he was a baby and he grew up with his grandmother, who was not religious. She is old and sickly now and Omar thinks she is losing her mind. She keeps forgetting his name, and she talks to herself.'

'Hmm… I think I should meet him.'

'Oh, Pa, you're not going to threaten him, are you?' 'He'd better not,' said Shanta.

'I'll leave that to your father', Valmiki said to Shanta.

'We can go into the city tomorrow – and we can meet him in the library,' said Radha.

'Does he live in the Library? Valmiki asked.

'No, Pa.' Said Radha.

'Well, you will bring him here. No more hide and seek!'

'I love you, Pa,' Radha said, as she left the veranda.

Shanta said nothing, but she took him by the hand and led him to the bedroom, the Wapishana looking on at their receding forms, like a lover spurned.

Chapter Twenty-six

The country had been experiencing a heatwave with daily highs of 42 degrees Celsius, and an unusually long drought, but the day when Omar came, the heavens opened, and it rained without stopping. The young man was ushered into the house, his carefully coiffed black hair all wet and matted, and his trousers all soaked with no sign of them ever having had creases. It was an inauspicious introduction for a suitor, but Valmiki, remembering his first encounter with Shukla, tried to put him at his ease.

'Nobody expected rain like this, I tell you.' Then he called for Shanta to bring a towel and a cup of tea. After she had come and gone, and Omar was seated, Valmiki cleared his throat, and said:

'So, you and Radha have known each other for a while…'

'Yes, Sir, we met at the library and I knew she was the only one for me.'

'So, you are thinking of getting married?'

'Yes, Sir, as soon as she has submitted her thesis and I have returned from my field trip to the interior – and if you give your permission, of course.'

'What kind of field trip?'

'I will be going to the interior to monitor the rate at which the trees are being cut down and trying to work out a viable replanting strategy. We cannot destroy the trees without replanting. It would be catastrophic for the environment.'

'It's not going to be that easy,' Valmiki said.

'I know. There are many pirates operating in the rainforest, so it's difficult to monitor the rate of cutting.'

'No, I mean the marriage.'

'Oh, I see. Radha did mention something about me being a Muslim and that it might cause some problems.'

'That is putting it mildly. I can't go back in history. All I can say is that Hindus and Muslims do not ever get married. Can you think of any Hindu and Muslim who are married? To each other, I mean.'

Omar's mind appeared to be scrolling through its files until it came upon one marked 'Hindu-Muslim Marriages'. He screwed up his face as if he was reading its contents. Scroll; scroll. He had once read a b

ook called, 'The Flora and Fauna of Ireland,' and under the Chapter entitled 'Snakes in Ireland,' there was only one line: 'There are no snakes in Ireland'.

'No. Not really,' he said.

'That's what I mean. Radha's grandfather is an old man and he is a Brahmin and a Pandit. It would kill him if she were to marry a Muslim.'

'But I am not really a Muslim, Sir.'

'No? What is your surname?'

'Khan,' replied Omar.

'Well?' Valmiki said, arching an eyebrow.

'Do you know any *Brahmin* named Omar Khan?'

'But it's only a name. I am not religious. In fact, with due respect to you and your religion, Sir, I think all the problems in the world have been caused by religion. Hindus and Muslims, Jews and Arabs, even the Christians divide themselves up so that they can fight against each other. What they don't realize is that all this fighting is futile, and unless they stop and work together, there will be no earth left to fight over.'

'That might be so, but it doesn't solve my problem,' said Valmiki. 'I love Radha very much, and her happiness means all the world to me.'

'I love her too, so what can we do, Sir?'

'You said that you are not religious. Have you ever worshipped in a mosque?'

'No, Sir.'

'How much do you love Radha?'

'More than anything in the world, Sir.'

'And would you do anything for her?'

'Anything! Anything at all.'

Seeing the devotion and steely determination of the young man in front of him, Valmiki began to think of ways of getting around this problem. He rifled through his memory for his special gene and, after a while, he found it. With the passage of time, the gene had become rusty for want of practice, but it was nothing that couldn't be fixed with a bit of spit and polish.

'Would you tell a lie for Radha?' He asked Omar.

'I would.'

'Would you tell a lie in a holy place of worship for her?'

'I would. I don't believe in fire and brimstone and karma.'

'Oh? Then what do you believe in?'

'I believe in the Earth. I believe we should live in harmony with each other and all living things, including plants and trees; that we should protect the earth, instead of poisoning it like they do when they burn the sugar cane plants.'

'No religion, eh? Well, leave this to me. I have to work out a few things with Radha's mother and we will let you know.'

When Valmiki floated his plan to Shanta, she hugged him and said, 'Val! You are a genius. How could you think up something like this?'

He looked abashed but said nothing.

The plan was simple, really: With Valmiki's coaching,

Omar would pretend to be a Brahmin and he would marry Radha in the *mandir*. As neither of them held religious beliefs, there would be no moral dilemma, and Shukla would be happy because he wouldn't know.

Shukla had not spoken to him since that day at the store, though Shanta had visited him many times, and while Valmiki had told himself that he couldn't pander to the old man's prejudices by grovelling to him, it was not in his nature to cause harm by wanting anything unkind, like sudden-death-caused-by-a-rude-shock, to befall him.

'You are worrying about whether my father will be happy, but what about you, man? You are a Pandit and if you marry them, what is going to happen to your *karma*? Have you thought about that?' Shanta asked.

'Nothing. Nothing at all will happen. How can I be punished for doing something that will bring happiness to my daughter, her husband, her mother, her father and her grandfather?'

'And don't forget Mother Earth!' Shanta said.

'And, above all, Mother Earth,' Valmiki agreed.

'You are right. But Pa must never ever know,' Shanta whispered.

When Valmiki outlined the plan to Omar, he willingly agreed, unshackled as he was by the promises and threats of eternal damnation. In the months that followed, he paid regular visits to the house to rehearse. In truth, he loved the idea because he saw himself as a film star playing the lead in a great romantic epic.

It was during one such rehearsal that the star stopped the director and said, 'But there is one problem, Sir.'

'What's that?' Asked Valmiki.

'Everybody knows that 'Omar' is a Muslim name, so I can't continue using it.'

'Hmm '... I hadn't thought about that. You're right of course – it's a dead giveaway. We must find a Hindu name for you,' Valmiki said.

'And it must sound similar because, if it is different, I won't answer when I am called – and that would look suspicious, don't you think? I mean, if they call me 'Vivekanand' or something Hindu like that, I wouldn't answer.'

Valmiki looked at Omar with respect. He recognised in him someone from his distant past.

'Let me see,' said Valmiki, and he thought and thought, trying to conjure up his deviant gene. And, as if he had rubbed Aladdin's lamp, the genie appeared.

'*What can I do for you, oh master?*' The pot-bellied djinn asked.

'*Find me a Hindu name that is similar in sound to the Muslim name Omar.*'

'*Your wish is my command, Master,*' the gene genie said, and after three puffs of smoke and one abracadabra, he pronounced:

'*Derived from the sacred syllable and spiritual icon of the Hindu religion, 'Om' is found at the beginning and the end chapters of the Vedas and Upanishads. Therefore, the name 'Omkar' signifies a name of the finest Brahmin pedigree,*' said the genie.

And so, Omar became Omkar and preparations for the wedding moved on apace.

In one of their quieter moments, Valmiki said to Shanta:

'You know, I think it would be a good idea if we asked your father to perform the marriage ceremony...you know...as a peace offering.'

'Why this sudden change of heart?' Shanta asked,

narrowing her eyes

'No reason. I just think it's time to make the peace. He is old and he has his prejudices, but we can't shut him out.'

'You're worried about what would happen to your *karma* if you performed the ceremony, aren't you?'

'Not at all. I am not afraid of such things. Your father is getting down, though, and…well, who can say how long he's got? I just think it's a good opportunity.'

'And what about Pa's *karma?* Have you thought about that?'

'His karma won't be affected because he doesn't know that Omar is a Muslim. As I said, it's simply an opportunity to make the peace.'

'I know you, Val. I think you have something up your sleeve. Come on, what is it?'

Valmiki smiled, but said nothing.

'Come on. Out with it!'

'Ok, I'll admit it, but it's nothing to do with *karma.'*

'What then*?'*

'I would love to watch the bigoted Pandit of Highbury marry a Beefeater into his Brahmin family.'

Chapter Twenty-seven

Before the marriage ceremony, Valmiki said to Omar:

'You are only allowed to reject my offer of a dowry twice and then you must accept it. I know of a case where a groom rejected the offer four times and that pissed off the bride's father so much that they didn't talk for years. You don't want to piss me off, do you, Omkar?'

'No, Sir!' said Omar.

Shukla performed the ceremony in a doddery fashion and after he had closed the Holy Book, he took the opportunity to make a speech, like priestly men have done since the beginning of time when presented with an audience that had nowhere to run. His voice was shaky, but loud enough for people to hear, as he traced the history of the Indians since they came to their new country. Some of his speech was about himself and what he had achieved, and some was lauding the greatness of the *Brahmins*, who, he described as the only true Indians.

'There are false religions from all over the world, but you must remember that Hinduism is the only true religion,' he declared, as the Muslim, the Christian and the non-believing guests shifted in their seats.

He said that Shanta and Valmiki had done him proud by finding such a fine *Brahmin* husband for Radha and he remarked on how far his own family had come:

'Three generations of *Brahmins,* our blood undiluted in our adopted country, and I am looking forward to my pure *Brahmin* great-grandchildren to continue the line. I have a book full of names for them. True *Brahmin* names.' He proclaimed, and everyone looked in a different direction.

It was a relief to all when he ended his speech. Valmiki

and Shanta were happy that he couldn't stay after the ceremony as it allowed them to go around and apologise to those guests who had been caught in the scatter of Shukla's shotgun - Indians of other castes, Christians, Muslims and non-believers. The guests graciously said that they were sorry that the Pandit was not feeling well and couldn't stay, but that they had understood.

After the wedding, as Valmiki and Shanta sat on their veranda, Shanta said, 'It was a nice wedding, Val, and I think everyone enjoyed it.'

'Yes. Except for your father's speech.'

'You have to excuse him. He's getting old, you know. I think he's losing his memory.'

'That's no excuse. He's always been like that - going on about the superiority and purity of *Brahmins* as if everyone else is inferior.'

'But it's what we were taught since we were children.'

'I know, but how can one person be born better or superior to another?'

'I don't know ...'

'Ok. Just suppose I said I was a *chamar* – an untouchable. What would you say?'

'I would say you had too much to drink.'

'Assuming that I didn't have anything to drink,' he said, taking a sip of rum.

'I would say you are talking nonsense. How could you be a *chamar* when you are a *Brahmin*?'

'Ok. If I take off my Pandit clothes and tell you I am an *untouchable*, can you tell the difference?'

'No, but then I would expect you to clean latrines and not read the Vedas.'

'Are you saying that an untouchable cannot learn to read a Holy Book?'

'I don't know what's got into you, Val. Talking all this

nonsense.'

'What if I said I am a Muslim?' Would you believe me?' Persisted Valmiki.

'Only if you dropped your trousers,' said Shanta, trying to lighten the atmosphere.

'That's what I mean. Looking at all of us you can't tell what the difference is. Yet some people, like your father, will argue that one is superior.'

'You sound like Radha and Omar.' Shanta replied, trying to change the subject. 'Which reminds me, Pandit Valmiki, do you have a book of true Brahmin names for our grand-children when they come?' She giggled and he smiled. He shook his head and hugged her.

Not long after Shukla's death, the grand-children came.

They were a trio of girls.

And they were called Gaia, Summer and Sky.

Printed in Great Britain
by Amazon